The Gatherer

The Gatherer

Colleen Winter

REBEL BASE BOOKS
Kensington Publishing Corp.
www.kensingtonbooks.com

Rebel Base Books are published by
Kensington Publishing Corp. 119 West 40th Street New York, NY 10018

All Kensington titles, imprints, and distributed lines are available at special quantity discounts for bulk purchases for sales promotion, premiums, fundraising, and educational or institutional use.

Special book excerpts or customized printings can also be created to fit specific needs. For details, write or phone the office of the Kensington Special Sales Manager:
Kensington Publishing Corp.
119 West 40th Street
New York, NY 10018
Attn. Special Sales Department. Phone: 1-800-221-2647.

First Electronic Edition: November 2019
ISBN-13: 978-1-63573-083-8 (ebook)
ISBN-10: 1-63573-083-X (ebook)

First Print Edition: November 2019
ISBN-13: 978-1-63573-084-5
ISBN-10: 1-63573-084-8

Printed in the United States of America

To Ron, for everything.

"Universal peace is a beautiful dream, but not at once realizable."

–Nikola Tesla

ONE

Storm paddled easily downstream, the cabin falling behind her, the hills on either side casting large shadows across the fast flowing river. Blue sat in the bow of the canoe, their self-appointed navigator, his nose lifted to the wind and whatever scents the river delivered. They hadn't encountered a single boat since they'd started out, and the swirling vortexes of the current took on an ominous feel as they drew them relentlessly downstream.

She steered into an eddy at the final bend before Three Rocks and caught hold of a fallen log to hold her place against the current. Blue shifted and circled, rocking the canoe as he tried to leap ashore. She felt the same agitation, her concern growing the farther they had come downstream without seeing another boat.

Three Rocks acted as a supply post for the more remote communities further north. Float planes used the wide, flat river as a runway, landing and taking off in an incessant roar of outdated engines. She should have been part of a consistent flow of boat traffic, her canoe rocking in the waves from the boats' wakes.

Drops of water fell from the paddle she laid across her knees and she flexed her fingers against the cold. Any other year and the river would have been frozen, yet this year winter hovered out of sight, refusing to come.

She stepped carefully onto the slippery surface of a rock ledge, grabbing a tree branch for balance as Blue leapt from the canoe. He positioned himself at the top of a low rise, head up, tail high. She stashed her paddle and lifejacket under the canoe and slipped on her backpack. A few steps from the river's edge, she stopped and listened. Or rather, she called it listening, but it was more than hearing, her nerve ends tuned for the slightest trace of electromagnetic fields. A few small animals skittered along branches.

A crow cawed in the distance. Underlying it all was an instability, as if something had shifted and left the woods off balance.

She followed the path along the curve of the river, staying close to its edge. She stopped every hundred metres to listen and to feel. It wasn't until the low warehouses were visible at the water's edge that the first traces of current rippled across her skin. Not strong, yet there was the rhythmic pulsing of a signal along her nerves where none had been before. Water lapped against the pilings from the old docks and a slack flag shifted in the breeze. She slipped off her backpack and signalled Blue to stop. He hadn't gone more than ten metres from her since they had left the canoe. She found her full suit of silver inside her pack, the material creased from being stored. It had not been worn in over a year since she'd first arrived in the Yukon. She removed her boots and coat, hunching her shoulders in the cold, and slid her feet into the fitted leggings, pulled the snug material up over her thighs, forced her hands out through the arms and flipped the hood over her head. She zipped it up and exhaled, feeling a brief pause in the tension that had grown since she had left the cabin.

The suit had protected her from the worst of the electromagnetic fields when she was still in Rima, but it hadn't stopped them from robbing her health, the muscle spasms so intense at times that she had collapsed to the ground. It would protect her from the relatively weak effects of any fields that were emanating from Three Rocks, yet it made her more uneasy since she couldn't gauge when their strength would overpower its thin protection. She pulled an opaque mesh over her face and the last tingling stopped. She slid her boots and coat over the suit. She looked like an alien. Blue whined.

"Hold on."

He continued whining, his nose pointed at a thick stance of tamaracks. She lifted her veil to get a better view through the trunks, hoping for the smooth flank of an elk or deer and not the bristling fur of a grizzly. No movement. She threaded her arms into her backpack and had turned towards town when she saw the boy.

"Leave it," she warned Blue.

He stood further away from the river, half hidden by a poplar tree. He was thin, wearing the same scuffed, worn blue parka from last year. The zipper was undone and the sharp bone of his wrist was visible below the too-short cuff. Straight black hair hung in his eyes.

"It's Jacob, isn't it?"

He turned away from her, his shoulders pointed towards town, the turn of his head over his shoulder his only sign of interest.

"You saw me last spring. When I came to your dad's store."

There was a wariness to him that hadn't been there when she had come into town over a year ago. It had been at night, soon after she'd arrived in the territory, when the stores were closed for the night and the town quiet. Jacob had watched from the window while she had met with Mac on the street. The quiet, solid man, the only person she could trust.

"I need to talk to your dad. It's important."

Jacob retreated further behind the tree, yet the trunk wasn't wide enough and his shoulder and arm peeked out the other side. She stepped forward, afraid that he would run. It had been almost six weeks since Mac had shown up with supplies, the days growing colder and darker as she had watched for his truck at the entrance to her clearing.

"Has he stopped making deliveries? Is that why he didn't come?"

He tossed his head to clear the hair from his eyes, a movement she didn't think meant no. She held up her hands, appeasing, needing to know what made him so wary, realizing as his gaze followed her hands that the silver gloves only made things worse. She yanked off the gloves to show her bare hands, a slight sting rising on her skin. She pushed back her hood, feeling the cooler air. The skin on her scalp rose. She shouldn't be reacting this far from town. She had thought she was getting better.

Jacob held his head high, his chin lifted, with an air of self-reliance that hadn't been there last spring.

"Is your dad okay?"

Something in the way he moved his hand stopped her. A tremor, slight but present. She tried to get a closer look, but he moved his hand behind his back when he saw her watching. She strode forward, not wanting to believe what she saw and needing a closer look. She was almost close enough to touch him before he ran.

Blue leapt after him.

"Wait!"

She ran even as she knew that chasing him would only make him run further. Blue matched her stride. The boy moved fast, flashing between the trees, disappearing and then appearing at disjointed intervals.

She was good at moving fast through the woods, but not as good as this kid. Already she was overheating, the silver suit creating a private sauna.

Blue shot ahead of her in beautiful long strides, effortlessly closing the distance. The boy looked over his shoulder, his eyes stricken with terror as Blue cut hard in front of him. The boy stumbled, almost falling, then redirected. Blue circled gleefully, head and tail high, nipping at the boy's heels. Jacob was panicked, frantically searching for an escape route. He kicked at Blue, who danced away from him. The boy found a stick and swung it. Blue herded the boy closer, strutting in circles, showing off.

"He won't hurt you."

She was winded from the short burst of running, her body unprepared for the exertion. Jacob spun to face her. He had made good distance towards town and she felt the tingling agitation on her face.

"Come."

Blue trotted to her side and she rested her hand on his head. Jacob watched them carefully, assessing his chances of getting away. The shaking was more noticeable up close but she needed to get a better look. Already her brain was drawing conclusions, fitting the final pieces into a puzzle that she refused to believe until she had more evidence.

"This is Blue. I'm sorry for scaring you."

He didn't answer.

"I'm not going to hurt you."

A rush of energy, like electric drops of water hitting her cheeks. She lowered the mesh. Poor kid, no wonder he was freaked out. She could see him through the thin weave, but she probably appeared like a faceless android. She slid off her backpack and lowered it to the ground.

The Mariners baseball cap she kept on top was lined with silver. It kept the fields from reaching her head and had been one of her first projects when she'd started getting sick. She had worn it continuously before she left the city, but she carried it with her now the way an athlete wears a favourite pair of socks, more for the emotional reassurance than any improvement in performance.

She offered him the hat.

"This will help. With the headaches."

If he had them.

She wasn't certain what she had seen or how it was even possible. She examined the rough stitching and the frayed ends of fabric that stuck out below the rim. He stood as still as the trees around him, poised to resume flight.

"I used to wear it when they got really bad."

"I don't get headaches."

He spoke defensively, though he had lost some of his wariness.

She extended the hat towards him and stepped the final two strides that separated them. He backed up and Blue rose to his feet.

"Try it." She laid it on top of an exposed rock. "I don't use it anymore." She gestured towards the suit. "I have this."

She retreated far enough from the hat that she would not be able to lunge for him. The boy's gaze moved between her and Blue, an awareness perhaps that she could have Blue subdue him if she wanted. She forced herself to bide her time and moved further back.

He turned it slowly, noting the same imperfections that she had. She had a sudden flash of the relief of sliding it onto her head, her self-made protective helmet against the world. She longed for that kind of simple solution now. Already the needling pain penetrated the suit, another reason not to go into town.

She stopped herself from telling him to try it on. She would know for sure if he was being affected once she saw his relief when he put it on, like cool water running over your head on a hot day. She signalled to Blue that he was released and, tail wagging, he sniffed a trail along the ground, peed against a tree, then sniffed his way to the boy where he sat and lifted his head. Jacob turned his shoulder towards him.

"Will he bite?"

His voice cracked when he spoke. He was older than he looked.

"He wants you to pet him."

He reached out a tentative hand and Blue lifted his head to meet it. A breeze shifted the remaining leaves on the trees like a tiny fanfare of applause. What she wouldn't do to have Blue's ability to engage people.

A slow ache spread over her body. She walked a few paces. At the movement, Blue returned to her side. The ache eased, washed away by the flow of blood to her muscles and Blue's presence at her side.

Jacob examined the hat for several seconds before he lifted it to his head. It was too large and sat low on his forehead, yet the tightness around his eyes eased and his shoulders relaxed. He tilted his head to look up at her from under the brim.

"How does it do that?"

He looked younger with the hat on, and she wanted to snatch it back, flee back to the isolation of the cabin, and pretend she hadn't seen this.

"It blocks electromagnetic fields."

She didn't tell him that the hat would only help for so long. A salve on a growing wound. It didn't make sense he would have these symptoms here.

"I need to see your dad."

The boy swallowed and she had a momentary glimpse into his fear and concern.

"Is he sick?"

He shrugged, pressing his lips together. This wasn't about a single missed delivery. She knelt in front of him, grabbing his hand before he could bolt. Up close the circles under his eyes were black.

"Has he seen a doctor?"

Water seeped into her knees from the earth, a gust of wind delivering a colder, sharper bite. His thinness shocked her, the bones of his wrists too small and fragile.

"They don't know what it is."

He pulled his hand from her and for a second she thought he would run. Instead he took the hat off his head and offered it back to her. A crease appeared between his eyes and his shoulders rose as if needles of rain fell on his head. When her first tremors had appeared, she had seen countless doctors who had provided her with suggestions on how to reduce her stress, sleep more, and take endless runs of antidepressants. She had questioned her own judgement, worried the shaking and fatigue was something she had created in her own head. She had finally made the connection to the electromagnetic fields on her own, after months of fatigue, aches, and sudden sensations of burning. She pushed the hat back towards him.

"Why don't we go see him."

She should turn around. Go straight back to the cabin.

"He could try the hat."

Jacob's hands weren't shaking where he held the hat and she wondered again if she had seen it at all. When he finally lifted his gaze to hers, his cheek twitched unmistakeably. The nerves in her cheek gathered to mimic it, the twitching ingrained from the months when she'd suffered the same reaction.

"Okay."

She cringed at the rise of hope in his voice. She had no right to offer him that, for after eighteen months of trying she still hadn't found a cure. What she didn't understand was what had caused his electrical system to get so out of balance. She had caused her own body's imbalance when she had been developing the Gatherer, but Jacob hadn't been involved in any testing and lived here in the Yukon.

Jacob turned and started towards town. When he wasn't running in terror he moved effortlessly through the low brush and spindly trees. Blue trotted beside him and occasionally. Jacob scratched the dog behind the ear.

They picked their way across a slick stretch of mud, holding branches and the tops of shrubs for support. As she followed the back of his heels, she wrestled with whether to turn around or keep going. Part of her grew increasingly frantic as they approached town and the ache in her muscles deepened. Another part grew stronger, overpowering the first, her need to understand what had caused Jacob's symptoms energizing her in a way she hadn't felt in months.

They followed a worn path through overgrown weeds along the wide, spacious back yards. Children's toys were strewn about without any sign of children and uncut grass twisted through the wheels of a boat trailer that hadn't moved in a long time. Even the well-kept yards had an air of neglect, as if the occupants hadn't returned from a vacation.

Jacob led her past all of them, his eyes on the trail. A few trace currents skittered across her cheeks and there was an increased agitation to the air that left her jumpy, waiting for a stronger attack. She ducked through a narrow opening between trees and raspberry bushes dragged against her leg. A thorn caught, opening up a small patch of itchiness on her shin.

She slapped her hand over the tear while slinging off her bag and searching through it with her free hand. After wrapping several layers of foil tape over the flap of fabric she sat back on her haunches, finally taking a full breath, her heart drumming in her ears. She needed to keep her anxiety in check. Deal with what was happening, not what she imagined.

When she started walking, Jacob stepped in front of her, maintaining his position as guide. They paused at a T-junction at the top of a road that led into downtown. She had never seen the town in daylight, the loose grid of streets dominated by the three rock cliffs that loomed on the opposite side of the river. The streets were empty at midday, absent of the cars and people that should have been collecting supplies for the winter. She should have been relieved, as it gave her less chance of being recognized, but the underlying instability was still there and she couldn't help but think that something was desperately wrong.

"My dad doesn't talk."

Jacob spoke so quietly it took Storm several seconds to register what he had said.

"At all?"

Mac was more of a man of action than words, bringing her something in her order she hadn't asked for, or shovelling out snow when she had been too weak. But there had been words, if not many, on his last delivery.

"How long has it been?"

They walked close together down the centre of the street. A sidewalk ran along the side, yet there was no reason to move off the road. The air of abandonment persisted in the blank windows, and the street was quiet but for the rush of the river's current running close beneath the surface at its end.

"Twenty-six days."

Twenty-six days that he had likely marked on his calendar, waiting for the time when his dad would return to him. An eternity for the person trapped inside their head; no reason, pattern or logic to the never-ending kaleidoscope of memories and sensations.

They passed a boarded up house, a plastic lawn chair overturned on the porch. On her worst days, hours had gone missing in the labyrinth of her thoughts, the images so consuming she had been unable to see her way clear. She paused, the flow of the river visible through buildings at the end of the street. She needed even more now to get to Mac, for a suspicion was forming in the back of her head that she only half understood. It didn't make sense that this boy and his father might have her same illness when she had contracted her sensitivity in an experimental lab so far from here.

"Curtis said he'll come around."

They had crossed two intersections, the houses turning into open stores with no one in them, even the shop keepers staying out of view.

"Who is Curtis?"

It was getting harder to breathe, a pressure building in her chest. She veered to one side, the ground not where she expected it to be. Jacob watched her from the side of the street where she had started, his gaze blank in disappointment.

A vibration rose up from her gut, streaming out into her arms and legs. She paused, Blue circling her legs. She needed to hang on until the next corner, make it down the block to Mac's store. She leaned against the wood siding, sweat sticking the suit to her sides. The grip on her chest was so tight she struggled on each breath. Already auras were shimmering at the edges of her vision. Jacob said something to her, the hum in her ears like a high voltage line running through her head.

When she stepped around the corner, she was hit with a full frontal blow, tendrils of pain tearing at her nerves. She clawed her way back around the corner, her arms responding with harsh painful jerks. Christ. The field was wrong. She'd become accustomed to the power of it entering her nervous system in its long alternating waves, but this one had been frenetic, the usual energies of it sharper like a chord with a single wrong note that sounded almost right but grew as it resonated, spoiling the entire chord.

"What's wrong with you?"

She sat with her back against the building, her skin pulsing from the damage. She tried to stand, stumbled, and fell.

"What was that?"

Her voice was distorted, echoing inside her skull. There had been a white box at the end of the street, in the central square, curved and open to the sky. Her ears popped, struck by the sound of Jacob's shoes scraping the bits of gravel and her lungs struggling for air.

Jacob looked around the corner. He should have been thrown back the same as she had been. When he turned back to her, he was smiling, excitement chasing away the wariness in his eyes.

"Don't you recognize it? That's the Gatherer. Three Rocks was the first community in the Yukon to get one."

A violent, reluctant understanding as the puzzle piece she had been refusing to acknowledge slammed into place. She leaned over and vomited in realization and revulsion. The Gatherer she had designed was small, compact, made to fit into a basement or a garage, and to draw energy well below the levels that would harm a human. That monstrosity in the square would be capable of drawing hundreds if not thousands of kilowatts out of the air.

She wiped her mouth.

"How long has it been here?"

A slight pinch on his smooth forehead, the brightness of the sky forming a halo around his head as she looked up at him.

"It came in the spring. Once the river was clear."

Six months and he was already showing symptoms. It had taken a year of testing the Gatherer before she had shown any deterioration.

She staggered to her feet and forced her cramped muscles to move. The road sloped upwards to a refuge of trees with several dozen curtained windows along the way. Her shoulders rose from the feel of their eyes on her as she passed. How many people waited behind those curtains too afraid to come out?

"Don't you want to see my dad?"

An earlier rain had carved a path in the sand on the road, the branches splitting and merging until they'd had enough volume to wash the sand through town and into the river. She wished the current were strong enough to take her with it, floating her out to sea, her body cleansed and vacant by the time salt touched its skin.

TWO

The lights of the railway crossing flashed in the darkness as the train clattered by, before the backdrop of Maria's reflection in the train's window descended back into darkness. The few passengers in the dim cabin slept, yet Maria resisted the gentle rock of the train, her gaze fixed outside the windows for the occasional yard light or headlights that broke the darkness.

The train's whistle blew, and they clattered through another crossing, more lights appearing as they drew closer to the coast. A few screens were lit on the backs of the seats and a digital sign scrolled advertisements at the front, the car and the sleeping passengers cast in a stark, restless light.

None of the passengers had noticed her when she'd boarded the train, and the foothills and most of the Rockies had passed while the cabin slept. Maria had been the sole witness to the few brilliant cities followed by diminishing stretches of emptiness. The larger patches of darkness would come once she turned north, the coordinates Havernal had given her placing Freeman closer to the Arctic Circle.

Maria's reflection was drawn and shadowed, the lights reaching only the ridge of her cheekbone and the brow above one eye, as if only part of her had boarded the train, the shadowed piece of her still back in Ottawa with Havernal. He had been weak, the hand that had held hers boney and dry like that of an old man. At one time, she could have held onto its warmth and strength forever.

A whoosh of air as the door between the cars opened, the vibrating hum of the train punching into the car. A man of around fifty beelined for the seat facing her on the diagonal. He wore a down vest over a worn khaki shirt, and he shifted and adjusted before settling into his seat. His boots were old and his jeans had the near black blue of a new pair. A civilian, yet she changed her position so she could see his reflection in the window clearly.

You won't be the only one looking for her.

Havernal had warned Maria as if she wouldn't know that there would be others with a vested interest in finding Freeman. The debates she had slogged through online, looking for any piece of evidence as to Freeman's location, had been endless. Some posts proclaimed Freeman to be a God and named the Gatherer a miracle. A few zealots claimed she was more important than Jesus. Each person had their own argument as to which group had been more devastated by the introduction of the Gatherer—oil and gas, renewables, terrorist groups—and which one was more likely to have carried out their revenge.

A second opening of the door, and the Electricline conductor stepped in. In his mid-thirties, he was fitter and had straighter shoulders than she normally associated with what was essentially a ticket taker. He nodded to her and the man before continuing on, resting his hands on each seat back as he passed, like a school bus driver checking off his charges.

"That's the third time."

The man craned his neck towards the conductor's retreating back.

"The third time he's been through the train."

"Is it?"

She had noticed the same thing. At least three passes through the cabin between every stop. The lights of a car stopped at a crossing came and went, the train a hurtling ball of momentum.

"They're checking for terrorists."

Irritation tightened across her shoulders at the ignorance of civilians who latched on to rumours and conspiracy theories with no real understanding of what was going on.

He drew in closer, his knee pressing into hers. His eyes were too wide, with a startling brightness.

"Al Qaeda. The Russians. Maybe the Chinese. It could be any of them."

True to her word, Freeman had released the Gatherer around the world, free to impoverished communities. It had changed people's lives overnight, moving from a subsistence level to starting small businesses, purifying water, and having computers and access to the internet.

The number of terrorist attacks had dwindled to their lowest levels in decades but the general population and nutcases like this guy had been less willing to give up their fear and apprehension, always believing the next attack was around the corner. She moved her knee away as the door to the next car slammed shut behind the conductor.

"Doesn't look like he found any."

The man nodded repeatedly, missing her sarcasm, his intense gaze locked on her.

"I'm Coulter."

He didn't offer his hand. No one did that anymore.

She nodded and didn't offer her name.

A single light appeared in the blackness, its pool illuminating a tiny farm yard that could have existed in any time. She watched its static simplicity as it passed out of sight behind them.

A jolt and she was flung forward, barely catching herself on the seat in front of her. There was a powerful pull in her gut as the brakes screeched, her hands braced against the seat. Blackness surrounded the windows.

When the force eased, she was on her feet, clambering over Coulter as he snapped forward from the recoil. Other passengers rubbed their heads in confusion after being woken. Using the backs of seats for support, she ran towards the front of the train, the windows still dark. There was nothing to explain why they were slowing down. She slid open the door between cars. The strike of cold, hard air hit before she stepped into the next car. The door didn't slide shut behind her and she turned, irritated that Coulter had followed her.

"Stay in your seat."

"I'm not a dog."

He pushed past her, falling against her as the train came to a sudden jarring stop. Using her as leverage, he got away sooner and, feeling ridiculous, she hurried after him. The few passengers craned their necks when they came in, their expectation turning to disappointment as they hurried past. She kept her attention on the windows for signs of light or movement as she catalogued the passengers. Not a single one was sick. A brief image flashed of when Havernal had first fallen ill. He'd been strong, measured and calm as they had discussed the phenomena.

Why some and not others?

Their unit had done studies and analyzed the data they could find.

There has to be a pattern.

Havernal's hand had trembled as he ran it through his hair, a symptom exhibited by around half of the sufferers. There hadn't been a pattern they could find. No underlying activity or location that could explain why some strong healthy people deteriorated into a wasted shell while others carried on. It had none of the contagion patterns of a typical disease.

The first glow of light shone outside the train, a low, orange flickering from flame. She pushed against the crowd at the front of the first car. Was there a fire in the engine? Was it that simple? The lights in the train were on, its systems running smoothly.

She had almost reached the front of the car when a woman carrying a torch appeared outside the window inside the train corridor's protective fence. She was middle-aged and stout, her gray hair cut in a bowl, a scarf tied tight around her neck. She walked with the slow casualness of a sightseer, lingering so the passengers would see her. A warning chill of fear down Maria's back.

"Open the emergency exit."

A man in short sleeves looked startled for a moment, saw the torch, nodded and pulled the first lever of the emergency exit. There was a rush of cold air as an alarm sounded. People streamed towards the exit and the pressure of the crowd eased. The woman climbed the bank of the tracks to stand within arm's reach of the window. Her face was so still she barely seemed alive, her eyes nearly lifeless. She drew her hand from her pocket and cocked her arm.

Maria ran, crouching against the expected rip of an explosion across her back. When it didn't happen, she glanced back, the car empty behind her, the woman's palm flat against the window. Maria recoiled at the woman's thin disjointed smile, like a damaged soldier that has taken refuge in their anger. The woman turned her head, like a dog that had heard its owner, and she was gone down the slope, the bobbing erratic torch marking her retreat towards the front of the train.

Angry shouts carried through the emergency door and Maria ran, instinctively pressing her arm against the reassuring bulk of the gun in its holster beneath her arm. Frozen, dried cornstalks crunched under her boots as her fingers touched down on cold, hard ground.

She ran close to the towering bulk of the train, through the spill-off light from the windows and into the shadow of the engine. The shouting had stopped and she pushed through the cluster of passengers. The conductor in his gray Electricline uniform faced off in front of a crowd of thirty men and women carrying rifles and burning torches. Most were hunting rifles, though there was at least one handgun. A single bearded man stood forward from the rest with the woman from the window behind him, the strange, lifeless smile on her lips. A massive combine, parked on the tracks, loomed over all of them, its green side gleaming in the train's powerful headlight.

"This is as far as you go."

The bearded man held a hunting rifle across his chest. It looked old, though likely powerful enough to do its job.

"The line is bought and paid for."

The conductor, or whatever he was, held his hands relaxed at his sides, the back of his uniform creased at the shoulders, an automatic revolver in a holster on his belt. This version of him made more sense than the amiable conductor taking tickets.

Most of the protesters wore muddied work boots and pants with worn coats on top. A smaller group stood thirty meters down the track, beyond the combine, their faces like pale ghosts with frightened eyes staring out of hollow sockets. The passengers murmured the word 'afflicted,' the name given to the sick as they snapped photos on their phones. Maria moved to the side of the crowd, away from the lenses.

"We aren't here tonight to let you contaminate our home."

"I got a schedule to meet."

"Get off the track!"

The voice came from behind her.

The bearded man spoke calmly, ignoring the outburst.

"You'll have to find a different route."

"Get your sorry asses off the track!"

Coulter was at her elbow, jabbing his finger at the crowd on the tracks. "You bunch of terrorists!"

There was a panicked murmuring behind her, the passengers stamping and shuffling like a herd of horses ready to spook.

The crowd on the track closed ranks.

"We're not moving."

"Federal law gives me the right to keep this train moving. Regardless of what stands in my way."

The front of the ElectricLine train had a steel plow on it, in the case of a cow or a tree blocking the railway line. She didn't know who would win if they tried to plow the combine off the track.

"Is that the same government that says the Gatherer isn't killing us?"

It was the woman who spoke up, stubborn and belligerent, a fight in her voice. The question hung above the shining rail line, filling the space between the conductor and the protesters.

The bearded man shook his head in reprimand and the woman clamped her mouth shut, glaring more ferociously at the train and its passengers. Some dairy farmers had reported losing their entire herds to the untreatable virus. Other bovine varieties were left untouched. It was the inconsistency that had made people so afraid. There was a movement from the group further down the tracks as a small, pale girl rushed towards them. She made only a few steps before she was pulled back. A group too frightened to leave their children at home.

"This is a major route west. This isn't the only train that will be coming through here."

The conductor's breath floated up through the beam of the light and escaped into the night above, as calm and unhurried as the man himself.

"We're prepared for that."

"Get off the track!"

Coulter waved a gun above his head and fired it into the air.

Maria lunged for him, taking out his legs as she yanked his arm, forcing his momentum down into the ground. He landed head first, the air bursting out of him like flour from a sack as she dug her knee between his shoulder blades. He squirmed, gasping with pain, and she eased off the pressure on his arm enough so that it wouldn't hurt if he remained absolutely still.

A piston hissed in the engine and blood pounded in her ears. A dozen guns pointed at her—the conductor's handgun, and every rifle from the blockade. Cornstalks snapped as the passengers fled back to the emergency exit, and the unarmed protesters peeked out from behind the combine. She lifted one hand in surrender as the other held Coulter's hand behind his back. His gun lay next to her knee.

The conductor stepped forward, gun still trained on her, and kicked the handgun towards the train. How easily she had taken out Coulter signalled military training as surely as his precise, controlled movements. Part of her settled. She understood this place, these people. Knew what to do and what not to.

"He's neutralized."

"Like hell." Coulter's voice was tight with pain.

She forced him up to his knees, resisting the urge to twist harder at his complaints.

With deliberate movements, the conductor picked up the gun from the ground and slid it into his holster. He slid his own into his belt and turned slowly, hands half raised. He spoke clearly and loud, his breath turning white as he spoke.

"We passed a junction three miles back. I can go back, take the Ashcroft line and rejoin the track at Basque. That work for you?"

The protesters' rifles held steady as Maria gripped Coulter's arms tighter. The protesters were ill-prepared and the conductor was giving in. It could have been the thin, wide-eyed children behind the combine or the knowledge that it was a fight he could win if he chose.

The engine ticked as the bearded man stared down the barrel of his gun. Every gun behind him was ready to follow his lead. Either this really was about keeping his people safe, or the conductor had made the wrong gamble.

With a nod, he lowered his rifle and the band around her chest loosened. There was a huff of disappointment from one of his group as they followed his lead. The tight ranks of the group behind the combine eased, and they expanded outside its protection. Several of the group leaned on others for support.

Maria had read the reports of the spreading numbers of the afflicted in the rural areas, with some of the first animal cases appearing in the upper Midwest in the cattle ranches of South Dakota—an area that Freeman had visited personally, glowing with benevolence as she had presented the shiny compact Gatherer, a gift to make their lives a little easier.

"All aboard!"

There was no one left to board, only her, her captive and the conductor on the ground. Coulter was panting hard and she eased further off the pressure on his arms, a strange burning from his skin.

The conductor extended a calloused palm towards her, sweat gleaming in the creases.

"I'll take your gun."

He would have seen it under her coat as easily as she had seen the training in his footsteps.

"I'm not a threat."

"You aren't getting back on my train if you're carrying it."

The protesters hadn't raised their rifles, but they watched from their positions in the same protective arc, the night a solid wall around them. She reached in slowly, the weight of the gun a security she didn't want to lose. It dug into her skin where she gripped the barrel as she laid it into his palm.

Keep a low profile. The fewer people that know you're on the move the better.

She was pretty sure this wasn't what Havernal had in mind, but she'd had to stop Coulter.

The conductor held the gun in his hand with two tucked in his belt as he turned back to the protesters. The group tensed, some of the men half-raising their guns. The conductor nodded once at the bearded man, who nodded back. He glanced disdainfully at her captive's bent shape.

"You can come with me. And bring him with you."

THREE

Coulter stumbled ahead of Maria, stopping several times on the way to the engine, bent double even though Maria no longer pinned his arm. The conductor walked behind them and she couldn't help feeling like a prisoner being taken into custody.

A set of steep, narrow steps and they were in the subdued warmth of the driver's compartment, the main light source the extensive bank of screens below the windows that wrapped around the forward half of the small room. Several bolts slid into place as the conductor locked the door and Coulter dropped into a black seat at the back of the room, next to the door that led back to the rest of the train. A tall, skinny blond stooped over the controls. His long fingers were more suited to a piano player, and they played over the screens and adjusted switches with the delicacy of a craftsman.

Maria stayed standing, her nerves too wired to let her sit. The conductor said something into a walkie-talkie below Maria's hearing before he slipped both Coulter's gun and hers from his holster and placed them in a cabinet flush with the side of the cab. The cabinet door was open only a moment before he locked it, but it was long enough for a view of significant fire power, including what couldn't have been a semi-automatic. He kept his gun in his holster.

Her agitation rose as her gaze slid to the protesters where they stood on the tracks, some of their torches having gone out. Volatile and inexperienced, she should have placed her bets with them and stayed on the ground. They looked small and frightened from the height of the compartment and she had the sudden fear that the men meant to plow through the bedraggled group.

With a deep hum under her feet the torches began to retreat and the empty track fell away, the powerful engine driving them back towards the junction.

The conductor turned to her from where he watched the process over the thin man's shoulder. The lightness in his step betrayed a formidable strength.

"Thanks for your help out there."

"You're welcome."

She felt a flicker of pride that barely ignited before it flickered out, wary of something in his tone.

"But next time stay in the fucking train."

She felt the hardening inside her, as she often did on missions, where she retreated deeper inside, letting her training and toughness take control. She imagined a veil over her face, letting the anger flow freely beneath it, even as she let her lips, cheeks, and eyes turn to glass.

"What are you doing on my train?"

The engine's vibrations ran up through her feet, pulling her into its resonance. She lifted one foot then the other, trying to break the connection, but the very walls were trembling, a deep, almost imperceptible frequency, as if the earth shook at its very core.

"Strictly as a passenger, sir. I'm on my way to Vancouver."

She had added the 'sir' intentionally. The flickering torches formed a small island of orange light beyond the cool beam of the headlight, its salvation growing weaker as they drew further away. He moved in closer and she forced herself to hold her ground. Up close his eyes were a darker gray than his uniform, his unshaven beard a shadow on his cheeks, and his tightly trimmed hair little more than bristles on a bare skull.

"A passenger who is a member of the military."

"Not anymore."

At least partially true, since only Havernal knew where she had gone.

A flicker of amusement showed in his bleak gaze as she engaged her legs against the pull of deceleration.

"We're approaching the switch."

The thin man had his hands on the controls, the spotlighted post of a railroad crossing coming into view on the largest screen.

"Once the engine is past the junction, activate the switch."

The man navigated the switch via the camera. She had seen soldiers like him before, kept on for their skills, yet slipping in and out of formal protocol as their focus drew them elsewhere. There were multiple cameras, judging by the number of different views he was using for the change. She wouldn't have thought it would be so difficult. Back up, flip the switch, go forward. Yet the man's creased forehead and hunched, tense shoulders suggested a much harder or at least critical maneuver.

"What is it?"

The conductor moved back to the console.

The man's gaze darted between screens as if he were wary of an attack. The footage of the surrounding fields showed frozen, barren emptiness, not even the light of a house in the distance.

Maria widened her feet for balance as the train slowed.

"Nothing sir."

He pulled a lever carefully towards himself.

"I'm just making sure."

Maria scanned the other screens, catching sight of a frozen image of her holding Coulter's hands. On the screen beside it, her military identification photo was displayed with her name, rank, and a large number of details that were too small to read. She felt the sudden tightness of the room, the space too small for all these people.

Without altering her stance, she broadened her search, her gaze flicking to screens on separate consoles. Three screens showed static images like that of a security camera. It showed the long interior of what had to be one of the cars, with two large crates secured to the floor. Armed soldiers stood at either side. This crew wasn't about protecting Electricline and its passengers. They were protecting that secured cargo. With enough military fire power that her palms began to sweat. She had missed clues she should have seen because she had expected this to be a passenger train.

You have to see what's really there.

Havernal's voice in her head, exasperated again.

Get out of your own head.

She'd been so busy thinking about him she hadn't noticed what kind of cars made up the train. Right in the middle there would be a freight car, probably small, made to look like a passenger car, but there would be fortifications if she had looked. The train coasted slowly along the rail, making no sound at all.

"We're past the junction."

The conductor lifted a microphone and made an announcement apologizing for the disruption, thanking them for their calmness, and saying they would be back on route shortly, once they changed tracks.

One of the guards on the screen nodded.

Maria looked for the light of the protesters yet their band had disappeared, leaving only the tracks splitting away from each other. The freedom of that open darkness would be so much preferable to this cramped dimness.

The train came to rest, and she swayed, momentarily off balance. She walked purposely to the door that led to the passenger car. In his seat next to the door, Coulter had slumped down, his head bent and to the side at a painful angle.

"Stay where you are."

The conductor was backlit by the glow of the console. The driver bent beside him as he repeatedly activated the same switch, his gaze focused on a schematic showing on a single screen. The view of the fields showed nothing but darkness in all directions.

"I was going back to my seat."

He shook his head and pointed to her frozen image on the screen, deftly touching it so the writing grew larger.

"Maria Kowalski. Special Operations Task Force."

He smiled.

"Current status—Absent without leave."

Tiny pricks of cold spread over her shoulders. The glare of the screens hurt her eyes.

"I'm on special assignment."

He laughed.

"First, you got off the train, then you subdue the crazy guy, and then come into the driver's cab. And the whole time you're AWOL?"

"I am no danger to this mission."

"That I agree with."

The train stopped, the headlight shining on a bare forest to the left, open darkness to the right.

"The switch isn't responding."

The conductor's face hardened in irritation. His second in command's bursts of typing were the only movement in the room.

"Can you reset it?"

The man pressed buttons, changed the camera angles and shook his head.

"It's an old model that hasn't been upgraded."

The conductor leaned into the screen and Maria looked at the security screen. The guards held the guns in low ready mode. Two large cube containers, twice their height, towered over them. On the closest one was the unmistakeable open hands symbol of the Gatherer.

A moment of incomprehension at the size of the crates. None of the Gatherers she had seen had even come close to that size and hadn't needed armed protection. She tried to look closer but there were only the upturned hands stamped on the outside. Agitation rippled across her nerves as her body shifted to high gear, aware of every detail and movement in the small room and on that screen. What the hell was the military doing with two oversized Gatherers? She dragged her gaze from the screen before the conductor remembered her.

"Sit down. And don't move."

Maria took her seat next to the foul smelling Coulter, cataloguing the information she had gathered on her way back to her seat. The door to the rest of the train lay behind her; the door she had entered through that led directly outside had a multi-stepped opening process.

The seat was hard against her back, the air in the room hot and stuffy, and she felt as if she were inside the barrel of a gun about to be fired into oblivion. The streamlined train clicked and shifted around her, uneasy at rest, the energy of the batteries that powered it flowing through the entire line of cars, searching for a way out.

Coulter was slumped in the corner. She had always marveled at and hated people like him. Serene when someone else was in charge.

The driver typed fast on his keyboard, interrupting the flurry to change viewpoints and consult an on-screen procedural manual. After several minutes of dreadful quiet, the conductor turned only half away from her as the driver straightened and lifted his hands from the keys.

"It's not responding. We'll have to do it manually."

Maria remained absolutely still, pushing back into her seat and making herself as small as possible.

The conductor put on a heavy parka, checked his gun in his holster and rewatched the video on the screen that showed a relaxed engineer demonstrating how to manually change a switch on a bright sunny day. His brow was furrowed and a lethal darkness had descended across his features. She dropped her shoulders and tucked in her legs as the conductor made a final check with the driver.

"Do you want one of the guys from the back?"

The man's gaze shifted to Maria, checking how much she knew. Maria maintained a neutral gaze out the window, on the web of bare branches highlighted in the headlight.

The two men lowered their voices. The camera views showed a sparse forest that offered little cover and an open, wilted field that offered even less.

The conductor moved to the outside door, passing close enough she could have grabbed his hand. She was about to release her breath, when strong, rough fingers grabbed her wrist, cool metal clicked around it, and the conductor clipped the other handcuff around Coulter's.

"I'm not that stupid."

His stale breath was warm on her cheek.

"I didn't think you were."

Cold air flowed over her as the door opened and the conductor passed through, only to have the hot air return fast and close when the door slammed behind him.

"Coulter!"

The driver had returned to his screens, his back turned.

She pushed Coulter's shoulder. His head fell forward, his weight pulling on her wrist where they were attached. He would have fallen forward off their bench if they weren't handcuffed together. She grabbed his shoulder with her free hand and shoved him upright. She had to strain to hold him straight.

Bile rose in her throat as she pressed her fingers into Coulter's greasy neck. His hand followed hers.

"All clear."

The driver spoke into the walkie-talkie.

She sat back, trying to get distance from the lifeless body, and it came with her, its weight continuing to follow where it was led. She forced herself to breathe and not panic. She had seen dead bodies before, it wasn't going to hurt her.

"Hey!"

The driver hunched over his screens. The conductor stood on one of the screens, gray and grainy bent over a low metal box. He looked repeatedly from side to side.

She yelled again.

He glared at her and turned back to his screens.

"Can you unlock this?"

She held up her handcuffed wrist and Coulter's. The smell of Coulter was intensifying, his gases oozing out through his skin.

"This guy is dead."

The man's mouth had dropped open when he turned this time, a decidedly unmilitary expression. The conductor reached his hand into the metal box and Maria took the opportunity to scream.

"Get him off!"

She pushed at the dead man's chest and tried to pull her wrist through the handcuff. The metal scraped open her skin and she pulled harder.

"Shut up!"

He had his back to her, focussed on the screen as the conductor gave a thumbs up.

"Help me!"

She stumbled towards him, dragging the body with her. Coulter's boots scraped along the floor. The driver typed a few more keys and pressed a button on the console. The conductor started closing up the box.

"Okay, okay."

He reached for his chain of keys, hardly even glancing at Coulter.

"Give me a second."

Maria sniffled and gulped as he turned the key in its lock, lifting her hand to strike him in the throat as the handcuff fell. He stumbled backwards onto the console, unable to breathe. She scooped up the handcuff and followed. He lifted his arm to protect himself, but he was a controller, not a soldier, and she had him handcuffed to the rail along the wall before the conductor had finished closing the box. She slipped his key ring into her pocket as she strode to the exterior door and slid the bolt into place, a lock strong enough to stop an armed attacker.

The driver wheezed, trying to talk. She moved to the console. Despite all the screens the system wasn't that complicated. Forward. Back. Stop. Fortunately he had left it in park. The conductor had left the screen and was picked up on another walking back to the engine. She hesitated for only a moment before sliding the train into gear and felt as much as heard the engine kick in. Once you went AWOL you had already reached the end of the line. She might as well find out what lay beyond it.

The conductor had begun to jog. Against the wall, the driver was making frantic gagging noises. His legs lashed out as he tried to kick her.

She accelerated harder and a shimmer rippled through the frame of the train. She planted her feet as a surge of adrenaline cleared out her veins. One of the most powerful engines ever made. The conductor slid out of camera range. By now he would have reached the door. Faint clicking noises sounded from outside, quickly lost in the growing hum of the engine as it picked up speed.

The engine crossed the switch, smoothly transitioning onto the line going north. There was a quick flash of the conductor running and stumbling in the light from one of the passenger cars and then he was gone. At least he'd been smart enough to let go.

"You are . . ."

The man's voice was barely a croak.

". . . so much trouble."

The headlight showed a clear straight line of track stretching into the night.

"I could say the same about you."

She glanced at the images of the guards who had stood down now that the train was moving. How long until they knew something had changed? She pressed the lever forward far enough that the engine trembled beneath her as it kicked into gear. The thrill of being in motion coursed through her, merging with her adrenaline so that it felt as if this surging, powerful path had been exactly what she was meant to do all along. She smiled, ignoring her photo that stared sullenly out of the screen, willing the words in her description to have nothing to do with her.

Past the next junction the line curved south, taking her away from her destination. She stepped over Coulter's body and barred the door to the rest of the train. On screen a tiny icon of a train made its way westward, the territory she was aiming for a large gray area at the top of the display.

FOUR

Blue shot into the woods the moment the bow of the canoe touched shore, the outline of the cabin and Storm's workshop forming darker shadows in the dusk of the clearing. It had taken hours to paddle back from town, the current pushing relentlessly against the bow, the bends of the river changing and morphing in the fading light so that she thought she'd reached the final turn multiple times.

Her legs were stiff and weak as she dragged the canoe up on shore. The silver suit chafed against the raw skin under her arms where the seams had rubbed with every stroke, its warmth against the deepening chill an inadequate consolation for the raw flesh.

She dropped her backpack inside the door of her workshop, made her way to her workbench by feel, and lifted down the case for the satellite phone. Her fingers burned as she powered it on and a searing ripple of current ran up her forearm. She typed in the number and pressed send before stepping into the protective enclosure she used when she ran her experiments.

Her message would be sent to a service that would forward the message to a different service. It would then be forwarded to a designated phone lying on a desk somewhere that would automatically notify her mother's assistant at the Gatherer's headquarters that her dry cleaning was ready. And sometime in the next hour her mother would call.

She lowered herself to the ground to wait, being careful not to lean against the cool smoothness of the aluminum walls. Set up as a Faraday cage, the radiation from the phone would be drawn along its path, leaving her in an inert shell at its centre.

Her arms weighed heavily at her sides from the hours of paddling, and hunger gnawed at her hollow stomach as her mind traced the elaborate communications path they had set up. She identified all the places where it could fail and which would explain why the phone wasn't ringing. She closed her eyes against the fatigue. As always the first images that rose in her thoughts were of her team and the few precious years when they had been together in the lab.

Callan had been the first one to arrive in the mornings. She would find him bent over the Gatherer's structure, his large worker hands carefully adjusting something in the braces supporting the crystals. It had been his job to collect the materials that would support the crystals without interfering with the sensitive Gathering process.

She and Daniel would arrive together, having come from one of their barely used apartments. They should have moved in together and saved the extra rent, but there had always been something more important to do at the lab.

Jana would stroll in mid-morning, coffee in hand, and slide into her chair without a word. Her ability to speak arrived somewhere around noon right about the time that Ari would wake up from the grungy couch next to his aquarium where he had fallen asleep again in the early hours of the morning.

It was when they would be finally all settled in the lab, working at their respective areas, that the brain power of the five would merge into something larger than all of them and the wonder at what they were creating would overtake her.

"Getting all misty-eyed on us again?"

Daniel often teased her, for it wasn't the first time her wonder had overflowed, fed by the closeness of the group and their ability to draw off each other's energy. Sometimes the ideas and breakthroughs came so fast, it was as if they were merely players orchestrated by some higher force. God or creativity or pooled energy whatever you wanted to call it. It was so palatable she often believed she would see it shimmering in the air around them.

"Storm."

The tone of Jana's voice when she'd called her over had been unmistakable. Surprise, excitement, and fear all mixed together so Storm had known even before they had all gathered around the convoluted crystal structure—for the others had heard the same note in Jana's voice—what they would find.

Several green bars glowed on the battery's display, indicating the first time they had been able to store the energy the crystals were collecting.

None of them had said anything as Jana had checked the connections, ushered them out of the test area, and ran the test again.

When the three bars had glowed green again, Storm, Daniel and Ari had all looked over their shoulders in unison, towards the unlocked door that led down three flights of the empty warehouse, as if the world's lens that had been so oblivious to them had suddenly turned in their direction.

"What's the temperature of the supports?"

It had been one of Callan's and Jana's biggest hurdles to control the temperature of any materials that came into contact with the concave dish. In their first designs the metals had melted into formless lumps, wood being the only substance that could come in contact with the Gathering process. The wood was at room temperature and they had all stared at the concave dish surrounding the crystal lattice in silent shock. It had been one thing to dream of finding free energy, quite another to see it come to fruition.

"What do we do now?"

It was Ari who had finally broken the silence, the fear and astonishment that had rendered them all speechless so evident in his voice that she had laughed and the others had followed. Deep guttural laughs that had banished any consequences that their creation might bring and left only the pure joy of their success. Soon they had been jumping around the lab like football players in the end zone, releasing the months of work and exhausted bickering, all of it suddenly worthwhile. Their excitement had filled the lab to the rafters, an insurmountable force drawing them inwards.

It was this moment that Storm remembered most. The sweetness of success strong on their lips. All of them healthy and brilliant and part of something larger than themselves. And so certain that what they were doing was right.

When their exuberance had finally calmed, they'd sat squished on the couch, bathed in the light from the aquarium, each of them having some new idea on how they could improve the Gatherer's performance and bring it closer to being a viable product. For from the beginning, that had been understood: this would be released for free, distributed into the marketplace before the government or OPEC got word of it. A small, simple invention that would change the world. She and Daniel had caught each other's eye while they had talked, their connection as strong as it had ever been.

The group had left the lab together that night, an outing to the pizza place as exciting as it would get since they all wanted to be at the lab early the next day. Daniel must have had his suspicions that it might not all go as they planned, for he'd carried the delicate crystal structure with him, tucked carefully in discarded packing foam inside the lunch box with the Buzz

Lightyear sticker. The others hadn't noticed him taking it, so wrapped up in their ideas and how they were going to spend all the money they made. Callan and Ari had been debating between Lamborghinis and Bugattis as they'd descended the stairs, despite the fact that neither of them drove.

Daniel had slid the padlock into place, the first time anyone had bothered with the steel clamp, and Storm had made some kind of joke about the value of the couch and the scavenged parts of their lab. Daniel had laughed and slung his arm across her shoulders in a rare show of public affection. They'd trailed behind the other three as they descended the stairs, weighed down by the lunch box tucked under Daniel's arm, though in the physical world it barely weighed anything at all.

Storm woke with her cheek cold against the concrete floor and a deep chill along her back and thighs. For a moment she was confused about where she was until the cylindrical form of her cage took shape in the flat light from the satellite phone's display screen.

She clambered to her feet, veering to the right so that her shoulder brushed against the side of the enclosure, a sharp burn as the current momentarily chose her as a path to ground. She stumbled away, her hand pressed against the burned flesh, the agitation of the phone's signal vibrating along her skin as she stared down at a blank screen. In a swell of anger and frustration, she powered it down and tossed it back into its case.

That had been the deal when she'd come out here. If someone had found her or if there was any emergency, she just needed to call. It would be worth risking the fields if it was an emergency. There would be an immediate response and help would be on its way. She'd never had to use it, though she had opened the case enough times during the winters when she had been willing to endure the burn of the radiation if it would have eased the ache of loneliness. The fear of being found was what kept her from turning it on, for the press of the button could have revealed to the world where she was hiding.

She navigated her way to the door in the dark, the remnants of her most recent experiments taunting her from the workbench. It was as if her ability to successfully create anything had abandoned her the moment she'd set foot in the Yukon.

The door swung inward when she turned the latch and she stumbled back. Blue's dark shape rose to its feet and pushed in towards her, rubbing against her and circling her legs. The air pushing in behind him carried the bite of winter.

"Sorry."

She touched the hard patch of fur between his ears, her cold fingers lingering in the warmth emanating from him.

She crossed to the cabin beneath a brilliant blanket of stars, the height of it making the clearing smaller, the outlines of the struggling trees like those of a miniaturized landscape.

Blue entered ahead of her when she opened the door to the cabin, grateful for the cool inertness of the sanctuary created by the shielded walls and windows. She stripped out of the silver suit in the darkness, only lighting the oil lamp she kept at the door once she was free of the suit's restrictions.

She touched the lighted match to the newspaper of her pre-laid fire, waiting only long enough to make sure it caught and it had enough wood to last the night. She tried not to think of her depleted wood supply that wouldn't get her through the coming winter.

The sheets were cold on her bed and she called Blue to her. A single turn and he curled up against her, his heat pushing back the cold. She adjusted the blankets over them and with her last bit of energy, turned the oil lamp to off.

FIVE

Maria splashed along the edge of the creek, her feet ankle-deep in icy water. The initial shock of pain had receded to an aching numbness and she looked ahead to the domed shape of the bridge that spanned the creek. She had been splashing in and out of the water for more than two hours, traveling beneath a canopy of dense forest, every moment expecting the sounds of a chase behind her. The driver from the train wouldn't be able to follow her, but the two guards with the guns would be able to track her down without breaking a sweat.

The image of those monstrous Gatherers on the train never left her. She should have stayed to prevent them from being delivered to their destination instead of leaving the train where the track turned south.

In the end it had been Havernal's words that had made the decision.

Make sure you get there first.

The water ran fast against the side of the bridge and there was no path along the bank for her to follow. She climbed carefully up, the grasses slippery in the morning dew, and emerged into a lighter, wider view of open fields bordered by thick patches of forest. A thin mist hung over the fields, dampening any sound. To the east, a band of yellow marked the horizon. She slid down the bank on the other side of the bridge, a strange warmth in her feet as she returned to the creek.

It was Freeman who would know how to stop the disease the Gatherer was creating. It could be as easy as a small, simple fix. Or even a limit to the size of the device so that it stayed below some limit of acceptability for humans. What worried Maria was why Freeman had been absent when rumours of the Gatherer's connection to the plague gained strength every day. Maria had read more than one post online that argued the connection, and Freeman's absence only fueled the possibility that it was true. Maria wondered whether she would find Freeman at all when she arrived at the coordinates. Or whether Freeman's death would explain the absence.

There was a movement along the bank, the animal's body hidden, its movements marked by the disturbed path it left through the tops of the individual blades of grass. It was hard to imagine the two men pursuing her without breaking the silent morning. Yet if they were good they could be within sight and she wouldn't know. She checked behind her, the bridge almost out of sight behind branches that bowed over the creek and a bend that twisted slowly south. She would need to turn north soon, though she was reluctant to leave the creek's protection. The GPS on her watch already indicated she had gone too far west.

The sound of splashing came from up river and she felt the iciness of the water rise to her chest. She strained to hear above the low murmur of the water pushing past her ankles. Had they circled ahead of her? She had seen no one since leaving the train, the rising hills and intensifying forests the only witnesses to her flight.

A gunshot cracked open the morning and she ran stumbling towards the bank, the water dragging at her feet. She tripped, her hands sliding through water before she recovered. On the solid ground of the bank she ran faster, until the steepness of the bank slowed her and she scrambled up, her hands clawing at partly frozen dirt, grasping at stalks of grass that broke off in her hands.

Another shot rang out and she heard splashing below her. She threw herself over the top of the bank. They had been so close—how had she not heard them? She risked a glance behind her, expecting the barrel of a gun sighting her back.

A deer, blood running from its left flank, hobbled through the water, the white light of its tail bright above the stain of blood. It paused, one ear cocked backwards upstream, the other flickering downstream, then towards her on the bank. Its head lifted in her direction, the dark bullet eyes meeting hers.

At the sound of voices upstream, she and the deer locked in an exchange that seemed to ask, *you or me?* With a leap it was gone, bounding downstream towards the bridge and the safety of the forest she had left behind.

The sleekness of the creek's surface was as it had been, any disturbance her feet and the deer's hooves had made absorbed back into the flow. The voices grew louder and Maria crouched behind the upturned roots of a fallen tree, her hand resting on the chilled wetness of the wood. The first man wore a ball cap and a hunting vest over an expansive gut. A smaller hunter, in a bright orange cap, followed. She tried to imagine that these could be the men from the train but the transformation would have been too great, the belly under the man's shirt and his thick jowls all too real.

They stood in the place she had been, the water running below the tops of their rubber boots as they lit cigarettes. The larger man seemed to be in no hurry, the smoke rising lazily from his cigarette as the water parted around their boots. The shorter man had a pointed, narrow face, his cheeks hollowing out with each draw of the cigarette. He smoked faster and flicked ashes, wanting to be moving.

A piercing ache shot through Maria's feet as the first flow of warm blood reached the numb flesh, and she bit her lip as the pain gathered strength. She opened her mouth to soften the sound of her laboured breathing. The smaller man lifted his head, his gaze panning the top of the river bank. She didn't move as he dropped his cigarette and lifted his rifle. As the barrel of the gun panned the bank, the rush of blood from her pounding heart radiated the pain of her feet into her shins.

The taller man took a final drag of his cigarette and lifted his rifle across his chest, his gaze focused on the creek beyond the bridge where the deer had disappeared. With surprising grace, the smaller man stepped towards the bank below her, his steps flowing soundlessly with the river, his gun trained on her tangle of roots. He would have to lower the gun at the steep section of the bank and she could escape then, if it wasn't for his buddy providing backup from the centre of the river.

He stepped up onto the bank and she wished she had gone with the deer. Wide open fields lay behind her, the top of the bank completely exposed for more than a mile off.

The larger man moved several steps downstream, stooping to see through the opening of the bridge. The man with the gun trained on her tangle of roots had reached the mid-point on the bank. She had a flash of hiding in the grass during hide and seek as a kid and the terror of knowing she would be found. A slightly higher mound of earth lay further upstream next to a group of bushes. If she crawled behind the trunk of the fallen tree she could run to its shelter without being seen. Maybe. She gripped the root, saying a brief prayer to Havernal and all the people who needed her to stay alive.

One. Two. Three.

She dropped to her stomach, her elbows pulling her forward through sharp blades of grass. There was a grunt from the man below her, the crack of a gunshot, and a cry from below.

She rammed her elbows into the dirt, pulling faster, waiting for a second shot, the butt of a rifle in her back, or the sudden pain of a bullet wound through the adrenaline.

She was near the end of the log, ready to rise to a crouch when a second gunshot echoed into the morning's quiet. Further downstream. On the other side of the bridge. She stopped mid-crouch and dared to look down to the creek bed. As empty as when she and the deer had fled, the water appearing to flow faster and smoother as it pursued the two men.

She shook with the beat of her heart, her panting low and shallow. The sky had lightened, emerging as a clear, pale blue. The sounds of splashing came down the creek and she had a brief moment of sorrow for the deer. She checked the river again and rose to a half-crouch.

She moved away from the lip of the embankment and ran parallel to the river. After a hundred paces, she turned north, rising out of her crouch and letting her breathing ease into full deep breaths. Her feet ached with the blood pounding through them, and she relished the pain and its confirmation that she was alive.

SIX

Maria breathed in deeply as she stepped onto the deck, the air's cold sharpness stripping away the hot stuffiness of her cabin. The air was still, the night over the ocean and boat in full darkness but for the lights on deck and the small town where they had stopped to pick up passengers. Her eyes were heavy, the cold doing nothing to enliven her dull, sluggish head, and she leaned over the rail, turning her face north to the wind.

A gull perched on the ship's rail and she was surprised it was there, the other gulls having departed when the passengers went inside. Its featureless gaze had hovered above her for most of the afternoon, dipping closer and floating farther back until with a few flaps it would pull itself back into the slipstream. She would like to have believed that it had waited for her and that this was the reason it hadn't screeched and dove for the scraps of bread the other passengers had offered. At one point she had reached towards it, and with a flick of its wing it had dipped away, its black eye unaltered, its beak pointed straight into the wind.

Cold crept along her skin as the work of the diesel engine emanated out through the hull as the ferry maneuvered into the small port. She hadn't felt the rumble of an engine in months, and its low vibrations grounded her to the deck. Only a few services had access to diesel these days, its use severely restricted once the Gatherer had established itself as the shining solution to greenhouse gas emissions. Only larger airplanes and a few boats had access to the strictly controlled substance. She had seen a digital sign at the terminal announcing the replacement of the ferry with a new electric version in the new year.

The gull's claws gripped the metal as it tucked its head into its chest. The light gleamed in the blackness of the bird's eye, and she had no idea if it watched her or not. When she moved closer, it shifted its feet away, its wings partially opening to show its discontent at being disturbed.

The port they had stopped in was less of a town than a single shack, its dark windows reflecting the ferry's image back at them. A single yellowed light cast a murky glow onto the sloping forest behind it and down onto the flatbed truck that was lined up to board. No sign indicated where they had stopped, an unreadable faded poster on the building the only evidence of what might have been the port's name.

Being careful not to disturb the bird, she looked back over the stern to where the flatbed's front tires had just crossed onto the ferry. A whiff of diesel floated on the wind as the stern dipped under its weight, pushing Maria into the rail, the deck stabilizing as the truck moved further in.

Its cargo was tightly strapped, the outline beneath the tarps square and straight. A draft of warm exhaust intensified the smell. Diesel vehicles had been officially retired six months prior, and she leaned out to get a better look at the tractor's side. No markings or government insignia identified where it had come from or whether it was authorized to transport the tightly controlled substance.

She stepped back from the rail, out of sight of the older crew member that solemnly followed the truck's progress. She was near the top of the British Columbia coast and that load of diesel barrels wasn't anywhere near the officially regulated supply channels. Her alert system clicked on, for the loading in the middle of the night and the small roster of passengers pointed to the Diesel Train—an aging, violent group that held the general belief that the Gatherer was either the devil's work or an instrument of the government to control their lives, and most likely both. She backed further away from the rail and when she was a safe distance turned to face into the wind. She rounded into a hard, wide chest.

She reacted instinctively, facing her assailant, her weight shifting to her toes and half lifting her hands. A nanosecond before she struck out, her brain kicked in. He was one of the crew she had seen on deck with the other passengers, stocky, round-faced and easygoing.

"Sorry if I scared you."

He didn't look at her raised hands but she knew he'd noticed her response. She lowered her hands and retreated to the rail as the ferry's gate closed.

"I wasn't expecting anyone."

With a trembling surge they were free of the pier, the engines pushing them out into open water. Her pulse refused to settle as the vibrations grew.

He laid his forearms on the rail where the gull had been, his bare hands hanging over the water, a hip cocked to one side as if he were at a rodeo watching a show.

"Did the stop wake you?"

She leaned her forearms on the rail, feigning the same casualness.

"I was already awake."

She realized her error immediately, as much as telling him she had seen what the transport carried.

"What was the name of that last town?"

He picked something off his lip and flicked it out over the water.

"It's hardly big enough to call it a town."

He turned his back to the water and took in the full breadth of the ferry for a long minute. He was older than she'd thought, his round cheeks having masked the loosening of skin around his ears and neck. He moved lightly, his rumpled uniform not hiding the easy strength more common in a younger man.

The moon passed out from behind a cloud, washing the ocean and deck in a still, blue light as she tried to gauge how much trouble she was in. Most passengers wouldn't have noticed or cared what was being loaded, but through her unit's work on energy security, she had known immediately, and her reaction had shown it.

"When will we reach Murdoch?"

Her voice sounded shaky and she cursed her body's refusal to stand down. He gazed west into the horizon where neither the end of the sky nor ocean were visible.

"We should be on time, barring any major storms."

"Is there bad weather coming in?"

Her voice sounded strained, doing nothing to convince him she was just an idle traveler.

He shook his head, his gaze still on the horizon as if there was something to see besides darkness. She prayed there wouldn't be a storm or fog, anything that would delay her in getting off the boat.

"What's taking you to Murdoch? You got family there? I know most everyone in town. Let me guess. The Pukkinens? Or maybe the Vasals? Unless you're by marriage, so could be the Hamlins or the Barretts?"

He had bantered with the other passengers, teasing them about their travel plans, cajoling them into telling him about their lives. Even facing her, his expression was unreadable: a slightly mocking grin, the shadow that had covered his face not having lifted from his eyes.

"Am I close?"

His uniform was creased at the elbows, worn more than one shift without being changed.

"Not family."

He frowned, pursing his lips. The same act she had seen with the other passengers. What would this group do if they found out who she was? She needed to hold her tongue. This group believed vehemently that the Gatherer was the devil's work and its link to the plague would only justify their brutal, unhinged violence.

"There isn't much else in Murdoch. Come on, you have to tell me where you're going, if only to satisfy my curiosity."

The gull had reappeared, floating far enough off the side that it was more of a flicker of white in the darkness than the shape of a bird.

"Sea kayaking."

"This time of year?"

She lifted her chin into the wind that blew cold off the bow.

He watched her, appraising, and for a moment the easygoing mask slipped away, leaving the focused tightness of his interrogation. Displaced water churned against the ferry's side, a white writhing strip against the black depths.

"I'm not afraid of the cold."

He nodded, his gaze casually falling to her shoulders and thighs.

"I believe that."

She stepped back from the rail, even as the bird dipped further out to sea, showing her an escape route if she were only to follow its lead.

"I should turn in."

"You can't go yet! I hardly know anything about you."

He was good, and she still wasn't sure how much trouble she was in.

"It's late."

She tilted her head towards the bow and Murdoch somewhere in the darkness ahead.

"And it will be an early morning."

He frowned with disappointment as she stepped further away, her senses tuned to any shifts in balance or readying of his muscles.

"You sure you won't stay?"

She turned into the wind with an apologetic grin as if she really were sorry she had to leave. She hunched her shoulders, breathing easier as she put distance between them. She would have liked to keep walking off the boat and onto the dark shore, whatever dangers might be waiting for her there preferable to taking her chances here with the diesel crew now that she had seen their cargo. At the door, she paused to take a final breath, the crew member watching her from the rail.

She nodded goodnight, hoping to look like another tired passenger heading off to bed.

The panicked beating of her heart was amplified in the narrow corridor, and she heard nothing but its heightened rhythm as she walked between the muffled walls, even the sound of the door closing behind her a distant clang. She checked over her shoulder for his stocky frame but the corridor was empty, nothing but the blank smoothness of the moulded walls and the warning on the back of the door to be careful of the wind.

* * * *

Clouds hung low on the coast, pushing the ceiling close to the water so that the ferry streamed into Murdoch in a narrow band between water and sky. Maria squinted against the glare, her sleepless eyes stinging in the growing light. She hung close with the other passengers as they waited to disembark, the pack and few belongings she had purchased before boarding heavy on her shoulders. She hadn't seen the crew member who had questioned her on deck, and she lifted her gaze to the shrouded mountains and gazed out at the lifeless ocean in an adequate imitation of someone who had come to see the sights. The escape to shore was so close her feet ached to touch the solid ground.

There were only a dozen other passengers, most of them looking as tired and disgruntled as she did after her torturous night below deck. She lowered the zipper on her parka to clear the remaining hot stuffiness and loosened the straps on her pack to allow the air into her sleeves, just like any overheated traveller who was enjoying the morning air. She noted the three trucks parked crosswise on the exit lanes, as if the three men that hovered restlessly at the front fenders had gathered for a tailgate party. The only other detail from her short glance was the disciplined stance of one of the men and the purposeful turn of his head as he surveyed the area. She would have liked the security of her gun beneath her arm, but there had been no time to break the locks when she'd left the train.

The deck vibrated beneath them as the ferry backed into its slip, white, agitated water boiling up around the stern. The town was larger than their stop in the night, stretching back from the boardwalk that lined the docks, with an aged clock tower rising out of the downtown, houses climbing the slopes of the mountain, and the only way inland a valley that split the mountains a half mile up.

Maria checked over her shoulder and found the man from last night chatting with a rumpled, gray-haired local next to the barred exit. He winked at her, the playfulness of it doing nothing to ease the sense that she was being watched and that she couldn't get to the safety of the shore fast enough.

She followed calmly as the passenger gate was opened, the man wishing passengers good journeys and godspeed like a tour guide on a vacation cruise. Several cars scooted out of the ferry below, bumping up onto the land, before skimming past the three trucks. She was almost at the exit when the engines stopped, the rumble replaced by a tighter grind below where the transport's grill had emerged out of the hold, its engine straining as it got its load moving.

"Have a good trip."

He hadn't bothered to smile, falling in behind her as she walked down the plank. She lifted her gaze to the clouds breaking up on the mountains, and looking everywhere but at the transport and the three trucks that had come to meet it. His boots shook the exit ramp, so close it felt like he would run her down. The smell of diesel was everywhere, coming from the transport's cargo, not the ferry's engines. She walked faster, a tourist eager to get on her journey, coming up against the painful slowness of the older couple in front of her, imagining she could feel the man pushing against her pack.

"Where's your ride?"

His voice was flat and sounded close enough to be almost touching her. The three pickups moved in, setting up to accompany the transport as she gauged the distance to the terminal and the steepness of the hill into town, noting the clutter of ships and cargo further down the boardwalk.

When her foot touched ground, she moved left around the couple hugging their ride, even as the man grabbed her pack from behind.

She twisted away and slammed into a teenage girl on the right.

"Hey! Watch it!"

The man yanked the pack and Maria keeled backwards until she wrenched open the buckles and the pack flew backwards. She ran, regaining her balance with each step, male voices shouting behind her. She left the protection of the other passengers and ran across open space, away from the bark of a command, waiting for the crack of a rifle or the shock of a bullet. The terminal and the boat warehouse lay thirty metres ahead. Boots pounded the pavement behind her, moving fast. She surged faster, the strong, tight power of her stride propelling her forward.

She had always been a fast runner. Her short legs were so fast the older kids had never been able to catch her, and it was one of the things she'd become known for in her unit. Her ability to run as fast as, if not faster, than the men was what had gained their early respect. She never felt better than when the ground flew beneath her feet, her soles barely touching earth.

The boots got closer and a second pair added itself to the first on her right. At the terminal she faked right before ducking left, running fast past benches and tourist plaques. Her boots rang hollow on the wood boardwalk, the pounding behind her like the crash of thunder. The rows of wood planks stretched before her. She pushed faster, reveling in her strength and the fleeting touch of her feet to the ground as the footsteps behind her faltered, then slowed.

She would have liked to give the fading men the finger for their underestimation of her. She imagined it instead, grinning, as the boardwalk ended and the echo of wood changed to the crunch of gravel. The path along the shore narrowed and she ran through the thick stench of trapped water against the wharf. The coastline stretched ahead, mist veiling the rounded hills above the gray water. An alleyway opened up and she turned, slowing to a fast, steady pace as she wound her way through the empty streets. She had been lucky they hadn't used their guns. Either the other passengers or the tractor full of diesel coming off the ferry must have restricted what the men could do.

The streets grew wider as she drew away from the docks, past locked doors of unopened shops, choosing laneways over streets. She left her pursuers far behind as the commercial section fell away and she moved into the sleeping quiet of residential streets, the occasional staccato barking of a dog the only notice of her passing.

At the top of the hill, where a street ended and the land began its climb upwards to the mountains, she stopped, breathing hard and exhilarated. The docks were hidden by the higher buildings of downtown, the tall structures smudged against the backdrop of the ocean by the morning mist.

She imagined the men scouring the alleys, searching for her hiding spot, not thinking that she could run so far or so fast. The boat's horn sounded far below, yet it felt close, as if she should be standing at the rail watching the wake froth and churn against the dock as she and it pulled away.

She would miss the sleeping bag in her pack and the food she had collected for the trip, but the men rifling through her belongings would find only the gear of a lone traveler planning to explore the North.

She turned her back on the town and the boat sliding up the coast. A footpath continued from the end of the road, winding up, and her first steps felt light and sure on the packed dirt. Freeman was out here somewhere, hoarding the knowledge that Maria needed. The same way she had from the beginning. A goose honked from above, part of a straggling v-formation of Canadian geese flying across the dead gray sky, heading north.

SEVEN

Birds dove from the tops of the dated buildings, their circular flights forming a frenzied, silent cloud above the white bulk of the Gatherer. Maria stretched her leg muscles, her heels aching with broken blisters, scanning the main street for a grocery store she might find a dumpster behind, or a restaurant ready to close that would have food they were willing to spare. Several of the larger birds, some kind of dove, lay dead or injured on the ground and she considered plucking one clean and cooking it over a fire down by the river, but she wasn't quite there yet.

The birds swooped and careened in a strange, erratic pattern through the lengthening shadows of mid-afternoon, the sun having already dropped behind the westernmost rock. The Gatherer loomed larger in the growing shadows, its clean, simple lines out of place in the worn exterior boards of the buildings and the streets that were more dirt than pavement. Not as large as the units Maria had seen being guarded on the train, it still dominated the square, the open glowing hands of the logo echoing the concave curve of the roof.

Screens mounted in the square flashed and changed in the growing dusk of the afternoon. Shining new signs hung above rundown storefronts and new streetlights had been installed on every block. The few vehicles she had seen had glided like silent ghosts through the mostly empty streets.

The town lay at the bend of the Yukon River, and the place couldn't hold more than a few hundred residents. Someone would have had to remember seeing Freeman. What she couldn't figure out was how Freeman had chosen here as her destination. It contained nothing of significance but for the spectacles of the three rock walls that loomed above the small cluster of streets and buildings that had seen their prime decades pass.

She winced as her socks pulled at the burst blisters, the blood having dried in the few minutes she had let herself sit. The square was empty and she considered lying on the bench and letting the distance she had travelled ease out of her legs. The bench would be drier than the moss she had slept on the past few nights, the flap of the birds' wings making her head heavy, her eyes close.

She lowered herself onto the boards, adjusting her shoulder blades between the slats, and looked up into the fading light of the day. A bird crossed within arm's reach and she turned her head to follow its soaring path when a brightness flashed from the far end of the street. She sat up for a better view of what was reflecting the light of the store signs as it moved in and out of visibility.

The person moved erratically, bursting forward before stopping to lean on a lamppost, the reflections coming from the silver suit that covered their entire body, with some kind of mesh blocking the face. A strange creature against the muted colours of the town.

She expected the person to stop when she saw Maria, or at least acknowledge the only human presence in the square, yet the veil didn't once turn towards her, the suit's pace growing slower and more faltering the closer it drew to the Gatherer.

The figure carried a backpack and a crowbar in one hand, and as it grew closer its shape was distinctly female. Maria had the unexpected thought that the woman had come for the dead birds, hunger the cause of her desperation, but she stepped over them like cracks on a sidewalk. There was something about the long-legged gait in between her frequent stops and the heavy clumsiness of her footsteps that made Maria rise.

The woman circled the Gatherer, an urgency to her steps. Maria flipped up her hood and matched her pace, reaching the smooth, featureless side of the Gatherer at the same time the suit disappeared around its curve. Maria had to stop herself from running, not wanting to scare her away, for it didn't make sense that she would be here, doing this.

Maria circled below the open wings, the exterior shell hard and seamless. A camera lens was fitted into the top edge of the wall and she kept her face turned away. The unit was larger than any Maria had seen before if she didn't count the ones on the train, its silent efficiency more powerful in this larger form. Its beauty was in its simplicity, the smooth lines of the outer shell protecting the crystal structure inside, an integral part of the design that drew an unseen energy into it and condensed it into a usable form. Freeman's smaller units had been rougher, yet they had elicited a sense of wonder that the simple device quietly tapped into something previously unknown, an infinite energy source that when offered up to the people had reduced poverty, ended wars, and improved lives. It was no wonder people had treated Freeman like a saviour. For the changes she had been able to achieve with the simple device had felt like miracles. People were convinced that this solution had come from a higher place.

The sound of scraping and hammering came from beyond her line of sight. She approached carefully, her fingertips resting on the Gatherer's side. Havernal hadn't been able to come near the Gatherer, its drawing of energy a poison that left him racked with pain. Maria felt only a distant restlessness, like raindrops tapping at a dark window.

The woman had her back to Maria, her legs planted wide as she struck the crowbar repeatedly at the Gatherer's side, the blows glancing off with no effect. She grunted with each blow, half-collapsing after each strike as if it would be her last. She was unaware that Maria was there, and Maria no longer needed the veil to lift to confirm who this was.

With a sudden fierceness, Storm Freeman jammed the end into the seam of the access door and pushed hard against the bar, the plastic cracking enough for Storm to slide her hand in, release something and spring the door open. The pause was infinitesimal, a momentary gathering of purpose, before she stepped into the interior. Maria followed.

A circular corridor ran inside the outer wall of the shell, leading around the outside of a second interior chamber. She heard no banging or tearing of a forced entry and the corridor was strangely muted but for a low sensation that wasn't so much a sound as a vibration just beyond her perception.

Storm was bent double at the second entrance, clutching a black box to her chest, the small access door opening inwards. She had lifted the veil, her face so drawn and gaunt as to not be Storm at all except for the distinctive red hair across her forehead.

Maria opened her mouth to call out, remembering all the words that she had rehearsed, as Storm stepped through and out of sight.

There was a crash of glass shattering and the clang of the crowbar to the floor. Maria reached the opening as Storm hit the floor and a high keening sliced through her ear drums. Its source was the concave dish of crystals covered with broken glass and the black box.

Storm's neck and back arched, each muscle triggered by the keening, her eyes rolling back, violent tremors jerking through her. Glass crunched under Maria's boots as she grabbed Storm, the keening changing to needles of pain inside Maria's head. Storm was so light Maria fell against the wall when she lifted her, the sharp corner of a metal junction box digging into her back as her vision blurred from the piercing pain. She lifted Storm over her shoulder, nausea joining the pain, and she had the sudden sense of Havernal beside her on patrol, the smell of burnt oil, and the cold wash of water down her legs as she stumbled to the door.

Her foot was on the threshold when the pain and sensations stopped, a clearing of the air, the sudden quiet complete but for the drop of a single fragment of glass to the floor. Storm trembled on her back, her arms striking Maria as they jerked and Maria turned back to the dish, searching for what had happened. A giant bird bath filled with an intricate web of crystals, the broken glass resting in the crevasses of the lattice, a black box perched on top as if it had been thrown. It hardly resembled the Gatherers she had first seen at Storm's lab—coarse, awkward things that hadn't looked like they could collect anything at all.

A moan emanated from Storm and Maria started moving, their breadth barely fitting in the narrow hall and too wide to fit through the final door to outside. She lowered Storm to the ground, leaning her against the side wall, but she kept slipping down. In the end she dragged her under her arms, her legs bouncing on the threshold, Maria feeling the outline of every rib.

She dragged Storm away from the Gatherer in deep dusk, keeping her face turned from the cameras. There was no point in hiding Freeman, she would already have been recorded. Night had arrived quickly and it was only when she paused to readjust her hold that she noticed the darkness of the town. The signs above the shops had gone out, buildings that had once had lighted windows now shadowy outlines against the fading sky. There came angry shouts in the distance, the erratic points of flashlights moving towards them from the end of the street. She lifted Storm, trying to get her to take some weight on her legs, but she flopped on Maria, almost all her weight across Maria's shoulders. More bobbing lights appeared in a separate laneway, a group of four or five. Maria hefted Storm onto her back, locking her hands behind her rigid knees.

The main street ran south from town, the only route she knew, now filling rapidly with tiny lights. To the north lay black hills covered in a thick forest, its shelter two, maybe three streets away. She turned into a laneway going north, the darkness complete between the high walls. She had no time to let her eyes adjust before charging blindly away from the square.

EIGHT

The adrenaline from the Gatherer had long ago worn off and Maria dropped to her knees, the muscles on the right side of her back spasming as she lowered Storm to the ground, her arms sluggish, and her head spinning with hunger. She collapsed to the ground and leaned back against a tree not much wider than a broom handle.

She listened for sounds of pursuit, hearing nothing above the low rustling of the river and the whisper of the breeze through the bare trees. It concerned her that no one had come after them, despite the cameras. You didn't shut down a Gatherer without consequences, which meant that they were either waiting for them somewhere or were silent, skilled trackers who had chosen not to show themselves.

The outline of Storm's silver suit offered the only visible shape, the rest of the woods sunk into darkness but for a lingering glow in the sky and a narrow brightness coming from the openness of the river. They had been following the river's flow since they had left town, the low murmur coming close and moving away. She had hoped the path would touch the river for a chance to quench her thirst, yet she had been stumbling along for over an hour, tormented by its taunting presence.

It was ironic that she was once again cold and hungry in the dark when she had so expected something to change as soon as she found Freeman. She freed Storm's arm from underneath her and slipped the small nylon backpack off her shoulders. Her limbs were heavy and lifeless and Maria felt a jolt of frustration at the woman's helplessness. She wanted to wake her and make her answer for what she had done. Yet there had been so little flesh on Storm's legs where she held her, the sharpness of her hip bones so near the surface.

She opened Storm's backpack, the click of the zipper's teeth a ratchet of noise in the quiet. She groped inside, touching first puffy softness that she pulled out slowly, the material taking the shape of a down coat she ached to slip over her shoulders. She tucked it tightly around Freeman instead. She found Storm's wallet and a glass bottle of liquid, half full when she shook it, smelling sweet and tasting bitter on her lips. She was so thirsty and hungry she took three gulps before she could force herself to stop. She returned the lid and placed it between her and Freeman as her body woke up to the sudden nutrients. She carefully opened a long, hard case, and when she felt inside, made out two tiny glass vials and the delicate cylinder of a syringe and needle. She wished for light and a closer look at the contents, to figure out if this was something meant for Storm or others. She placed it next to the drink, finding only a pair of canvas gloves left in the bottom, too large for Maria's small hands, though she kept them on, already feeling the creep of cold now that the heat of the walk had left her. The pack still held weight, tilting forward when she lifted it, her hands wrapping around a nest of webbing and plastic that she pulled from the narrow front pocket, hoping it would untangle into what she desperately wanted. She slid the straps onto her head, adjusting them over her ponytail, shocked at the sudden closeness of the tree trunks when she clicked on the light. The reflected brilliance of the silver suit and the deeper darkness shone around them. She stood, the head lamp bringing the closest dangers into focus: animals, fatigue, and cold.

She ran the light up and down Storm's still form, thinking irrationally that the light had the power to wake her, the rush of the river enticingly close. She swung her head to light the southern path before she pushed between the thin trunks, Storm's canvas gloves protecting her as she parted through branches and stumbled towards the openness of water.

The trees ended suddenly and stars shone above a steep sloping drop to smooth silty water. The river's swirling surface extended beyond the reach of the head lamp, the opposite shore little more than a formless shape. There was no easy access to the water, its heady smell making her thirst so wild that she grabbed the trunk of a tender, pliable poplar. She bent it towards the water, lowering herself hand over hand, bracing against its branches. Shoving a glove in her waist band she scooped handfuls of icy water into her mouth, tasting grit and sand in her teeth and the overlying sweetness of the water. Her hand turned numb, her face and coat soaked, her single arm on the poplar holding her out over the water. She stayed longer than she should have, her arm weakening, even as she took just one more scoop.

When she pulled herself ashore, her belly full with water, she felt sated and strangely wild, wiping her mouth as she took in the breadth of the river and the expanse of black sky above that had grown darker and more remote with every step north.

She moved back to Storm, keeping her back to the river, moving faster when it took longer than she remembered. She stumbled abruptly on the narrow trail and panicked when Storm wasn't there. Her first thought was that their unseen pursuers had got her, until the light picked up a flash of silver to the north. She jogged along the trail, the water sloshing in her gut, the liquid returning life to her limbs.

Storm was no longer prone on the ground but propped against a tree, eyes closed, her hood pulled back to expose the cropped red hair. When the light touched her face, Storm held a hand up to block the light. Maria removed the head lamp and held it in her hand to create a small pool of light between them.

"You're a long way from home."

Storm's voice was rough, slow from either drugs or fatigue. Her left hand curled around a syringe, the open case held in her right, like a drug addict who has taken a hit.

"You too."

Storm half-smiled, placing the needle back in its case before sliding it into the pack. Maria wrapped her fingers tightly into the webbing of the head lamp, set on edge by Storm's subdued disinterest.

"What did you do back there?"

Storm lifted her chin and let her head rest against the tree, skin so pale as to contain no life at all.

"Did it work?"

Storm's gaze slid to Maria's, the challenge there undeniable, the circles under her eyes like caverns. They had been on opposing sides since the first time they met. Storm hell-bent on releasing the Gatherer, and Maria ordered to stop it at any cost. The change from the young woman who had outsmarted her was stunning, as if every drop of energy the Gatherer had collected had come from her flesh.

"If stopping that Gatherer was what you wanted."

Storm pulled the bottle Maria had drank from out of the pack and lifted it to her mouth, her lips stained red when she lowered it.

"You should have stayed out of it."

The cold gathered thick against Maria, sitting deeper in the dampness on the front of her coat. The flare of irritation was familiar, the woman's half-truths and side-steps returning her to the days when Storm had claimed they were running more tests even while she sent the device out to energy bloggers to review and stocked retail stores.

Storm returned the bottle to the pack and zipped it up, a heavy stillness on her but for the careful movement of her hands.

"Why would you destroy a Gatherer?"

She knew why Storm had destroyed it. The proof that the Gatherer was linked to the plague was undeniable, but she wanted Storm to say it. A part of her was unable to resist that need for vindication.

Storm pulled her knees in and, bracing against the narrow tree, staggered to her feet. She gripped the trunk, swaying as if pushed by a strong wind, her legs like the fragile sticks of a young bird.

"How far are we from town?"

A stand of trees lay behind Storm, the closest trunks all that were visible of the tangled mess.

"They'll be looking for you."

Storm released her hold on the tree and stood for a moment, testing her stability. A pure stubbornness had always driven her. Combined with her unique intelligence it had allowed her to see and do things no one had before.

"How far?"

Storm looked back into the darkness of the path, scanning the shadowy outlines of the hills. She took one shaky step towards town, then another. The headlamp reflected off the suit, a shining, unreal beacon in the heady earthiness of the forest.

"Do you want to know why I'm here?"

Storm had walked far enough that she was being absorbed into the woods, a ghost roaming lost in the open lands. With the head lamp secure again, Maria approached close enough to bring her back into the pool of light.

"Havernal sent me to find you."

"Still doing his bidding are you?"

Maria let the insult roll off her. She was used to Storm's derision for hierarchies and a chain of command.

"I do what needs to be done."

Storm grabbed a tree trunk for support, forcing Maria to stop. She turned her face back towards the light.

"How did you find me?"

Maria hadn't known where the coordinates of Storm's location had come from, only how long she had been searching, unsuccessfully, for that information.

"You were the person we thought could help us."

"You wasted your time."

Maria's agitation grew as Storm continued back towards town. She could physically stop her but that wasn't going to help. She was relieved when, after less than a hundred meters, Storm stopped at an intersecting trail that Maria had dismissed as a deer track when she had passed it earlier. Storm pointed a finger down the short lighted patch of path that followed the river.

"That will get you back to town."

"You think I'm just going to leave?"

Storm lowered herself to the ground, her back against an outcrop of rock.

"I don't remember asking you to come."

"You would have died back there."

The animosity was familiar, easy, but the time for it had passed. For both of them.

Maria lifted her chin so the beam of the head lamp followed the smaller track into a criss-cross of branches blocking the path.

"Where does that take you?"

Storm retrieved the drink and took a small sip, the hand that held the bottle steady. Maria tried to ignore the intoxicating sweet smell of the juice that sent pangs of hunger deep into her gut. She crouched, her face level with Freeman.

"There were cameras in the square. They'll know it was you."

Storm's eyelids were half-lowered, and she seemed in no hurry to answer.

"What is it you want?"

The head lamp pulled at Maria's hair as it came off, the pool of light where it hung leaving her and Storm mostly in darkness. Maria thought of the long days getting here, the driving need to find Freeman dictating every decision, every choice. Yet she hadn't expected to find this.

"Havernal's dying."

Storm barely reacted, a deepening of her frown the only indication the information had registered at all. She stared into the darkness behind Maria's left knee.

"How long?"

"How long what? Until he dies?"

Maria's voice was high and raw, the harshness of it betraying her.

Storm's gaze lifted to Maria's, so intense it felt like an accusation.

"How long has he been sick?"

Storm and Havernal had had a wary respect for each other, though this inquiry felt more factual than personal. Maria tried to remember when it was she had noticed the memory lapses, the sudden flinches as if he had been poked with a pin.

"Nine months...maybe more."

Storm's gaze was distant, intent on how this new piece of information fit with what she already knew. What Maria wouldn't have done to have Storm's knowledge and understand the world as she did.

"You had one of the first Gatherers."

It had been small, one of the first models—a slap in the face at the time, Storm having released the Gatherer under their noses and sent them one of the first production models as a gift. It had been installed in the central control room to feed the banks of computers and the entire administrative complex.

"Did you know then?"

Storm stood, staggering slightly. She grasped a branch to steady herself. Her free hand was held to her forehead as if there was a great pain there, and for a long time, the rustling of the river spoke for them.

Cold settled onto Maria's shoulders, into her buttocks and the backs of her legs. Storm held an open hand out to Maria, demanding the light.

Desperation tightened Storm's features and the pain curled her body inward.

"Give me the light."

Anger, or pain, cracked Storm's voice.

Maria's grip around the light's case tightened. The toll the plague had taken on Storm was heartbreaking, rendering her such a weakened opponent.

"I'm coming with you."

Storm withdrew her hand, the effort it was taking her evident in each shaky movement. She opened her arms wide, displaying her pain-ridden, emaciated body.

"I can't help you."

Storm threaded her pack onto her shoulders, struggling to get her arm into the second strap.

There was a memory of Havernal overwhelmed by the effort to put on his shoe, and Maria stepped forward to help. Storm turned away from her.

"If you slip through town, you could be far from here by dawn."

Maria's path along the river had been quiet, her route keeping her away from the main highways. No one would know she was here.

"I didn't come all this way to be sent away."

The suit shimmered as Storm readjusted the pack, its weight looking more than it should.

Storm stepped away and her foot caught on the edge of a large stone. She stumbled, falling hard to the ground. She swore and rolled onto her back, eyes closed against whatever renewed pain coursed through her.

Maria stood over her, her disappointment gathering inside her. The air felt colder in this new place they had moved to, the cold digging deeper into places it had not yet reached. When Storm opened her eyes, Maria extended her hand. Storm could have gotten up without Maria's help, squirmed her way out of the narrow space between Maria's legs and the underbrush along the path. Maria could see that she wanted to, the offered hand an admission to something she didn't want to accept.

A wolf called in the distance, and Storm cocked her head as if she had heard more than its simple plaintive cry. She gripped Maria's hand, all sinew and bone, her strength failing halfway up so that Maria had to lift her to standing.

Would she even be able to do what they needed her to?

The trail climbed steadily, carrying them out of the river valley, the stars that had come out as they walked spread in a dense, distant blanket that stretched beyond the horizon. The Yukon was a vast place, probably part of the reason Storm had chosen it—as good a place as any to disappear.

Storm stumbled frequently, though Maria shone the light directly in front of her. The first time she fell, Maria helped her up. The second time, she slipped under Storm's shoulder. Storm initially resisted the support, but after a few steps her weight fell onto Maria.

"How far is it?"

Storm mumbled something that Maria thought sounded like 'forever.'

"How far?"

"Twenty k."

Maria faltered, nearly sending the two of them sideways into the scrappy underbrush. She tightened her grip beneath Storm's ribs and lowered her head to the task, the ache of hunger and fatigue already creeping through her.

NINE

Maria lowered Storm onto the rock outcrop and the tension from carrying her the last few kilometres released from her back muscles. Storm slumped onto the rock, curling in, consumed by the shaking that had overtaken her as they walked.

A dog's wild incessant barking reverberated out of the woods to the south. Turning off the head lamp, she placed her feet carefully through the stones and boulders lit by moonlight and climbed the low ridge. A clearing spread below with the dark shapes of two buildings, a vehicle, and what could have been the crouched figure of a man disappearing into the trees. The barking came from the smaller of the two buildings and the cause of the animal's agitation was visible at the larger, further building. Flashlight beams bobbed inside the windows, a window growing brighter as one of the beams explored into the corners. Whoever they were had wisely avoided the smaller cabin, choosing to search or wait for Storm in the larger structure.

Maria made her way back to Storm and crouched beside her.

"There are people waiting."

Storm didn't respond immediately and Maria leaned in closer, unable to see whether she was still conscious.

"We'll have to wait until they leave."

Storm pushed herself to sitting, her movements slow and heavy.

"I can't wait."

She paused on her hands and knees, her head hanging low below her shoulders.

"You can't go down there."

Storm stood and started picking her way to the top of the ridge. Maria could have tackled her, held her down until the searchers gave up and left, yet this show of strength was the first sign of hope she had seen. At the top of the ridge, Storm looked back at Maria, her face gaunt and skeletal in the moonlight.

"If I don't make it, the door is unlocked. Carry me to my bed."

She started walking.

"Please."

A path led down to the clearing, one that Storm appeared to know well. The pace and strength of her strides increased as they neared the bottom, the grass swishing against their ankles.

"We should keep to the edge. In case—"

The lights panned inside the barn, a beacon amidst the cold darkness of the clearing. Storm walked straight for the cabin, barely lifting her head to the lights. Halfway across, the dog's bark changed from an intruder alert to an excited welcome home. Maria waited for the searchers in the barn to hear it. They were twenty paces from the cabin when the door of the larger building opened and a flashlight beam cut into the dark. Maria ran forward, her arm around Storm's shoulder rushing her faster to the cabin. They reached the cabin as all three lights swept into the clearing. Maria pushed Storm against the rough wood, the searchers' view blocked by the corner. Storm leaned heavily on her, her body trembling. The dog's barking reached a frantic pitch, and the wall shook from where the animal launched itself at the other side. Storm freed herself from Maria and slipped to the door. Maria could hear nothing of the approach above the dog's frenzy. The latch clicked and the dog's barking abruptly changed to joyous whimpering. Lights panned across the grass at Maria's feet. Storm spoke softly to the dog as Maria stepped in front of the open door. The beam of a flashlight ran up the front of the cabin, across the peak and ended on Maria.

"Ms. Curie?"

The dog barked twice, returning to his intruder alert, but a short command from Storm made the barking stop. The men stood behind the halo of the flashlights in the sudden quiet, the light reflecting on a high forehead, outlining a bushy beard, and catching the long, straight line of a nose above a uniform.

Behind her, a match struck and a yellow glow flooded the porch, casting her shadow over the men. A constable with a gun in his holster stood beside a tall wiry man who had left three attack points open. The bearded man hung back two steps, his large gut hanging over his belt. Three men with a fourth potentially still in the woods.

"We'd like to question Ms. Curie on what happened in town tonight."

She could feel them taking in the rumpled clothes, their wariness at what her role was and how dangerous she was. She settled into a wide stance, feet planted, her muscles taut with anticipation.

"She needs to rest."

The sound of pants being pulled off and a parka hitting the floor.

The Constable was mid-forties, broad shouldered, and thick at the waist. He kept one foot on the first step of the porch.

"This isn't a choice."

She bristled at the assumption of authority. If she had been in uniform it would have been different, her status unquestioned.

"Her name's Freeman." The bearded man spoke casually, with all the time in the world.

The Constable looked to him for confirmation and Maria took the opportunity to glance back into the cabin. Storm stood next to a long, silver rectangular enclosure. She had stripped down to an unlikely peach lace bra and underwear, the underwear hanging loose on boney hips and her breasts barely filling the cups.

"I came here with Mac once, on a delivery."

The tall man frowned and started forward.

"Wait. That's Storm Freeman?" He leaned sideways to see in the door.

"What are you talking about, Alan?"

The Constable's hand shifted to his holster.

"I never thought she'd be here."

Alan knocked into the Constable as he tried to catch a glimpse through the window.

Maria placed herself in front of the door.

The Constable moved his foot up another step.

"You need to let us pass."

"Can't do that."

The Constable's gaze hardened, re-assessing her.

"Disabling a Gatherer is a federal offense. I suggest you get out of the way."

A door slid shut inside the cabin.

If she was operating under an official order, it would have been easier. As it was there was no reason for her to be here other than to make things right and she doubted that qualified in his list of acceptable reasons.

"Ms. Freeman is in no condition to see you right now."

"I don't care what state she's in."

The porch shook as the Constable's unhurried steps struck the stairs. The bristles on his beard showed dark in the full light of the lamp.

"You need to get out of my way."

The threat was implicit. If she didn't move he would make her. But she wasn't going to let them take Storm away. No when she had finally found her. She leaned forward onto her toes.

* * * *

Storm pulled the blanket up to her chin and turned on her side, each movement requiring focused attention to complete. A drunken surge of fatigue rushed through her muscles, the burn in her eyes easing as her lids closed. The sleep of this kind of fatigue would be complete and she let go of her hold on the room and the voices outside. She would need a day, a week, maybe a lifetime to recover from this.

"She is in no condition to see you right now."

The voice tugged Storm back from sleep, like a fish caught on a line. She would gladly destroy all of them if she could. And the schematics and test results that could ever lead someone to build a Gatherer again.

"We'll go down in history!" Callan's flushed, excited face floated out of the fatigue.

"I don't care what state she's in."

Storm felt a reluctant response of adrenaline to the aggression in the Constable's voice. Her heart beat slowly, each beat a struggle as it tried to respond. Could they not leave her alone? She fought the weight of her eyelids enough to see Kowalski's silhouette blocking the door, her unwanted, self-appointed protector.

"You need to get out of the way."

The Constable's voice was louder, his bulk towering over Kowalski, Alan and Curtis crowding in behind. She had guts. Storm would give her that.

"Let them in."

Her words sounded raspy and thin.

After a long pause, Kowalski stepped to the side. The three men filed in, crowding into the tiny area of the kitchen afraid to get too close. Blue barked twice before positioning himself at the head of her bed. Kowalski positioned herself between Storm and the men.

She felt them taking in the room—its functional design, her strange setup inside what looked like a woven metal incubator, and the absence of any of the electrical gadgets that the era of light had brought.

"Are you working on a new Gatherer?"

Alan stepped forward, almost bowing in reverence.

"Is that what you're doing out in the lab?"

"That's none of your business."

Kowalski's pants had streaks of dirt down the back and a round dirty circle on her ass. She held herself straight despite her legs having buckled countless times under Storm's weight.

"I wasn't asking you."

Alan moved to push past Kowalski and she blocked him. He pushed her aside and with a sudden twist and jerk Kowalski had him bent over, gasping in pain, his arm twisted behind him.

The Constable stepped forward, hands held out in supplication. His hair was cut close around a square forehead, his eyes, eyebrows, and the bridge of his nose all unrelenting, straight lines. Kowalski's blonde hair had fallen out of her bun and she had the peaked, delirious look of someone too long without food or rest, yet her hands were steady where she pinned Alan's arm.

"There's no need for that."

Kowalski frowned, looking back for confirmation. Storm nodded and Kowalski released him, shoving him towards the Constable as she did. Curtis caught Alan as he stumbled.

"Are you Storm Freeman?"

The Constable had apparently figured out what Alan was talking about.

"I should have recognized you."

Storm wriggled her toes against the nylon bag, the tension easing along the top of her feet. She no longer felt like the Storm Freeman he would know, who had been so sure of her creation and professed a victory for humankind.

"Are the rumours true? Is the Gatherer the source of the plague?"

Alan had crept forward again, like a tourist at the zoo hoping for a better look.

She pulled the blanket closer, Kowalski and the three men staring at her like she was on trial. Was it true? The signs had been there, if she had bothered to look.

"Mac lives right next to the damn thing."

Curtis had remained in the shadows of the kitchen, his grim, bearded face visible in the lamp light.

"It's a rumour. Nothing else." The Constable had raised his voice, using volume to banish the very idea. "Do you all want to go back on the generator? No one—not even the hospital—ever really having enough?"

His hand was back on his holster again and he had moved closer to the bed, his gaze sliding down the sleeping bag, along the shining frame of her shelter, and returning to her face. There was a low growl from Blue as he rose to his feet.

"You'll need to come with me."

"It's okay, Blue."

Storm closed her eyes against the pressure pushing at her skull. Was this it? The world finally coming to drag her back in?

"The Gatherer in town was misfiring. I disabled it before it self-destructed."

There had been Gatherers that had misfired. Though this wasn't one of them. The battery overcharged so that it had burned up in the newer models where they had expanded the Gatherer's original function far beyond its capabilities. The Gatherer in Three Rocks had worked fine; she had felt it in every burning wave that had rolled through her body.

"Are you telling me you shut it down?"

She met his gaze, hating his certainty and his strength.

"By shutting it down I saved the mechanism. Otherwise it would have been irreparable."

The mechanism had been saved—physically—but it would never again latch onto the elusive shards of energy it was meant to collect.

"Do you have any identification?"

"I need to stay in here." She lifted her chin to indicate her shelter.

"I'm not too concerned about where you think you need to be. What I am concerned about is that you halted the Gatherer that supplies power to the entire town. I'm going to need some identification saying you are who you say you are."

"It's her alright."

Alan moved into the light looking like he would hand her a photo to autograph at any moment.

The Constable stopped his approach with an outstretched hand.

"I'm going to need something more official than your starry-eyed confirmation."

"She's—I'm not being starry-eyed. It's her. My God. Wait until I tell—"

"You won't tell anyone."

Maria's words came out as an order, and forced open a crack in what Storm had been denying. It was too much. Her fatigue, the men, the understanding that the world would once again know where to find her.

"I can do what I like."

"Back off Alan." The Constable turned back to Storm.

"I'll need that I.D."

Storm tried to sit, her arms slow to respond. She'd be exhausted just getting out of the bed.

Kowalski picked up Storm's pack that lay on the floor beneath her discarded pile of clothes, and withdrew Storm's wallet from the side pocket. Kowalski handed over the license that showed Storm with longer hair and a beaming, world-conquering smile.

Storm tried to think what else Kowalski would have found in the pack. Her jacket, the head lamp. Anything important had been left at the Gatherer.

The Constable spent a good minute examining the license, lifting his eyes to Storm several times before handing her the card.

"You'll still need to come back to town. The Gatherer needs to be back on line and you're going to do it."

"You need someone from head office. Someone with tools."

The Constable moved in close, one side of his face lighted by the oil lamp. "You're coming back to town. Now."

Blue growled, though he faced the door, not the Constable. The bed shifted and rolling waves of fatigue swept through her.

"Pull yourself together."

She pushed herself to sitting, the weight of her head falling to her chest. Heat from the stove mixed with the cold air from the door that no one had bothered to shut.

"It'll kill her."

Storm sat for a moment letting the dizziness subside. Did she look that close to death?

"She made it here. She can make it back."

The cold passed right through her. The fire popped and she looked up to their shocked, averted gazes flicking away from her thinness. The fatigue pulled stronger like the bow line of a moored boat.

"You're not taking her."

Kowalski's hip brushed Storm's shoulder, blocking her from the Constable.

"You're obstructing justice."

Curtis and Alan fell in behind.

"I'm not moving."

Storm lowered herself back to the bed. She would rest while they argued. The chink of metal and the flash of handcuffs. The Constable stepped towards the bed and Kowalski met him, her small chin lifted in defiance, his powerful shoulders leaning over her.

Storm let her eyes begin to close. A crash and Blue started barking wildly. Kowalski and the Constable spun around, their bodies a frame for the distressed human that had come out of the dark. He was panicked, with unfocused eyes in a pale, tortured face, a torn open coat, with one boot gone, and lips that moved in a stream of suffering.

Blue backed off at her command, the man's words emerging as a low drone. He staggered forward, his movements sudden jerks out of a constant trembling.

Curtis caught the man before he struck the floor, the big man falling to his knees beside the convulsing man. Curtis laid a large hand on the side of the man's face, the man's eyes rolling as he tried to focus. His lips moved in a continual mantra as his legs spasmed and the one boot clunked against the floor.

"Help me."

The horror of it was unbearable. Mac, her steady, quiet contact with the outside world, who had not once told the world she was there, writhing on the floor, his agony turning him to a creature she no longer recognized. It was a pure, unfiltered accusation of what she had done. Mental symptoms worse than anything she had, the weight loss and terror in his eyes paralyzing her. He had to have been hiding his symptoms, not knowing what was happening.

There was a shifting beneath her as if she were on a raft at sea, the waves crashing across the boards enough to tear her free. She gripped the rough wood of the shelter.

"What do I do?"

Curtis, helpless above the convulsing Mac, gripped the man's hand to keep him there.

"Bring him here."

She slid to the back of the bed, opening a spot wide enough for Curtis to slide Mac in. A trembling mass of jerking limbs and the sour smell of sweat and piss.

She wrapped her hand around his, squeezing hard enough to cause pain. "Hold on."

She was rewarded by his gaze sweeping across hers before lifting to the roof of the enclosure.

Kowalski pushed through the bulk of the three men crowded at the bedside, handing Storm a filled syringe. She checked the dosage level—more than she would have given, but the extra wouldn't hurt him.

Curtis lowered Mac's pants while Kowalski held him steady. A red, weeping rash covered his upper thighs.

There was no response when she jabbed the syringe into his buttocks, the pain of the needle not even registering in the maelstrom that was his body. The tremors started to subside as she handed the empty syringe back to Kowalski. The pop of the fire was the only sound as Mac slowly calmed, the rigid grimace on his face relaxing as he slid from his place of mental cacophony into unconsciousness.

She pulled the blanket up to cover both of them, feeling a strange intimacy with him. Curtis tucked the edge around Mac's shoulder, a heightened flush of red across his round cheeks.

"What was that?"

Small twigs rested in Mac's straight black hair, dirt streaked his cheeks, and blood had crusted his fingernails where she held his hand.

"The injection will stop the attack. And let him sleep without any more seizures."

Her own fatigue was unrelenting, and she longed for the oblivion of the syringe.

The men hadn't moved, frozen in the helplessness and fear of men accustomed to taking action who suddenly don't know what to do.

She lowered herself off her elbow, the wafting dizziness buffeting her even as she lay still.

"But what was it?"

There was no denying the fatigue, its tendrils firmly wrapping around her. She tried to think of an answer, flipping through the available options, their clarity blurring each time she tried to pick one. The heat of Mac's body drew her towards him and the sweet release of sleep. Before she went under, Kowalski spoke, her abrupt, no-nonsense voice clear and plain in the silent room.

"That is the plague."

TEN

The rising sun set the copper roof of Storm's lab on fire, the steel sides shimmering walls of reflected light, a beacon amidst the stunted shrubs and dormant brown of the clearing. Maria ran her fingers over the surface of the window, feeling the tiny ridges of the mesh attached to the inside. She hadn't noticed it the other times she had checked the window.

Curtis's steady breathing disturbed the silence of the cabin with Mac's low snores beside Storm in the enclosure. She envied their sleep, the dull heaviness of exhaustion still clinging to her as she crossed to a second window above the sink. Two tire tracks led to the road and the stretch of the river that was beginning to reflect the sun's rays back to her.

Curtis had stayed behind when the Constable and Alan had left, promising to keep an eye on things. As Storm and Mac had slept, it had become clear that Curtis was more concerned with Mac's well-being than anything the Constable wanted him to do.

The thud of an elbow against wood drew her back across the room to Storm's enclosure. The copper that covered the bed was cool to her touch, strips of it forming a web with thinner strands of silver. A blanket with copper threads woven through it lay over both of them. Mac lay closest to the edge with Storm on her side in the narrow space against the back wall. Storm's eyes moved beneath her eyelids as Maria slid open the door, but Mac's slack facial muscles didn't register the disturbance.

She shook Storm's shoulder twice and Storm reacted, her eyes wide with confusion and fright. Maria hated her vulnerability, her fragility feeling like a betrayal.

"Time to get up."

Storm struggled to focus, disoriented by Maria's presence until her memory kicked in and her confusion tightened into a frown. Storm lifted her head enough to check if Mac still slept as Maria slid the door fully open.

"We should have been gone by now."

Storm pulled up the blanket to cover her bare shoulders and curled her head into the pillow next to Mac.

"They have you on video. They're going to take you back to Three Rocks."

Storm opened her eyes reluctantly, her gaze fixed on Mac's shoulders.

"I'm no good to them."

"They don't know that."

Storm lifted herself onto one elbow, her red hair smashed against her skull, the blanket held close though the room was warm from the fire.

"What is it you expect me to do?"

The floor shook and Maria moved to the window, but it was only Curtis bumping his chair as he shook the sleep out of his mane of hair. Her concern turned to irritation as he scraped the chair further across the floor. The clearing lay still, the increased reflection of the sun off the river the only change.

"Can you help me get some supplies together?"

It was a gamble but she thought she had read him right. He would be happy to see them go. He didn't respond as he rubbed his hands over his face and pushed his fingers along his eyebrows, struggling to free himself from sleep. When her words finally registered he nodded and picked up the bag she pushed towards him without a word.

"Pack whatever you can find. It won't be long before they're back."

Storm was lying down, her chin tucked into the cover when Maria returned. A thin band of dirt showed around the base of the bed posts, the wood frame buried directly into the earth.

Maria shook her shoulder again. Storm's eyes opened, her anger deepening the blue.

"Go away."

Maria leaned in, hovering above Mac and Storm's wasted bodies, trying to fit what she had found here with the hope that had propelled her across the country.

"You need to fix what you started."

Storm rolled onto her back, her gaze locked on the underside of the enclosure.

"I took out the Gatherer didn't I?"

The bang of cupboard doors sounded as Curtis searched the kitchen.

"There are thousands of them."

Storm traced a pattern on the roof of the enclosure.

"My point exactly."

Maria waited for the sound of a vehicle in the distance even as the morning stillness remained unbroken. Storm traced her hand again across the roof, a moment of grace in the slow movement. She licked her lips before she spoke, the corners cracked and dry.

"I didn't know."

Storm dropped her hand to her chest, her fingers bunching the blanket into her fist, the tips disappearing into its folds.

"Didn't know what?"

Storm held her gaze on the roof of the enclosure, her focus on something farther away.

"That anyone else was sick."

"You thought you were the only one?"

There was a quiet, bitter laugh from Storm at either Maria's surprise or her own blindness.

"How could you not know?"

Storm extended a long, thin arm from under the blanket, her palm open to indicate the entire room.

"How could I?"

Maria followed the sweep of Storm's hand, to the wooden furniture, the water pump at the sink, and the click of the propane fridge. There was no computer or screen, not even a radio, the stack of newspapers next to the wood stove the only sign of the outside world.

"No one else was sick when I came here."

"What about your team?"

The question came out as an accusation, but Maria didn't care. Three of Storm's team had died within six months of her disappearance. There had been rumours they had disappeared with Storm, but during her search Maria had learned of each of their slow deteriorations—Callan from brain cancer, Ari and Jana's illness unexplained.

"I didn't have the information I needed to fully understand."

Storm spoke with a fury out of sync with the frailty of her body, its force directed entirely inwards.

Mac exhaled, reasserting his presence and Storm suddenly looked crowded by him. She climbed over him, all white boney limbs and the pale peach of her bra and underwear. The row of ribs, the bumpy notch of each vertebra, her heels cracked and dried with blood. She was up and moving immediately to her discarded pile of clothes. Maria and Curtis looked away but they needn't have bothered. Storm was dismissive of their embarrassment, as if she had long ago detached herself from the degradation.

She walked barefoot to the sink once she was dressed, the dog circling excitedly around her. Storm used two hands to pump the water.

Maria moved next to Storm as the water rushed into the glass, spilling over the edges.

"We need to go."

Storm had her back to the window, the glass at her lips, its sides beaded with water. She gestured towards the door where the dog had disappeared through its flap.

"I'm not stopping you."

"Not without you."

Curtis had his head in the fridge and dropped several containers into the bag.

"I still don't know what you expect me to do."

Storm glanced down at her wasted body as she spoke, as if it were something outside of herself.

"The same thing you did before. Solve the problem."

Storm took a long, slow sip of water, each swallow visible in her thin throat.

"That person doesn't exist anymore."

"Like hell."

Maria's palms were sweating, her jaw aching from the force of her clenched teeth.

"You need to talk to head office. They're the ones who know where all the Gatherers are located and how to recall them if there's a problem."

It was a rote answer, Storm once again speaking through the Corporation that had taken over the distribution of the Gatherer.

Curtis had come to stand next to Maria. He smelled of animals, cigarettes and the residue of gun shots.

"They aren't acknowledging that the Gatherer is the cause."

A splash of water landed on the floor between Storm's bare feet. Storm didn't notice, her attention fixed on the leg of the woodstove where it touched the floor and the fragments of wood and bark that lay around it. Maria had seen her withdraw before, whatever was going on in her mind so intense that she forgot the rest of the world.

"Neither is the government."

Storm's brow tightened at Maria's words as if she could deny what they were telling her.

Maria had felt the same chill of realization across her shoulders when she and Havernal had first made the connection and understood that the government knew what the Gatherer was doing but wasn't doing anything about it. Maria pointed to the half-filled pack hanging in Curtis's hand. He nodded and resumed his search in the closet next to the door. She strained to hear any change in the morning's suffocating quiet.

"Is she telling the truth?"

Storm directed the question at Curtis, who paused in front of the cupboard door. He looked like a thief caught red handed, the pack in one hand, a hat in the other. Yet his expression was of resignation, of a truth that couldn't be ignored.

"There's been talk online and articles in the media. But nothing official yet."

Storm finally looked up to meet Maria's eyes, the clarity in them one Maria hadn't seen since finding her. Yet pain underlay the clear blue, deeper than any physical pain Maria had seen her endure.

"And I destroyed the Gatherer in Three Rocks."

Maria nodded, the tightness in her shoulders easing as Storm put the pieces together.

"On camera."

The glass thudded dully as Storm set it on the counter. A log shifted in the wood stove and the fire hummed louder, drawing the oxygen from the room. Maria waited, her nerves agitated. She could feel the awareness of Storm's attack on the Gatherer propagating out into the world. There would be phone calls, people organizing to come for her.

There was a slow lift of Storm's head to look out the window, back lit by the gleaming metal of the lab, her focus following something. Maria thought the Constable must have arrived until the dog burst through the flap in the door, eyes bright and tail high. The dog went straight to Storm, who crouched down in front of him, her fingers buried in the fur around his neck, her forehead lowered to his. It was a gesture of such sad tenderness that Maria had a sudden longing for Havernal.

Storm spoke quietly to the dog, her voice too low to hear, the dog's ears flicking forward and back until it let out a long plaintive whine. Storm pulled her head back, looking into the animal's eyes, and it stopped whining.

"Come."

Walking stiffly, Storm led the dog to Curtis's side and commanded him to sit.

Maria moved to the window. The shimmer of the sun off the water reflected throughout the clearing, its vibrations cracking the calmness of the morning.

Storm pointed to Curtis and the dog's shoulders slumped, his whine a desperate plea. She repeated the gesture. The burly man looked down at his new companion and raised his shoulders in a companionable shrug. The dog's tail wagged briefly, and Storm's shoulders sagged.

"You'll look after him?"

The tremor in Storm's voice was more desperate than the dog's.

Curtis bent to ruffle the dog's fur and the dog braced his paws against the man's easy strength.

"He'll be good with the team."

Storm moved with measured determination as she put on her parka and slipped on her boots. She stopped briefly at the enclosure where Mac slept, flattened a piece of metal that had risen out of the protective mesh, and held on to the wood frame with both hands before letting go.

"What do I do for him?"

Curtis had moved beside Storm, his bulk increasing her frailty.

"Keep him here. It'll help with the symptoms."

"Will it cure him?"

A twig that had escaped from Mac's hair lay on the floor outside the enclosure, most of the others still hopelessly entangled in the long black strands.

"I don't know."

Maria put on her coat and boots, her need to move rising as she slipped her arms into the backpack. Storm handed her the silver suit, the case for the syringes, and a collection of small bottles out of the fridge that Curtis had passed over.

She was about to ask for another bag when Storm opened the door. Whether it was to get something from the lab or to test the temperature Maria wouldn't know, for with a warning yelp, the dog bolted through the door towards two white Suburbans entering the clearing. Storm closed the door and put her back against it as the dog's barking reached the vehicle.

Storm looked towards the lab, seemingly unable to move.

Maria pulled her away from the door. Storm moved slowly, looking around the room as if she had only just understood that she would have to leave.

The engine grew louder, its determined, steady grind already halfway across the clearing.

Maria pulled on Storm, towards the small bathroom at the back of the cabin.

The vehicle was in front of the cabin, the dog's barking frantic.

Curtis moved towards Storm, a cast-iron frying pan in his hand. Maria stepped between them, her arms raised, a coil of energy ready to spring. He was three times her weight and as slow moving as a bear.

"It's not for you."

He flipped the pan casually in his hand.

"It has to look like you overpowered me."

Maria relaxed, the spike of adrenaline flowing into relief.

"We don't need that."

She reached for his neck as a door slammed. Blue was snarling as a man, not the Constable, swore.

"Wait!"

Storm held out her hand, finally coming alive.

"You'll need to get Jacob. He's been hiding his symptoms."

The shock and understanding was immediate, Curtis's genial expression melting into renewed fear. He nodded.

With a quick step, Maria laid her hand against the warmth of Curtis's neck.

"Ready?"

Curtis lifted his gaze briefly to Storm.

"I'm with her." He tilted his chin ever so slightly towards Maria. "If you can fix this. You have no choice."

A quick, hard pressure behind his ear and Curtis and the pan dropped to the floor. The impact shook the cabin. A fist pounded the door as Maria and Storm crowded into the bathroom. They levered open the window. It wasn't a huge space but it would be enough for two thin women to squeeze through.

As soon as her feet touched the ground, Maria started running, crouched low, towards the spindly poplars that backed the clearing. Storm followed in a weak run, and Maria slowed, grabbing her elbow to help propel her forwards. The dog's crazed barking echoed behind them, answered by a man yelling for them to open up.

Maria kept her head down, looking forward as they entered the sparse woods. Storm stumbled beside her, her face pale and grim. They had entered a thicker stand of trees when the unmistakable whine of an electric jet filled the air. Maria tackled Storm to the ground as a sleek, white plane entered the clearing from the north. It was private, its insignia unreadable from this distance. Maria kept a tight hold on Storm as it deftly lowered down between the cabin and the lab, a whirlwind rising up around it.

The smooth slackness of dawning comprehension spread across Storm's drawn features before it abruptly tightened into angry understanding.

"We've got to get out of here."

Two men in black combat gear jumped out of the cab before the runners touched down.

"Do you know who that is?"

But Storm had already slipped from Maria's grasp and was running further into the woods, several strides ahead of her. Maria looked back only once as the men from the jet were met by the ones who had pounded on the door.

ELEVEN

Storm stood on a rock outcrop close to the water's edge. Brief glimpses of trees appeared and vanished as quickly as the mist shifted.

"Can you see anything?"

Maria adjusted the weight of the pack on her hips and clicked the buckle around her waist. Her eyes were red rimmed and she looked as tired as when they had stopped the previous night.

"No, but they can't see us any better than we can see them."

The mist muted Storm's voice, her words traveling no further than their few feet of rock. She peered harder, wondering if someone else beyond the blank wall of mist was staring back at them. A patch of tall grass broke through a momentary opening, the mist curled around the base of its straight, brittle blades.

"That doesn't mean they aren't there."

Maria frowned. Strands of hair hung loose from what was now half of a ponytail, and there was a heaviness to her eyes that matched Storm's, a poor night's sleep on hard ground intensifying the lingering weakness from the seizure at the Gatherer.

"Are we continuing in the same direction?"

They had spent the previous day pushing through endless swamps, taking refuge on higher ground when they could. Every moment she had expected to be caught or corralled into a corner. They hadn't spoken of where they were going or the unlikelihood that they had ended up together. It had been about getting away. But even without discussing it, there had been a direction, their trajectory leading them decidedly southwest.

Maria's answer was to choose the shallowest section and step off. Clouds of organic matter erupted around her foot as she entered the water, a larger bloom spreading behind her. Storm followed, hating the return of the icy water. She longed to be back in her bed, curled up next to Blue until she remembered that Mac would be there with shaking hands and panicked, pleading eyes, unrecognizable as the man he had once been.

It shocked her that she hadn't faced her pursuers. Choosing to flee with Maria, the woman who had haunted her following the Gatherer's release.

This is larger than you are. It's irresponsible to release it without proper testing.

She hadn't cared. She had been more worried about it being taken from her control than she was by a few side effects. In truth, she hadn't believed there would be any. The Gatherer and the principles behind it had felt so right, like she had been meant to find it.

By the time Maria stopped on a higher patch of land, Storm's feet were numb. She stepped up beside her, the earth soft underneath.

"How many people are sick?"

They stood on a high point above the marsh's teeming surface, the thinning mist providing glimpses of an endless watery expanse.

"It's hard to say."

"Make a guess."

Mist drifted in front of them, its tendrils trailing along the water's surface.

"A lot of them drop off the radar once they're sick. Go into hiding."

Storm's irritation rose. She needed data to understand what had happened.

"A hundred? A thousand? What are we talking here?"

If the larger Gatherers were making people sick, it would be an easy fix. Manageable.

"Tens of thousands. More by now."

She felt her heart constrict as if it meant to stop.

"How is that even possible?"

Maria looked to her feet as she repositioned them, the ground beneath Storm giving way at the change in pressure. Maria pressed her lips together, a grim resolution to her features.

"You tell me."

Storm felt the pull of the Gatherers that had been delivered, an intricate web over the world with every branch leading back to her.

"Has anyone tried to stop it?"

Her raised voice echoed back at her, asking her the same question. If it was as extensive as Maria claimed, how could the corporation deny it? The company was unrecognizable from the entity she had hoped to create.

"No one wants to give it up."

The truth of it was another cut into a body that was hardly set to bear anything at all. Hadn't that been the whole point? Delivering free, limitless electricity to everyone so their lives would be easier?

"How far has it spread?"

"Everywhere there's a Gatherer."

A noise across the marsh. It could have been a branch falling, an animal plopping into the water, or footsteps moving through the woods. Their breath rose in white clouds as they listened. No sound but the push of tiny waves against the decaying stalks of grass.

Maria led, her steps soundless through the water that reached their shins while the splashes of Storm's feet echoed around them. The enormity of her task had expanded to encompass the endless marsh, each footstep not even registering in the elaborate network that the Gatherer had created. Storm's thoughts circled around a single question, returning to it and retreating. Her mother had taken over the operations of the Gatherer corporation when Storm had been forced to retreat to the Yukon. She had done a better job of it than Storm ever could have done, the distribution of the Gatherer spreading faster and wider under her focused attention. Her mother had never missed an opportunity to donate a Gatherer to a struggling community, or to skillfully navigate the obstacles and lawsuits thrown up by their opponents. So how would she not recognize that the Gatherer was linked to the plague?

"What has headquarters been saying?"

Maria didn't respond immediately.

"They issued a statement that it was another smear campaign from the fossil fuel industry."

Water had soaked above the knees of Maria's pants, her feet and calves likely as waterlogged and numb as Storm's.

"And?"

"The only real response came from the government. Saying that the Gatherer had undergone extensive testing and that there was no risk to human health."

"Do people believe it?"

The Gatherer had in fact been tested, except the tests it had undergone had been totally unconnected to how the Gatherer functioned. The electromagnetic fields around the Gatherer were nonexistent. It didn't send radio waves into the atmosphere. There was no test for what the Gatherer did.

"A farmer released a video of the effects on their cattle at the same time a journalism student released a documentary called 'In Plain Sight.' It covered the contamination of a village in Peru."

"Which one?"

"Rumira."

She had a memory of high expansive mountains and thin, cold air.

"How many are sick?"

Maria only shook her head, the number and the names of the people who had been afflicted not part of the documentary. Storm had been inside these people's homes, shared their scant meals. And in return, she had given them sickness.

The shelter of the trees lay a hundred metres ahead, and she wished their pursuers would step from the trees and take a quick, clear shot. A fast, cowardly end that would deliver some kind of justice.

Maria waited for her with a look that went straight into Storm's shame and her desire to escape.

"We have to keep moving."

Maria's usual abruptness was replaced by a trace of warmth.

"When we get to the trees, we'll take a break."

The water pressed cold around Storm's shins, the mud drawing her down further the longer she stayed in one place, the marsh all too willing to take her in, forever if she wanted.

Water splashed as Maria came back to Storm and stood next to her, the two of them standing side-by-side facing in the same direction. They stood together for only the briefest pause, Maria's body providing a warmth where the wind had been. Low clouds lay in the west and the damp taste of rain or maybe snow hung in the air.

"You take the lead."

The pull of mud was strong until the suction broke, the resistance of the water easier in comparison. On her second step Maria fell in behind. The mist parted as they walked, thinning and dissipating so that Storm's shoulders rose. They were more of a target than ever.

"Were those your people at the cabin?"

They had stopped on a small patch of solid ground and had heard nothing despite listening for several minutes. Maria's fatigue was evident in the drop of her shoulders, the exhausted stillness of her planted legs.

"If those were my people, we wouldn't have gotten away."

Maria continued walking, keeping to the higher ground. Storm followed close enough so she could speak in a low voice.

"Who then? Do you know? You have to have a suspicion."

"The same ones that you do."

Maria's response felt like an accusation. As if Storm would somehow know. There had been threats before she left, but she had been completely isolated up here and had assumed the world had forgotten about her.

"If the Gatherer is the cause of the plague, then the people who were after me no longer care. They'll be back in business soon."

Storm almost ran into the back of Maria when she stopped. They were twenty metres away from the shelter of the trees. Far enough to be an easy stationary target. Maria stared up at Storm in suspicion, crow's feet at the corners of her eyes where they hadn't been before.

"How can you not know this?"

A disturbance arrived on the air, faint like a bird lifting off in a distant tree.

They turned together and looked up at the sky.

The thick low lying clouds seemed to shift, their connection to the ground severed.

They ran, covering the distance to the trees as the piercing whine grew more distinct, a pulsing beat penetrating into her chest.

The trees were thin and too far apart to provide any real protection. They ran to the only dense section of underbrush and crouched beside it. Maria pulled at the contents of her pack, the black puffiness of the sleeping bag reluctant to pull free. Maria laid it over them as the white shape of the electric jet appeared at the far side of the swamp, sleek and white and sweeping low over the water.

"They're going to see us."

"Not if we don't move."

Storm stopped breathing as the jet flew straight towards them, pushing a wave of dark churned up water ahead of them. It felt as if it were barrelling down on them, its navigation system locked on their exact location. At the last minute, when Storm was sure they would pull up and land, it veered upwards, giving them a clear view of the call letters on its underbelly. The letters didn't mean anything to Storm. The open hands of the Gatherer logo on the side did. She could have stood up and waved them in. Let them take her back to the headquarters or somewhere safe where she could meet with her mother and find out this was all a mistake.

The trees shook with the power of the jets as it passed over, stirring up the wet leaves into a wilted frenzy. She stayed where she was, stomach pressed flat to the damp earth.

The sound of the jet faded and they didn't move, both of them expecting its piercing buzz to return at any moment.

The trees settled and the leaves calmed, but Storm's heart pounded in her chest. Her hands shook with the force of it. She had seen the jet's prototype before she had left the city. This version was larger and faster with none of the fragility she had seen in the original model.

"How did they know we were here?"

Maria had rolled from out of the sleeping bag and stared down at her.

"I have no idea."

"Of all the marshes in this vicinity they just happened to come to the one we were crossing?"

Storm pushed the bag off her legs and stood up, brushing wet leaves and dirt off her pants.

"How would I tell them? Some magical communication device that doesn't emit radio waves or electromagnetic fields? Or maybe I sent them my coordinates from the cell phone that I've kept tucked inside my coat this whole time?"

Maria's eyes were bloodshot, dirt smeared on the front of her coat, her pants wet to the knees.

"Then how did they find us?"

Storm looked to where the jet had appeared, following its path over the water.

"Maybe they know how you think. Could guess the route that you would take."

"Those weren't my people."

Maybe it had been the jet barrelling down on them or the adrenaline that pulsed in her veins, but Storm could now see the inconsistencies she hadn't noticed before.

"You were running from that jet faster than I was."

There was the smallest shake of Maria's head her gaze steady with its telltale hint of defiance.

"I don't want them to catch you."

"Why not? That jet was from the Corporation. If I went with them I could see my mother. Find out what the hell is going on."

"You wouldn't survive in the city."

"This journey isn't going to end anywhere else but there."

She recognized the truth in that instance. They were headed to Rima, the southwesterly path they were on already taking them towards it. She would arrive, not as a guest of the corporation but as the inventor of the Gatherer. The solution to this lay in her connection to it and her ability to understand it like no one else.

"Can you help me get there?"

She couldn't pretend she could get there on her own. If she wanted to survive, she would need Maria, and all her exceptional skills.

"That's why I'm here."

There was a simplicity to her response. Not that it had always been her plan but that this was where they had landed and what they needed to do.

Maria's fingers uncurled, as if she were physically letting something go. The swell of her chest and the long slow exhale hinted at the battle going on inside her, looking to get out.

Maria smoothed her hair back from her face and pulled the elastic from the remains of her ponytail. In a quick twist, her hair was tight and smooth against her skull.

"When the government refused to acknowledge the damage the Gatherer was creating, Havernal and I decided we had to find you."

The clean lines of her hair accentuated the high ridge of her cheekbones and the hollows beneath.

"No one knows where I've gone but him. Though by now I'm sure they've begun to suspect."

"Are they looking for you?"

Maria shrugged, or at least tried to, ambivalence not a gesture Storm had ever seen her pull off.

"I haven't done anything wrong."

A strong vehemence, and Storm wondered if Maria was convincing herself as much as her.

"We had to get to you first. Convince you of the data before someone else told you otherwise."

Maria's use of the word 'we' made her unbearably sad. She was using it to make herself feel that she and Havernal were still a team. That she hadn't risked her entire military career.

"No one 'tells' me anything."

It was why Storm needed to remain on her own, outside the influence of the naysayers and those who would deny what she created. It was the only way to keep her thinking clear.

Again there was an unconvincing shrug.

"You hadn't shown your face, even though people had been getting sick for months. We had to assume that you were either complicit or couldn't see the evidence."

"You know me better than that."

A look of irritation as Maria bent to collect the sleeping bag.

"You might not have as much control as you think. The corporation has changed since you left."

Maria shoved the bag back into the pack, glancing up at the low-lying clouds. She stood, the precise control of her movements easing.

"We should keep moving. For all we know they did see us."

"Wouldn't they have stopped?"

"Not necessarily. They may want to pick us up later. Wait for us to show our hand."

"There's nothing to show."

"They don't know that."

Maria's straight shoulders led Storm through the trees, her pace steady, though Storm sensed she had slowed her natural speed for Storm's benefit. She wished Blue were walking next to her, weaving in and out of the trees as he scouted ahead and behind.

"It was Havernal who noted it first. Once he started reacting to the fields, he started paying attention. Figuring out what caused his symptoms and what didn't."

Maria placed her hand lightly on a narrow trunk and stepped around it, their path becoming more convoluted as the forest thickened.

"At first he didn't understand what was happening. He tried to work through it, but no matter how much he rested or looked after himself he couldn't shake it."

Her voice was flat and factual, her professionalism giving her a distance from the emotions that occasionally broke through in short pauses or truncated words.

"He first suspected the Gatherer when he would be symptomatic at the office and almost symptom-free at home. He and his wife lived on an acreage outside of town."

It surprised Storm that Havernal had a wife. With Maria's protectiveness, she had assumed she and Havernal were together.

"I found him curled up on the floor of his office one morning. His jaw clenched like he was having a seizure. By then we had started tracking the illness. Trying to see if there was a connection to the Gatherer."

A branch brushed along Storm's arm, and a sudden softness to the ground made her question whether they had truly left the marsh.

"Did you find it?"

They had reached a more open area, giving them enough room to walk side by side.

"It was hard to establish a pattern when the corporation wouldn't divulge where the Gatherers were installed. Plus, some people show symptoms and others don't."

Maria had her head bent, her gaze unfocussed.

"They wouldn't tell you where they were?"

"Shortly after the symptoms started appearing the corporation closed ranks. No interviews. Only official statements espousing the great benefits the Gatherer had brought to the world. They claimed the rumours of an illness were fear mongering from the traditional energy industries that weren't ready to embrace the new world."

Storm tried to imagine the meeting that would have led to that decision. The open inclusiveness of the Gatherer flipped on its side to become a secretive organization. The company she had created was unrecognizable.

"Havernal and I went to the headquarters. Waited in the lobby until your mother agreed to see us."

Maria slowed and Storm matched her pace, grateful for the slower speed. Wind rustled through the tamaracks, the tiny vibrations filling the air, better than the vibrations from the jet.

"And?"

There was a reticence in Maria as if she were physically forcing the words out.

"Your mother knew her rights. At that point we were still investigating so we had no official decree."

"What happened when you went back?"

Their pace slowed further.

"We didn't."

A flash of heat traveled down Storm's front like a spotlight panning across her. Her step faltered though she recovered quickly. Her nerves sometimes echoed earlier attacks, the exertion of the hike triggering a response.

"We were given a strict directive that the Gatherer was not the cause of the plague. I was reassigned to a different case. Havernal went on sick leave."

Maria's words carried her disappointment, the bend of her neck giving her a vulnerability Storm had never seen before.

Storm started to speak, her words cut off by a sudden wave of agitation. She drew a deep breath, waiting for the pain to subside. These echoes of being so close to the Gatherer were the strongest she'd ever had.

"Are you okay?"

Maria's concerned face appeared in front of her, her grip on Storm's arm.

"What's happening?"

A deeper, searing ripple of pain raced down the front of Storm's face. She grabbed a too narrow branch and tried to turn back. It was like being caught in the undertow of a massive wave that drew her in when she got too close. The field was so strong, crashing over her with a relentless force.

She heard a panicked cry inside her head and froze in place. She had the thought that this couldn't be here and she was reeling backwards, the taste of metal on her tongue.

TWELVE

Maria grabbed the top of Storm's coat and dragged her back towards the trees, one meter into the woods, then two. Maria pulled as fast as she could, pursued by the soldier-like towers that rose out of the low grasses, their steel arms and humming wires as lethal to Storm as any gun. The coat pulled at Storm's armpits, lifting her arms awkwardly at her sides so they caught on tree trunks and fallen branches. Storm's heels dragged leaves and sticks along and left two shallow trenches behind them.

There was no time to readjust, not knowing how far she needed to retreat from the lines or how much Storm would be damaged for each second she stayed within the fields that must vibrate at a lethal frequency. Maria was breathing hard, hot inside her coat, when they passed the place where there had been enough space to walk side by side and there had been no signs of physical distress. Maria kept pulling, once or twice looking to the towers visible through the tree tops, dominating the entire sky if they had only lifted their heads to see.

When her forearms ached and her hands threatened to open she slowed, lowering a now quiet Storm onto what she hoped was a drier patch of ground. Her features were in the same still absence as Mac's had been when he'd lain in Storm's shelter.

She found the silver suit and laid it over top of Storm's motionless frame like a blanket, followed by the sleeping bag. The contents of the pack had spilled out and she lifted the Tupperware with Storm's emergency stash of medication from the pile. What Maria didn't know was whether this was an emergency. Storm was pale, her red hair brighter against the colourless skin, yet a slight tension below her eyes made her look like she wasn't as far away now, sleeping instead of unconscious. Maria returned the vials to the pack.

She sat down, her back against a thin poplar trunk, prepared to wait. She allowed herself to rest, acknowledging her tired muscles and the growing thirst, but more than anything the force that had been stalking her since she had left Ottawa.

It had been easy to ignore the grief when she had been in motion, first finding Storm, then getting her away from the cabin. But today, as they had walked directionless through this relentless landscape she had been unable to escape the truth of Havernal's illness. She wasn't going to be the white knight in shining armour, arriving back in Ottawa with Storm and a cure that would miraculously whisk him back to health. Any hope she'd had of bringing home a cure had died the moment she saw Storm holding the empty syringe on the path north of Three Rocks. More in need of help than being able to offer it.

The forest was silent, the tree branches devoid of scurrying animals, the life force of struggling shrubs and the careful determination of lichen having drawn inward, protecting itself from the winter that should arrive in weeks or days. Maria picked up a dried brown leaf, its curled edge damp, and let it disintegrate through her fingers.

She wouldn't be going back to Ottawa. She could see that now. There would be obstacles worse than this hydro line before this would be fixed. If it even could. She thought of the afflicted who had huddled behind the combine on the railroad tracks, of Mac's terror when he had fallen into the cabin.

Storm rolled over, her cheek resting on a pillow of matted leaves. At least she was asleep now and not unconscious. But would this shadow of the once formidable Storm Freeman even be able to stop this?

She stood and brushed off the seat of her pants, turning towards the hydro line that waited out of sight. There shouldn't have been any current travelling through the wires, yet Storm had reacted as if a strong, powerful field emanated from them.

It took less than five minutes for Maria to return to the power line, its faint hum reaching her before she left the trees now that she knew to listen for it. The steel towers extended north and south. With their outstretched arms they looked like a line of resigned soldiers marching towards a far-off battle.

It was like assessing any obstacle or opponent. Exploit its weaknesses; come at it from an unexpected angle. The multiple wires that the towers supported carried the current creating the fields that were so lethal to

Storm. Maria would have been standing in the field, yet she felt nothing. Her cells could have been compromised, or the electrical balance of her body under attack, yet she heard only its gentle hum, felt the light breeze on her face. The towers extended south, continuing indefinitely in a long unbroken chain. Unlike a river there would be no bridges to find if they followed its banks or a wildlife corridor over a highway to guide animals away from deadly traffic. The only way through was immersed in the full strength of the electromagnetic fields until they escaped its range on the other side.

She followed the gouges of dirt from Storm's heels and the broken branches back to the beacon of Storm's hair against the faded brown forest. It was darker beneath the trees, the early night already siphoning the light from the land. The hydro lines had been the first signs of civilization they had seen, and not the one they had been hoping for. A road or some place with food would have been better. Any animals or berries that this hardy landscape had to offer had departed with the long days of summer.

Storm slept with her hand beneath her cheek. The sleep of the exhausted. Maria nudged her three times before the first signs of reluctant consciousness played across her features. Storm's presence had added weight to Maria's travels; she moved slower, had to stop more often and encountered obstacles that Maria would have already left behind. Maria shook her shoulder and felt the warmth beneath the sleeping bag. It reminded her of dragging herself out of her sleeping bag into a bitterly cold pre-dawn patrol in Kandahar province. They had known the enemy was waiting for them, just not where or how strong.

When Storm opened her eyes, they were blurry and confused, taking several seconds to take in Maria, the trees, and the sky before she remembered at least partially where she was. She used both arms to pull herself to sitting, her movements slow and stiff.

"Is it morning?"

Storm pulled the sleeping bag closer around her, exposing the bottom of the silver suit. She frowned, looked at Maria, then the suit again, and took a full circle inspection around them.

"What happened?"

Maria sat down beside her, feeling her own stiff muscles and growing hunger. As the light retreated, she told Storm briefly of the power line that blocked their path and what she hoped to do.

Storm's pale face grew whiter against the darkness, even her hair seeming to lose colour. It gave Maria hope that she didn't argue. For it meant that despite the physical deterioration her brain still functioned at a frequency well beyond that of the normal person, assessing and discarding options until she arrived at the inevitable conclusion. She hoped this plan wouldn't change that.

Storm hung her head and for a moment Maria thought she was crying, her shoulders giving way under a weight that must have always been there. Maria stood and offered her hand.

"We might as well get it done. Before it's dark."

They didn't speak as they walked towards the hydro line. Maria tried to sense when they arrived in range of the field. She smelled the damp rot of the forest and felt moss give way beneath her feet, but other than the dropping temperature the air carried no other signal. She checked on Storm frequently in case it did for her.

"It doesn't make sense that it's here."

There was real fear in Storm's voice, a recognition that death had taken a step closer, eager for her vulnerability once the strength of the power line's electromagnetic field had done its damage.

"It could be part of the grid that's still operational. Carrying electricity from a dam operating north of here."

"The Gatherer has replaced all this."

They stopped before they reached the spot where they had been earlier. Storm's lifted face shone in the stronger light from the open meadow. Her expression was one that Maria recognized from exhausted men going into battles they expected to lose. Resignation, fear, and yet, underneath, a relief that at least the ordeal would be over.

"Can you feel it?"

"Can't you?"

THIRTEEN

The woods on the opposite side of the wires were four hundred metres away, if not more. Maria examined the pattern of shrubs and grass, looking for the most direct, unblocked path through the meadow. At one time she could have sprinted four hundred metres in close to a minute. With Storm on her back it could be three times that long, which would leave Storm exposed for that full time. Maria swung her arms, rolling her shoulders. The field would be strongest directly below the wire so she would need to pace accordingly. Start slow, sprint in the middle, ease up if she needed to when she approached the opposite trees.

"You'll be fast?"

Storm threaded her legs and arms into the silver suit. It would provide some protection, but ultimately there would be damage.

"I'm going to put you in a fireman's carry now so I don't have to waste time if you collapse."

Storm fitted the silver hood over her head, her face round and childlike, the growing darkness robbing the dark circles beneath her eyes of their force. She pulled the sleeves over her hands and drew a mesh veil over her face, blocking herself off from the entire world.

"The vials are on the top of the pack. If you need them."

"How will I know?"

Storm's breathing was shallow and fast.

"If I look anything like Mac did when he got to the cabin. Or you think I'm dying."

Maria couldn't tell if Storm was making a joke. She didn't think so, but she had heard enough dark humour before missions to understand the response.

"You'll need to go at least three hundred metres away from the lines. Can you carry me that far?"

The sky behind the towers was a dull, faded yellow, the sun barely having the strength to linger above the horizon.

"No problem."

Maria's heart pounded as if she were already running, her legs surging with the power that arrived with the adrenaline.

"Take a deep breath."

She leaned her shoulder into Storm's waist, tackling her. Storm didn't bend.

"Lean into me."

Maria's head was next to the boney point of Storm's hip, her forearms braced around the back of her thighs. Storm's weight was tentative at first, until Maria pushed up and lifted her hips. Storm grunted as she was forced upside down on Maria's back, her legs jutting out stiff in front of Maria.

"Relax!"

This position was so much easier when your victim was unconscious. Her core muscles engaged and she pulled down on Storm's legs, forcing them to collapse. She adjusted the weight, her legs solid and stable as she started to jog. Storm was trying to brace herself against Maria's back, the stiff bouncing painful for both of them.

"Be a rag doll."

She needn't have bothered. Storm's weight collapsed when they stepped out of the trees. Maria held on tighter, running faster and pushing farther into the field. Storm cried out, the terrorized bleat of an animal in inescapable pain. Maria ran faster, Storm's cries urging her on as Storm's body gave way, bouncing limp against her back. She had expected resistance to be greater at the centre of the field, yet her legs pumped as hard and the ground moved beneath her as fast as it had in the woods. The waves of Storm's seizure convulsed against her back, muscles firing of their own accord, her legs bouncing and jerking so that Maria had to grip hard to keep from dropping her.

Maria preferred an enemy she could see, meet head on, and defeat outright. Not one that waited it out, knowing that eventually you would come to it. The fear of being in the enemy's front line pushed one foot in front of the next faster, yet there was no enemy to see. Nothing to strike down but the unbreakable steel towers, the porters of the enemy's strength.

She ran directly beneath the wires, the meadow falling into darkness as Storm's body fell heavy against her. She pushed harder, frantic that the field had been too much and that once again she had rushed into a plan without thinking it through and would have another death on her hands.

Fifty metres from the edge of the woods, Maria stumbled on a depression hidden by the grass and shot forward, Storm flying ahead of her. Maria's knees struck earth as Storm's heavy thud sounded ahead of her without a cry of pain. She scrambled forward and found Storm partially curled on her side. Her suit glowed dully, the mesh over her face turning her into a lifeless mannequin. Maria rolled her onto her back as a pressure pushed on her ears and a vibration ran over her skin. Was this the field? Slowly electrocuting Storm as Maria wasted time? She tried to lift Storm but her knees buckled each time she tried to stand. The corridor of the towers drew out on either side of her and for a moment she was disoriented, thinking she needed to go back and run in the opposite direction.

Think.

Havernal's voice sounded in her head.

The sky glowed in the west where the sun was setting and where she wanted to go. The shelter of the trees drew farther away as the light faded, the towers growing darker and higher. She grabbed Storm under her arms, hooked her elbows at the joints so Storm was tight to her body, and pulled towards the trees.

She collapsed onto a dark patch of what she hoped was moss, leaving Storm spread eagle on the ground. Had she come far enough? The towers were out of sight and she had been hauling Storm's unresponsive body through shrubs and tangled branches for what felt like hours. She rolled Storm over and ripped the pack from her back. Maria's hands shook as she undid the rope and fumbled with the latch on the plastic container.

Stupid. Stupid. Stupid. Why had Storm let her do it? Had she wanted to die? The zipper stuck on the silver suit and Maria yanked to get it open. She plunged the needle into Storm's thigh. No response. She waited, wanting Storm to suddenly sit up, tell her the plan had gone better than expected when in truth it had gone much worse.

Tossing the needle aside, Maria slipped off the silver hood. Storm's neck was slightly sweaty, a good sign, as Maria searched for a pulse. She had a moment of anguish when she couldn't find it, then the relief of a faint, erratic beat, far beneath the skin.

A slight rise in the earth provided a small amount of shelter and Maria positioned Storm next to it. She had difficulty fitting the sleeping bag around her, her limp arms and legs wilfully falling to where they weren't put. There was no resistance, not even the hint of a muscle flexing. Storm was in a place so deep that it was like she had abandoned her physical body. Storm's description of what it felt like repeated in Maria's mind.

It's an ambush of emotions, like you're high on ecstasy, your mother has just died, and you're being chased by a rabid dog. Until a curtain of black oil oozes over all of it and you wake up sometime later wondering what happened.

When she had Storm zipped in, and confirmed her pulse still beat low and faint, Maria lay down next to her, spreading her own sleeping bag over the both of them. The stars shone through the bare branches above them, as far from earth as Maria felt from Storm. Maria tucked her arm around Storm's thin frame, willing the energy and health she carried to drain into her and replenish the stores that had been so brutally depleted. If the Gatherer could take energy from the world, there had to be a way to put it back. It was just a matter of figuring it out.

FOURTEEN

Storm's eyes opened and closed, returning to sleep for brief periods before they would open again and her bleary gaze would try to focus on Maria's face. Maria held a bottle to her lips, getting her to take small sips during her moments of consciousness. Storm was barely able to lift her head off the ground.

When her eyes finally cleared, she lay staring up into the sparse tree branches, her face drained of blood and hope and anything beyond utter exhaustion. Maria handed Storm a bar and she ate it lying down, only lifting her head to take the smallest of bites. Maria's stomach was tight with hunger but it was their last bar and Maria doubted Storm could go anywhere without it.

"Do you know where—"

Storm's voice was slow and slurred, and Maria hoped it was the effects of the injection and not any damage from Maria taking her beneath the wire.

"More or less. Do you need another injection?"

Storm shook her head though the motion obviously pained her. Storm tried to sit up and Maria crouched next to her to support her back.

"You need to help me up."

Storm held onto Maria for several seconds once she was standing, waiting for whatever waves were crashing through her to stop. When she let go, Storm leaned against a tree, looking too hungover for words.

"I can carry you."

"Not for long."

Maria collected their sleeping bags and garbage, the only trace of their stop a few disturbed twigs and branches.

When she had the pack loaded, she lifted her chest and let it settle onto her shoulders. Storm still hadn't let go of the tree.

"Ready?"

Storm's fingers released and after a glance behind them, she took a hesitant step forward. Maria stayed beside her. They started slowly, covering barely two kilometres in an hour. They walked through sparse forests and across spare open areas of low brush and grass. She expected any moment the return of the jet, or even a member of her unit stepping silently in front of them. Yet as the sun peaked low in the sky and started its fast descent, nothing interrupted their trek. The landscape was so empty of movement it was as if they walked through a world already gone quiet, one they hadn't been able to save.

The first headlights appeared at the top of a low rise a few moments after the sun had dropped below the western range. A river valley fell below them with the straight line of a highway crossing over it. It was the main artery connecting the north with the south and she had originally crossed it further north. The glow of a gas station shone a kilometre up from the river with the lighted windows of several houses spaced around it.

Storm slumped to the ground. It was too dark to see the details of her face clearly but Maria had witnessed her peaked exhaustion throughout the day.

"We'll stay here tonight."

She handed Storm the final bottle. The lights of a transport moved slowly south as Storm drank and offered the bottom half to Maria.

"I'll get something at the station in the morning."

The station glowed stronger as the day darkened, a bright spot in the dark bowl of the valley.

"We can't go in there."

"I'll go on my own. There'll be less chance of being recognized."

Or she hoped there would. If it was her, she would be watching every point on the highway going south. Her only hope was that they would be looking for two travellers, not one, and if she could get in and out fast enough they might get lucky.

They slept side by side, their sleeping bags zipped together, their combined heat barely keeping them warm. Maria woke frequently, thinking she heard footsteps or the approach of a jet, and was tired and cold when the slightest lightening in the east hinted at the new day.

She slipped carefully out of their bag, tucking it around Storm before she left. She might just catch a sleepy cashier at the end of a night shift, too tired to care who came in the door.

FIFTEEN

A wide expanse of broken pavement surrounded the station, with space for three or four semis behind it. The space was empty in the morning dusk, the only signs of customers a pickup parked at a shiny island of electric charging stations where the pumps had once been. Maria hadn't seen the Gatherer from the top of the hill, the white concave box tucked on the far side of the old station—a smaller size, enough to power the charging stations and the building that housed the store.

The open space gave Maria an easy view of who came and went, but it also meant she would be wide open between the entrance to the store and the dry, shallow ditch where she lay. A single surveillance camera hung on the corner of the low building, directed towards the charging stations. A younger man, his fluorescent safety vest reflecting in the lights, clomped to the pickup and slammed the door behind him. It was several minutes before he finally put the vehicle in gear and rolled back onto the highway, allowing the morning to settle back over the station.

There was likely only a single cashier in the store, hopefully tired enough after the night shift to not care much about the hitchhiker who wandered in. For without a car and her rumpled clothes, that would be their assumption.

The morning was brightening, the glow of the rising sun getting stronger in the east, drawing away what little protection the dusk could provide. She pulled the elastic from her hair, letting it fall around her face, and pulled Storm's ball cap down tight. She checked a final time for arriving vehicles.

She walked fast, not running, imagining eyes on her, the lookouts posted above the station waiting for this very thing. She kept close to the building and out of range of the camera.

A bell rang as she stepped through the door into an onslaught of her senses. A bank of drink coolers lined the back wall below a digital sign that flashed through a cycle of brightly coloured testaments to the choice of drinks below. Pop music played at a level just below where you could hear the words, overlaid by the blare of a loud weather forecast on the screen mounted high in the corner. The pallid, obese woman at the cash register nodded to her as she sorted through the lottery ticket display, her surprisingly small hands filing tickets into each slot. A surveillance camera was mounted behind the counter and there was a second in the far back corner.

She kept her head bent so her hair hung close around her cheeks and the hat's brim blocked the cameras' view. She swerved towards the far aisle where rows of what were presented as the healthy snacks crowded the shelves. She ripped open a box of granola bars, and bit into the soft chewy bit of heaven. As she chewed she checked ingredients on some of the other bars, all of them too sweet or filled with too many chemicals for Storm to tolerate. Keeping her face away from the cameras, she scanned the store for other options.

The woman shuffled down the aisle and Maria smiled as she passed. Her response was a blank, ambivalent smile and Maria felt her anxiety ratchet down. Maybe it was possible for her not to be recognized, that the whole world wasn't looking for her. She tucked three boxes of bars under her arm and moved to the coolers, scanning for the tomato juice Storm had requested.

A news story of a coyote nipping the heels of a jogger came on with an interview of a shocked, fit young woman in a sports bra. Once they had asked her way more questions than necessary, a less attractive middle-aged man came on to try to explain the extremes in temperature and volatile weather on the west coast.

"Choose Coke!" chirped a female voice as she opened the cooler. She took three apple juices off the bottom shelf and a half dozen of the tomato juice as the clerk passed her again on her way back to the counter. Maria added chips, five packs of beef jerky, and several suspicious-looking apples to her collection.

"What kind of smokes you want?"

The woman had opened the shelf behind the counter, exposing the rows of colourful cigarette cartons.

Maria dumped her goods onto the counter, keeping her face turned from the camera.

"I don't smoke."

The woman finished sliding three lottery tickets into the display under the clear plastic countertop, and after unlocking the register began an excruciatingly slow process of scanning each item.

The weather man beamed on the screen and clasped his hands together before the view changed to a thin, athletic-looking news anchor sitting behind a desk.

"A new Gatherer has been installed in a test laboratory at Berkeley in California. Researchers plan to look for new ways to access the energy that supplies the revolutionary device."

Maria turned to watch the screen, like any normal person watching the news.

The image showed a unit as large as the ones she had seen on the train being lowered by crane onto a concrete pad in the centre of a sunny green space. Storm's mother shook hands with half a dozen university dignitaries, everyone beaming optimism and good will.

The face of Alicia Freeman suddenly filled the screen, a microphone held before her by an intense, eager reporter.

"Why has this Gatherer been provided to researchers now, when previously all research on the devices had been prohibited?"

The cashier slapped a carton of Du Mauriers on the counter beside Maria's purchases. Maria was confused, distracted by Alicia's face on the screen.

"Providing the energy that the world needs is the Gatherer Corporation's number one priority."

She had the same red hair as Storm, though darker and styled in a smooth, slick bob. Her delivery was as seamless as any politician's and Maria marvelled at the transformation of the woman who, before the Gatherer, had been a difficult, failed academic.

"I don't smoke."

"Sorry I didn't hear you."

The cashier grabbed the Du Mauriers and shuffled back to the cabinet where she slid them neatly into place.

"If we can work together to find new and more efficient methods of accessing this abundant energy, there won't be any energy need we can't meet."

Alicia flashed a dazzling smile.

The woman placed a carton of Player's Lights onto the counter.

What was the woman doing?

"How do you respond to the accusation that the Gatherer is the source of the plague?"

The woman was about to scan the Player's and Maria finally looked up into the cashier's passive face. Behind the woman, the door of the cigarette cabinet blocked the surveillance camera's lens.

"The Gatherer has been put through stringent tests, and the larger ones in particular, like this one—"

Alicia pointed towards the shining new Gatherer.

"—Will provide a new level of energy supply that will make so many things possible."

The woman laid the carton of Player's down without scanning it through. Maria didn't understand what was happening, which meant she needed to leave. She rifled through her bag for the money Curtis had given them, and laid barely enough to cover the bill on the counter. She shoved her purchases into the bag as fast as she could, keeping her head low in case there was a camera she missed. She hoped to God the woman hadn't already pressed the burglary button under the counter that went straight to the local police. A bag of mixed nuts burst open in her haste to force it into a space too small. She kept packing, torn between the need for the supplies and the freedom of the door less than five steps away.

The woman slowly counted out Maria's change as the announcer moved onto a new story. When she turned from the cash register, the woman laid a newspaper face up on the counter. Storm's face filled the front page under the headline, "Freeman Comes out of Hiding."

The woman held her hand above it, waiting for Maria to take the change.

Breathe.

Maria extended her hand as casually as she could manage. The woman's soft warm fingers briefly touched Maria's as she laid a wad of twenty-dollar bills into her palm.

"Have a nice day."

Maria looked up in surprise at the woman's calm, determined gaze, making contact for only an instant before she turned away and opened a second cupboard of cigarettes that would block the view of Maria's path to the door. Maria jammed the money and the paper into her bag and lifted her pack.

"You too."

She ran, across the horrible openness of the tarmac, and the meagre bushes on the flats that led to the base of the hill. The store fell behind her, but no matter how far she went, she felt a long tether clipped to her back, reeling her in. The pack bounced heavily, its weight a reminder of what that visit could have cost them. The food and adrenaline spurred her on, so she climbed the hill where Storm waited sooner than she expected.

"You came back."

The relief on Storm's face was blatant, her pale waxiness making her look all the more vulnerable.

"Of course I did."

Maria didn't bother to hide her irritation. Storm's look of vulnerability closed in and Storm nodded, her show of fear tucked away. Storm made to open the bag.

"What did you get?"

"Lucky. We need to keep moving."

Storm's fingers stopped where she'd undone the pack's knot, her hunger turning to alarm.

Maria pulled the paper from the top of the bag and shoved it at her. A hard veneer slid over Storm's features as she read the article.

"They're looking for both of us. Not just me."

A sudden spike of adrenaline and Maria checked the valley below them. It had been a huge risk going into the station. Storm was rising to her feet, already tucking the paper into the bag.

"You knew, didn't you? When you ran from the jet? That it wasn't just me they wanted."

The question didn't need an answer. Maria loaded the pack onto her back, feeling the sting of the raw places where it rested on her hips and shoulders.

"What else does it say?"

"There are riots in the streets. That they've had to put armed guards around some of the Gatherers in larger cities."

Maria's shoulders rose, feeling the pressure of the escalating situation, aware of how lucky they had been to make it this far.

"Where do they think we are?"

Storm stared down into the river valley with the intensity of a commander about to launch an attack. Maria had a breath of hope, for the energy that enervated Storm's frame reminded her of the force that Storm had once been, for whom nothing had been impossible.

"On the run. And that we're dangerous."

Maria felt a strengthening in her core, that someone had recognized the damage that they could do if everything went right.

"We are dangerous."

Storm smiled suddenly, then laughed. A sound that did more for both of them than any food or water.

"I guess they'd better watch out then."

Storm moved faster than she had since they left the cabin, keeping up even though Maria would be jogging if she moved any faster. They kept the road to their right, watching for flashes of metal and waiting for the low vibrations that traveled through the earth when the larger vehicles passed. There wasn't much traffic, and if they timed it right they would be able to cross without being seen.

"Are you sure she recognized you?"

"She gave me two hundred dollars in cash. Showed me the cover of the paper."

Storm had returned to a paler version of who she had been at her peak, her presence always seeming to draw more light to it than anything else within view.

"I gave her forty dollars. She recognized me. I'm sure of it."

They were climbing a small slope, dislodging small stones that fell behind them. The sun had risen higher, and with no signs of pursuit Maria allowed herself a moment of celebration. The station had been a risk and they had gotten away. Storm slowed to navigate a section of uneven ground, and for a moment they walked side by side, the valley and the river bed below them.

"The paper says you're wanted for murder."

Storm's calmness startled her, showing such faith in Maria that she assumed it wasn't true.

"Who?"

Please don't let it be Havernal.

"Something to do with a train?"

She couldn't be sure but she thought Storm was amused. That it was somehow humorous that Maria had been accused.

"I didn't—"

But then she remembered stepping over Coulter's lifeless body. The driver had been alive and cursing her when she'd abandoned the train at the track's northern peak. But Coulter's death would have been all too easy to pin on her, giving them evidence of the violent radical who had gotten away with their train.

The thought of bars holding her in made her surge forward, Storm's breathing falling behind her until she came to the top of a rise, the sudden shock of a cold, damp wind and a full view of the mass of clouds gathered on the western horizon. A solid line of darkness inched its way east, consuming the tops of low mountains, sucking light out of the sky.

Storm stopped below her, her face tilted up towards Maria. A hint of colour had appeared on her white cheeks, the food and the walk chasing away the grayness that had arrived after her seizure. Maria wondered if that cabin had been the best place for Storm, as much of a cage for her as a jail cell would be for Maria.

"He was a civilian. I wouldn't kill—"

"I didn't say you did. I was just telling you what it said in the paper."

Storm held out her hand, asking for help over the final knee-high ledge up to the flat crown of the hill.

"We'll be able to cross down there."

The highway crossed the river that flowed smooth and brown, enough of a space along its edge that they could pass under the bridge without being seen. A car bumped up onto the bridge, going north, the sound of its tires the only noise but for the faintest of whines from the electric drive.

It was a steep climb down to the river bed and Maria slowed her pace, offering her hand to Storm through the trickier footing. At the river's edge, Maria waited for Storm to catch up, staring into the fast flowing silt of yet another body of water. Once they rounded the bend they would be in plain sight to anyone crossing the bridge. Maria listened for the hum of a vehicle or the bump of tires, cursing the silence of electric vehicles.

"I would have no reason to kill Coulter. He wasn't even a threat."

Storm had brightened the further they descended into the river valley.

"It won't matter to them what really happened. It just makes a good story."

Maria understood that. She had seen it happen countless times with the coverage of Storm, many of the actions and motivations attributed to her blatantly wrong. It was different when it was you being maligned, the injustice of it so much sharper.

The water downstream ran sleek and fast. A boat could find them as easily as a car. They moved forward, Maria aware of every sound, the shift of the air, placing her feet carefully. When she could see the bridge and anyone on it could see her, she ran, her eyes darting from the bridge to the sloped bank, her attention hopping from every possible viewpoint to the sloped path under her feet with the water waiting below it. No sound but their footsteps hitting the muddy bank. She wanted to help Storm, pull her faster, but there was no room on the narrow path and she focused on reaching the shelter of the bridge.

Maria reached the bridge first and turned back to check Storm when wheels bumped on the opposite side of the bridge. Storm was ten metres out and, if the driver was watching, in plain sight.

"Run!"

A surge of speed and Storm fell into Maria. Maria steadied her as the vehicle slowed above them and the tires pulled onto the gravel. There was a moment when their gazes met, an understanding of what would happen if they were caught, the thump of a door, and footsteps on the gravel. Their chests rose and fell in the utter stillness, all of their awareness on the crunch of the footsteps.

A frozen stillness hung as they half held each other, gazes lifted to the underside of the bridge. She could win a fight against a civilian, but there was no point in killing him. The vehicle, the body. There would be no time to cover their tracks.

A man cleared his throat and a zipper opened. A faint moan of relief. Maria took a deeper breath as the sound of water hitting the earth reached them with the acrid stench of piss.

Storm's eyebrows shot up as Maria pressed her finger to her lips.

A stream of urine ran down the bank, spreading and absorbing into the earth before it reached the water.

Storm leaned in close to Maria's ear.

"His truck."

Storm released her grip and moved away from Maria, towards the bank, straining her neck for a better view of the man.

Maria pulled her back. Storm tried to shake her off and Maria held on, trying not to dislodge any earth or stones that would give them away.

She squeezed Storm's arm and Storm whirled on her, the shock of pain on her face. Maria mouthed the word, 'No.'

Storm tried to pull her arm away and Maria squeezed harder.

The man did up his zipper, cleared his throat and spit into the dirt.

"Okay."

Storm mouthed the word, pulling her arm back when Maria let go and cradling it next to her chest. The footsteps retreated, a door opened and the whir of the engine sounded as it continued north.

"Why not?"

Anger added real colour to Storm's cheeks, her body vibrating with a new energy.

"A stolen vehicle is too easy to find up here. There aren't enough places to hide."

She had considered the same idea a dozen times on her way up, when her blisters had seeped and bled.

"We can't walk all the way."

Maria understood Storm was saying she couldn't walk all the way. That she wouldn't make it.

"You can't drive in a car anyways."

Storm's feet scraped on the gravel as she walked to the water's edge, her illness another kind of cage.

"It was a pickup. I could have ridden in the back away from the battery."

She ran an agitated hand through her hair.

"With the suit."

Maria made a note of Storm's desperation, and the urgency that would make her even consider this. At their current pace they would be traveling over rough terrain for well over a week before they reached Rima. Probably more.

"We'll figure something out. But that's not it."

The river flowed behind Storm's straight, solitary figure in its quiet, relentless push towards the ocean. Maria gave her the time, knowing that soldiers in the field needed a few moments to collect themselves after the action. Maria looked up the river, towards its source, wondering how far they would make it before something gave: Storm's body, their cover, or the resolve of those who knew where they were.

SIXTEEN

Storm braced herself on the faded hull of the canoe, the muscles in her arm pulling as Maria lowered her to the ground. A foot above the cracked pavement Maria lost her grip and Storm hit the asphalt hard.

"Sorry."

Storm's body shook with the beat of her heart and breath, each trying to recover from the new pace of their flight, their notoriety pushing them faster than her body wanted to go.

Maria walked the row of canoes, yanking on the rusted chain that locked them together. The chain rattled and clanked each time she pulled it. The boat launch sloped down to the river, the twisting, curling disturbance on its surface evidence of the powerful current running beneath.

Storm closed her eyes against the burn but opened them immediately at the intensity of fatigue and dizziness that waited there. She should have gone down to the river, splashed her face with icy water, and drank frigid gulps. Yet she stayed sitting at the end of the row of old canoes, her feet splayed before her where they had fallen when Maria dropped her. A row of single room cabins sat back from the river, with a larger, abandoned house at the top of the hill. Weeds grew around the porches and the dull light reflected off streaked windows. She lay down onto the split asphalt, crushing the weeds that pushed up through the cracks. Tiny blades of grass grew out of the sand accumulated at the edge of the launch, the larger weeds like tree trunks next to them.

Maria swore to herself in time with the rattling of the chain, the rustle and swirl of the river providing the constant, unsettled background. The chains clinked close to Storm's head.

"Who's going to steal these things way out here?"

Maria dug into the pack and placed a handful of crackers into Storm's curled, upturned hand.

"We are."

Storm nibbled on the crackers, the edges sharp inside her cheek. She'd had trouble matching Maria's pace since the gas station, Maria almost running now that she knew she was being chased. She had mostly carried Storm the last several kilometres, her frenetic energy enough for both of them.

If anything, Storm was calmer than Maria now, used to being pursued and the world taking notice. Maria had likely spent most of her time in obscurity, hidden behind her uniform and her unit, outside even the norms of society. The full glare of the world's attention on her had her running hard away from its beam. Storm couldn't blame her. There had been many times when she would have given anything for its beam to be focussed somewhere else.

Maria set off towards the river, in the direction of the collapsing boat house, the side facing the current buckled under its ceaseless push. Storm closed her eyes again, the dizziness better, the fatigue calmer after a few moments of rest. She let it come, floating in its current, the sleep it brought deep and complete.

She woke to the shadow of a man leaning over her, his outline darker than the heavy clouds pushing down around him. She pulled her feet in and sat up, away from his steel toed boot that was kicking her shin. The day was darker than it should have been, an artificial dusk having arrived while she'd slept.

"Did you think you'd be able to get past me?"

She pushed back against the smooth side of the canoe. His work boots were worn, a gut hung over faded blue work pants, and he glared at her with a pinched, small face distorted by a loathing that felt personal.

"I heard the chains clanking. That's how I knew you'd come back."

He held a rifle with both hands.

"I've never been here before."

Unshaven, gray whiskers surrounded the mean slit of his mouth. She tried to draw back but there was nowhere to go. He jabbed the gun into her thigh, the skin still tender after the hydro line.

"Get up!"

She stood, all weakness in her legs having vanished at the sight of the gun. He made a great show of brandishing it, as if they were a party of three. Without turning her head, she tried to search for Maria, the open area as void of life as when they had watched from the trees. He pushed her towards the larger cabin higher above the river. The yellowed backs of curtains blocked every window, the wood bleached by wind and sun.

"I knew you'd come today. With that business up north."

She slowed for a chance to look for Maria but moved faster at a push from the rifle. The mountains rose high and steep behind them, funnelling anyone who had to go anywhere down to the river.

They followed a faint path, leading from the boat house to the large cabin. She was unable to shake the feeling that the place was abandoned. They had watched the old camp for over an hour and there had been no telltale clothing hung on the clothesline or any of the care taken by people for where they lived. A large fender truck that looked as untended as the house was parked behind it, next to an overturned garbage can and hundreds of pizza boxes stacked in disturbingly tidy rows. They were from the same pizza place—Anthony's Italian—and the logos lined up.

"They can't tell me it's not happening, now that I've caught you."

A wooden screen door was slightly ajar, dim shadows and dark spaces all that were visible through the torn screen. A rank smell of boarded-up life and closed-in death drifted from it. The kind of place thousands of women had gone into and never come out of. She lifted up her hands and faced him.

"I only stopped for a rest."

He lifted the gun higher, his face pinched with unhinged frustration.

"I'm sorry for disturbing you."

She could barely breathe for the force of her heart in her throat.

"I'll leave."

She stepped sideways.

He laughed, a high pitched bark. He backed her towards the door.

The stench of rotting pizza caught in her nostrils and her throat thickened as if it meant to close. The outline of a hawk circled on the currents that fell off the sides of the mountain. If she went in that cabin, she would never come out.

"I can help you."

"You're a thief."

"I haven't stolen anything."

His hands were shaking, the face behind the gun flushed so red it was almost purple.

"They'll believe me when they see you this time."

A terror deeper than anything she had ever felt froze over her. All her movements shut down except for her ability to follow his commands. He pushed her and spun her back towards the door.

The door frame had more exposed wood than paint, the edge completely bare from a lifetime of hands. The handle was coarse and thick, the latch heavy under her thumb. As the latch stuck, her brain pushed through the terror, and she saw the whole scene before her as if she had drawn it in her notebook with the forces and reactions calculated to two decimal points.

She turned, swinging at anything and everything behind her. Her forearm struck part of the barrel, and she ran her hand straight at his wind pipe. The retaliation was so fast as to be unseen, a vicious crack on her head and the pain spreading hot and fast through the shattered bits of her skull. She fell, meeting darkness before she hit the ground.

* * * *

Maria's legs felt like lead as she kicked the boathouse door, the stubborn old wood requiring five kicks before the lock split away and the door swung inward. The bottom edge caught on the warped floor and, moving slowly, Maria leaned her shoulder into the sun-baked wood and pushed it open wide. The smell of decaying wood and gasoline lingered in the closed space. The sound of the river pushing against the moorings was louder inside. She ducked at the sound of scurrying feet in the rafters, claws scratching somewhere above her. Testing the sturdiness of the floorboards, she stepped into the darkness to let the light from the outside penetrate further into the interior. Something gleamed in the dusk and the square of light from the door reflected in a pane of glass. Relief eased the tension across her shoulders as a boat took shape, a chrome rail along its bow and its wide hull barely fitting into the narrow slip. Boards creaked as she inched further along the deck, the faint smell of leather and pipe smoke breaking through the rot and gasoline. With enough fuel it could carry them all the way to Rima.

The faintest of sounds came from outside.

She slid back to the door, her feet placed along the silent ends of the boards. The landscape was pressed flat by the clouds, no noise but the rush of water and the small rustling of grass in the growing wind. She strained to hear, a steep section of the river bank blocking her view of Storm. Had it been a voice? Or an echo of her footsteps?

She stepped outside, on high alert, and had started up the hill when the wind slammed open one of the shutters on a neglected cabin. She felt a wash of relief and could breathe again. She turned her back on the looming hills and returned to the shelter of the boathouse.

The outline of the boat was easier to see now that she knew it was there, and she stepped carefully along the deck, alert for any weakness in the old boards. The whole structure shifted with her movements, the light breaking through the cracks in the boards, betraying the slant of the walls, the entire structure leaning upstream against the current.

The boat rocked beneath her as she stepped onto the stern and released the latch on the back door. The doors screeched, caught by the wind, and banged repeatedly against the sides, the wind determined to wake this place from its slumber.

A blue heron, disturbed from the far side of the river, flew downstream with long powerful strokes of its wings.

She turned carefully back to the boathouse, the water cold and black beyond the stern. A gleaming, one-hundred-and-fifty-horsepower motor was mounted on the flat boat's transom. Her fear solidified at the pristine canvas stretched over the boat's interior. The bow shone white and blue, the newly polished chrome rail gleaming in the dim light. She scrambled off the boat, nearly falling into the dark space between the boat and deck, her foot breaking through the wood when she landed so that she fell into the fishing nets and old rods propped against the side wall, the tackle clattering down in a cascading disaster. When the last pail lay still, the echoing silence felt alive, the place and the people she was now certain were there fully awake.

She heard Havernal's voice.

Get out of there.

She twisted her foot to free it from the wood and climbed to her feet, her brain cataloguing the clean windshield, the shine of the snaps that held the canvas tarp, and the absence of any watermarks where the hull touched the water.

One step. Two. There had to be other signs that she had missed. A worn path. An open window. Something would have hinted that this was here.

She had almost reached the door when a shadow fell across the opening. An older guy, overweight but strong and looking like he knew how to use the rifle in his hands. The walls pulled in closer, and the cold coming off the water deepened.

"Caught two birds in the trap today."

He moved closer, the point of a really old gun trained on her. His clothes were loose and dirty, his body distended from years of abuse, and he had the classic redneck swagger boasting that they had got it right and everyone else had it wrong. But there was something wrong in the way he moved—perhaps the heightened aggression that was too much for the situation, or the fact that he didn't really seem to see her. There had been guys like this in training. The ones she had tried to stay away from.

"Is this your boat?"

"Get out!"

He waved the gun like he was some guy on a SWAT team, the ones you saw on TV, not the real ones. A wannabe who'd been isolated in the woods for too long. She doubted the thing even fired. She held up her hands at her sides. He was coming too close, but with a gun he probably figured he had the advantage.

"How many others are there?"

"Just me."

She was going to lie, hoping that Storm had gotten away until she remembered he had said two birds. Not one.

"And my friend."

He stopped moving forward and glanced quickly at the boat, making sure she hadn't touched anything.

"I'm sorry. I didn't realize anyone lived here."

"So you thought you'd just break in. I heard you kicking at the door. Just another thief with no respect for people's property. Well, you got more than you bargained for this time."

There was an excitement to his energy that was rising the longer he kept the gun trained on her. His words were threatening, yet he sounded happy. He stepped back onto the deck that ran along the front of the boathouse. He waved the gun at her, towards the door.

The gun had to be fifty years old. But he had taken care of it and at this range it would be more than enough to do the job.

He prodded her up a faint path that was barely used but that she should have noticed earlier. They passed the row of overgrown cabins, shingles caught in the grass at their base. Every curtain in the large cabin was closed and the grasses grew above the railing of the veranda.

"Is this your place?"

The stacks of pizza boxes and the dank reek of the cabin ratcheted up her alarm. Her mind raced through the thousand ways this could unfold. She could slam the door back in his face, turn with an arm and a foot directed at his throat and crotch. She almost didn't hear him when he directed her around the side of the cabin.

"In there."

The smell of decay rose from the opening to the cellar, the two wood doors flung back from the entrance. A new padlock shone on the door. Fear surged through her and she turned, her leg swinging out and up with full force. He ducked and came at her with the butt of his gun, too fast for his age and fitness. She blocked the gun and the butt glanced off her forehead. He used the momentum of the redirected blow and swung the back of his elbow into the side of her head. She was dazed, backing away from him, but he kept coming after her with a rawness that made him stronger than he should have been, like he had practiced this particular fight a thousand times and knew what she would do before she did. In an instant, he had her arms bent behind her back and pushed her headfirst into the black rot of the cellar. She twisted and struggled, the pain in her arms fuelling the rage at her helplessness and her weakness. He released her and she flew, landing on all fours on the sticky dampness of the cellar floor. The doors slammed, and the padlock clicked with the satisfaction of a plan well carried out.

She pushed against the doors above her head. They were heavy and solid and didn't move no matter how hard she pushed. She slammed her fists, feeling for a latch or an edge to get a grip on amidst the overpowering smell of rotting vegetables and her ragged, panicked breathing. She stepped back and silence swarmed out from the dark corners of the places she couldn't see, like it too had been waiting for her with its well laid plans. She closed her eyes, calmed her breathing, blocked out the terror, and listened. No sound of retreating footsteps, or of any movements above ground. She could never know if he was still out there.

There was a scuff of dirt out of the darkness. Someone was down there with her.

She had a sudden revulsion that there would be others down there, captives in this horrible, decaying place.

She remained still, listening and feeling for any signs of attack. She heard a sigh and the faintest of moans.

"Storm?"

Her voice was sucked into the walls, the syllables barely heard before they were gone. She edged towards Storm's voice. She found a foot first, bare, the toes cold. She got no response when she shook it, and she felt further up the calf, recognizing the length and thinness as Storm's. She shook harder, not knowing whether Storm had been knocked out or had passed out from her own demons. She no longer wore her coat. Maria felt her cheekbones protruding beneath her skin and the large welt swelling on the side of her head.

There was a deep, more irritated moan and Maria sat back, knowing that if Storm had the strength to be annoyed, she would be all right.

A strip of light around the door saved them from complete darkness, and as Maria's eyes adjusted, other shapes took form. Wooden crates were crammed next to old barrels and a large stash of empty bottles. The dirt walls formed a three metre square cave, the ceiling sloping away from the door to the back wall at waist height. She stooped to avoid the ceiling as she explored the cell.

An old lawnmower was crammed beneath the far wall, missing all its wheels, the handle attached on only one side. Buckets and containers of unidentifiable liquids and decayed solids and a spool of sharp-edged chicken wire lay along the base of the wall.

She pushed on the door again, tried to kick it out, and landed hard on the dirt. An engine started, a muffled rattling that vibrated through the ceiling. It pitched higher, slowed, and surged before fading. The silence it left behind mocked her. The maniac who had locked them in felt so secure in his prison he didn't need to stand guard.

She circled the room again. There had been extensive travel in and out of the house. The gravel drive was worn and packed from long usage and there had been the traffic leading either to the drive or down a path that led over a rock cut down to a place she couldn't see. They had come in on the unused side of the camp, the place untouched but for that damn boat in the collapsing boathouse.

She had been too focused, determined to find another way to travel that didn't involve carrying Storm.

Another moan came from Storm, sounding awake this time. She sat up, her hand held over the welt on her head.

"Shit."

Maria crouched down next to her.

"Are you okay?"

Storm's forehead creased, her eyes squinting against the pain.

"My head hurts like hell."

At Storm's words, the throbbing from the blow to Maria's skull pushed into the forefront.

"You should lie down."

Storm waved her off, gently touching her fingers to the wound. She pulled her feet under her and rose. She stooped beneath the low roof.

It was colder in the cellar than Maria had first realized, the cold beginning to make itself known in the chill across her shoulders and a tightening of her skin.

"Take my coat."

Maria unzipped her coat and started to remove the sleeves.

Storm pushed up against the bottom of the door, the same way Maria had, her thin white arms no match for its solid thickness.

"You need it more than I do."

Storm turned away, leaving Maria holding the coat between them, touring their small cell, spending longer looking into the decaying matter and peering deeper into the corners.

"Would you just take it?"

But Storm wasn't listening, her face pinched in concentration as she poked at one of the bins of unidentifiable liquid.

"I don't think he knew who I was."

Maria put the coat back on. At least one of them would be warm.

"I heard him leave. Got the impression there was someone he was going to tell. That he wanted to show us to someone."

Storm had finished her tour and returned to her original spot on the floor. She brushed some of the larger debris from the ground and sat back against the wall.

Maria didn't want to sit, the close walls making her skin itch, the dank air thick in her throat. They couldn't just sit here and wait for him to return. She found a flat stone the size of her palm and scraped at the dirt beside the door. It was packed hard, almost as solid as the wood after years of compression. She threw the rock back where she had found it.

Storm had her face lifted, the light glinting on the goose egg the welt had become.

Maria pushed against the solidity of the door again. There was no noise from above, not even the wind penetrating into their cell.

"How long have we been down here?"

Maria stepped past the vile stench rising from one of the buckets, coughing as it stuck in her throat.

"Half an hour. Maybe more."

Already time had begun to attenuate, and it was difficult to gauge how much had passed.

Maria scavenged a thin piece of metal the length of her forearm and tried to jam it in between the door and its frame. The fit was too tight, the metal doing nothing other than tearing skin off her palm. It made a muffled thud when she tossed it to the ground.

Storm retrieved it and used the sharp edge to draw in the dirt. Tiny incomprehensible symbols that barely stayed in the packed surface.

"Can I get some help over here?"

Sick or not the woman could do something other than make hopscotch squares in the dirt.

Storm's gaze was unfocused, most of her mind concentrated on some problem they would never get to if they didn't get out of there.

"Hold on a second."

Storm held up a finger. Her concentration so intense that it made Maria want to shake her. They didn't need her fancy formulas now.

Maria considered one of the barrels, gauging its height against the height of the door. If they wedged two on top of each other it might apply enough pressure to the door to loosen the hinges. And then ten years from now they'd be free when the hinges finally popped off. The passage of every second vibrated along her nerves, the return of the man only a matter of time.

Storm rose to her feet and began circling the outer edge of the room. She unscrewed the cap on the lawn mower, sniffed and screwed it back on. She tore lids off of crates, sniffed half full buckets and muttered to herself. It reminded Maria of seeing her when they had first tried to limit the production of the Gatherer, the final tightening of that freedom focusing Storm's entire intellect on making it go away.

"There aren't any tools, I already looked."

Storm pulled buckets away from the wall, sticking her face into open pails.

"Ah!"

With a cry of triumph, Storm pulled a crate towards the door, moving it no more than an inch at a time.

"What are you thinking?"

Storm waved Maria towards the crate.

"This needs to be under the door."

"The door won't budge."

Storm moved below it, indicating exactly where she wanted Maria to put it.

"So that the flat side is parallel to the wall."

The low roof forced Storm to stoop as she stepped out of the way, the typical mad scientist muttering to herself.

Without a better idea, Maria put her shoulder against the crate and shoved.

"Okay. That's far enough. We need to put this one in that corner."

Storm had her hand on a second crate and pointed to the corner farthest from the door and where she had woken up.

"But put the contents in this one before you do."

She touched the crate below the door.

Maria gagged at the reek of rotting vegetation as she stood over the open crate. At least four patches of darker material formed a splotched pattern on the straw. She wiped her palms on her thighs. The stench was so thick she doubted she would smell anything else ever again.

"We don't have all day."

Storm sounded like she had when she would direct her team, confident in what she was doing. Maria felt the intoxicating desire to follow someone who knew where they were going.

Maria plunged her hands into the first sticky blackness, releasing a powerful, dizzying stench as she scooped handfuls of the dripping mess into the crate below the door. Storm came over and sniffed.

"Perfect. We'll need all of it."

Storm poured the contents of a bag into the crate with Maria's pungent slop. It smelled of dust, chemicals and manicured lawns in the spring. Maria didn't think about what she was digging into, happy for the dim light.

Storm added more bits and pieces to her soup, and Maria began to understand what she was creating, annoyed with herself that she hadn't recognized it sooner.

When Maria's crate was empty, Storm pointed to another reeking bucket and Maria transferred its contents into the central crate.

"We'll need to pack whatever we can around it. To force the explosion upwards."

Storm frowned at the crate for several seconds before she nodded.

"Good idea."

Storm was doing a damn good impression of being healthy and engaged. Maria couldn't figure out what had changed, or if Storm was even aware of it.

They worked together, Storm pulling and tossing as much of the clutter as Maria into the huge pile around the crate.

"Leave that."

Storm pushed the lawnmower back against the wall.

When they had collected everything they could find, Maria wound the roll of chicken wire around the mess, the mass appearing as a great volcano opening towards the door above it. Storm stood with her hands on her hips, breathing hard, the sliver of light striking across her lifted shoulders.

"Give me your t-shirt."

Maria removed her coat again and handed Storm a slightly sweaty ball of crumpled cotton. Storm fed the shirt into the opening of the lawnmower's gas tank. Fumes of gasoline made small intoxicating ribbons through the stench of rot and earth. Storm nodded towards the crate in the corner and Maria crouched behind it. Storm placed the soaked cotton into the filled crate and thumped the lid into place. The space between the wall and the crate was so narrow Storm had to pull her legs close to her chest when she crawled beside Maria. All she heard was the sound of their breathing and the occasional pop or creak as the pile settled.

"How long?"

Maria whispered though there was no one there to hear. She strained to hear the rumble of an approaching engine.

"Cover your ears."

Their shoulders and hips pressed together, their hands over their ears, their heads bent as if in prayer. It was impossible to hear if anyone arrived, but it no longer mattered. They sat, so close their hearts beat to a single rhythm. Maria squished closer, the walls pressing inward, anticipating the explosion. She lifted her head, thinking the walls had shifted when the world exploded in sound, pain, and dirt.

SEVENTEEN

A thick fog of dirt hung in the air and Storm felt as if she was back in the fire. She bent low, her back brushing the sloped roof. There was a gulp of smoke and dirt, and she doubled over in a fit of coughing. She pulled her shirt over her nose, her eyes burning as she tried to see whether the bomb had worked.

A beam of light streamed through the dirt and smoke. One side of the door hung into the room, the other an empty ring of splintered wood. She tapped on Maria's hunched back, a thick coating of dirt across her shoulders and hair.

A crash sounded as something hidden by the smoke dropped and rolled, accompanied by the first whiff of clear, fresh air.

Storm bent over to yell into Maria's ear and saw Maria's hands grasping her leg below the right knee. The unattached handle of the lawnmower had jammed into her calf, a metal claw hooked into her skin.

She crouched down, marvelling at the strength in her legs and the clearness in her head, even as she recoiled at the sight of the wound.

"What can I do?"

Storm sounded a thousand miles under water, the echoes of the bomb ringing in her ears. She didn't hear Maria's response, but the shape of the words on Maria's lips was enough, her competent, capable veneer stripped away.

Take it out.

The rod had gone in at an angle, the edges around the wound ragged. It made her gag to look at it and she would have turned away if it weren't for the rigid grip of Maria's hands around her calf. Without letting herself think, Storm pulled.

The feral scream pierced through the ringing as blood gushed from the hole. Maria clamped her hands over it, and Storm laid hers over the top. Hot blood ran through their fingers.

"Your shirt."

Storm took off her shirt, feeling its small warmth leave her skin, and wrapped it tight around the wound. Maria sat with her head bent, her hands pressed over the shirt.

"Come on."

Storm offered Maria a hand, this time her voice not quite so far away.

For a moment Maria didn't move, the look she gave Storm a struggle against pain. Storm hated to move her but she knew their wide open escape to the outside could close at any time.

The blood stuck their palms together as Storm pulled her up, Maria's grip at least still strong. Maria gasped as her foot touched down and Storm looped Maria's arm over her shoulder, stooping to bring her shoulders to a level that Maria could reach.

Storm staggered under Maria's weight, her head and shoulders brushing the low wall so that a small shower of dirt added to the thickening fog. Torn pieces of chicken wire tangled around their feet as they picked their way through the splintered wood and the smouldering piles of hay. Four of the seven steps had been blown away, only the top two intact.

"Leave me here."

The cold air swirling in the raw opening chilled Storm's bare skin as she carefully lifted Maria's arm from her shoulder and placed it on the edge of where the door had been. Maria's ragged breathing combined with the rattle of the wind above ground.

"And then what?"

"You keep going."

Storm put her shoulder behind Maria's uninjured leg, bracing her body the way she had seen Maria do. She didn't know if she'd even been able to get her off the ground, let alone over the lip of the opening. It angered her that Maria thought she would leave her behind. As if she were still the person who had left her team.

"You can't carry me."

Storm pushed upwards against the back of Maria's thigh, testing her weight. Not as bad as she thought, and her anger added to her strength.

"How do you know?"

Storm knew it was true, yet she felt different. Not cured, but better than she had, the inertness of the earth letting her body operate without interference.

"What do we do once we're out of here? I can't walk."

"I'm not going to leave you behind."

Maria grunted as Storm lifted for real, Maria sitting on Storm's shoulder like a chair, her hand clasped with Storm's for balance. At first Storm's muscles shuddered under the weight, but a dormant and forgotten strength rose from deep inside her, rising through the sickness and weakness to lift Maria up and over the ledge. There was a truncated gasp as Maria rolled out of sight.

"Maria?"

The wind whipped through the trees. Storm called again as she struggled to pull the crate they had used as shelter underneath the gaping hole. She coughed in the smoke, tasting burnt hay on her tongue. She imagined Maria being dragged away, the others waiting to grab Storm the moment she poked her head out. She crouched on top of the crate and slowly peeked over the lip. She wished she had more of a clue of how to do this.

The scrawny trees bent and twisted in the wind, the dried grasses pressed against the ground in the gusts. A strange twilight lay over the scene, the wind drawing the encroaching clouds with it. Maria lay on her back in a small hollow below the opening, a ghost in the twilight, a dark stain spreading through Storm's shirt.

It took several tries to pull herself over the lip, her stomach scraping over the cool, moist earth as she finally climbed free. Her once white bra was gray in the full light, her ribs visible in neat rows above the hollow of her stomach. It repulsed her to see all that was left of her, like a creature that had lived without light and warmth for much longer than the hour they had been below ground. She listened for the deeper sound of an engine returning above the hum of the wind.

"Are you okay?"

Maria panted in her battle against the pain, her chin jutting up from the force of her clenched jaw. She gripped hard to the bunches of grass in her fists.

Storm was unprepared for this. She had no experience or first aid to tell her what to do. No understanding of how to relieve Maria's suffering.

White caps pushed down the river, every leaf and blade of grass caught up in the approaching storm, save for the looming bulk of the cabin behind them.

"I'll be right back."

She checked the laneway that headed along the base of the mountain and the wider branch that led down a slope into the woods. The footpath from the door disappeared into the same woods, its edges smooth and worn from the countless feet that had trod its path. An electrical cable the width of her thumb connected to a freshly installed junction box on the house, its trail leading in the same direction as the path and road. She jumped over it, feeling only a short burn on her shins and toes.

She listened at the cabin door. There were no signs of inhabitants other than the stench of old pizza stirred up by the wind. Any sounds from inside were lost in the buffeting gusts. She grabbed the rusted latch, checking the road a final time.

The door opened into the kitchen, the laminate counter and off-white cupboard doors all tinged yellow by the filtered light of the closed curtains. A few empty beer bottles sat on the counter, the shelves empty in one cupboard with its door ajar. It had the closed-in feeling of a shuttered house, the air stale and old, as if no one had been there for a long time.

She checked outside the screen door again before following a dirtied trail that led through the dust, ignoring the old phone hard wired into the wall. Heavy curtains blocked the light of the high windows in the main living area, the dated sofa and worn carpets tinted yellow. A frightful wooden chandelier hung above the center of the room and an unbroken layer of dust lay on the low side table.

She breathed in, trying to slow her slamming heart. She needed to be able to hear if anyone arrived or waited down the dark hall where the trail led.

No lights. No movement. But as she moved further in she recognized it was not empty of human activity, for several bedrooms had unmade beds with clothes discarded beside them. A bathroom showed a smudged half-filled water glass and several crumpled magazines beside the toilet. It was the absence of caring or any feeling of love that she was feeling here. There were echoes of it in the selection of the drapes, and an old plaque that hung above the fireplace. But it had been a long time since anyone had truly lived here and called it their own.

She searched the medicine cabinet behind the discoloured mirror and shoved the medical tape and safety pins into her pocket, though the tape was barely enough to wrap a finger. Back in the hallway, she smelled the acrid, pungent smell of gasoline.

She stopped on the threshold of the final bedroom. Three shirts hung on hangers in the open closet and a rack of guns hung on the wall. There were no personal possessions other than a pair of glasses lying beside the bed. Nothing that spoke to any kind of humanity. Her coat was draped over the back of a plastic chair, her shoes tucked beneath. A new style walkie-talkie sat in a charger on the bare desk, its red LED light a beacon in the tiny room. She approached carefully, knowing it couldn't hear her but wary of its presence. The room reeked of body odour.

She chose the least offensive shirt, a blue plaid with a torn sleeve, sliding her coat over and slipping on her shoes. She took the remaining shirts for Maria. She placed her hand on the bottom rifle, choosing it not for her knowledge of guns but for the box of ammunition positioned next to it. Maria would know how to fit the pieces together. She fitted a faded ball cap over her head as the walkie-talkie crackled.

She grabbed the rifle and stopped short before entering the hallway. There was no sign of life but for that brief burst of static. She ignored the reek coming from a closed door at the end of the hall and tore the liner from a curtain in the main living area on her way past. When the screen door slammed behind her, she felt again like she had escaped from a long confinement. She found Maria shivering violently where she had left her, great plumes of smoke rolling from the exploded opening.

"You're going to have to leave me here."

Storm's anger rose.

"I brought you something."

Storm laid the rifle carefully next to Maria, not knowing enough about guns to tell if it was loaded.

"That isn't going to fix my leg."

Storm shook off the dust and tore the curtain liner into strips. Tendrils of smoke from the cellar wafted past them. Maria inhaled through clenched teeth as Storm unwound the bloody shirt. The calf had already swelled up and blood flowed freely from the wound.

"They'll be accusing you of every unsolved crime on their books by the time they're done with you."

Maria ripped grass from the ground as Storm redid the bandage.

"Can you sit?"

Storm levered Maria up to sitting, worried about her shaking and drained whiteness. At the sight of her, Storm recognized her own fatigue, it having slipped back in the moment she had kneeled down. She looked upwards as if to find the cause, the deepening banks of cloud providing no answers. Fury coursed through her, her few moments of strength making its return all the more devastating.

Maria's hand pressed on her arm.

"There's a boat, if I can get there."

The wind blew harder through the trees, the tops bending towards the river. Storm breathed and ignored the heaviness in her limbs.

"Can you stand?"

Storm wrapped her arm around Maria's waist, feeling Maria's core strength as she stood on her good leg.

"We need a key."

"I'll worry about the boat. You worry about getting there."

They hobbled towards the sagging shelter of the boathouse, several drops of rain striking her hands as Maria hopped and paused, her hand locked on Storm's shoulder. Thirty meters to the door and Maria was getting slower, the new bandage already soaked with blood. Storm couldn't risk carrying her, her legs already struggling to keep moving forward. It would be impossible to hear the truck returning above the noise of the wind whipping around them. The reek of the man's body odour on the shirts never left them.

Storm gripped Maria's waist tighter.

"Almost there."

She left Maria at the door near the splintered lock, her face as gray as the sky. Wind swept over the slope pushing against Storm's cheek, the raindrops striking faster and harder. She was panting by the time she scooped up the pack from where Maria had left it against the first canoe, hardly recognizing herself in the depleted person who had lain down to rest only a few hours earlier.

The full force of the rain rushed in as she hurried down to the boat launch, her shoulders soaked, the brim of the hat the only thing that allowed her to see. When she ducked through the door, Maria was on all fours, crawling through fishing nets and rods along the edge of a shining new boat. This was what he had thought they were stealing.

Maria trembled as Storm helped her into the boat, the fingers that gripped hers cold and clammy. The roar of rain on the roof surrounded them as Storm lowered Maria into the passenger's seat. Maria slid down onto the floor and crawled under the bow, collapsing onto her side.

"You'll need the gas."

Maria pointed towards the front of the boathouse where two red gas cans sat on the deck. The pervasive smell of gasoline could have come from here, the toxic scent impregnated into the man's clothes like his sweat and skin.

When Storm had the cans in the boat, she took off her coat and laid it over Maria before turning her attention to the motor. A 150 horsepower. Enough to practically fly them down the river. She wiped her wet palms on her thighs before she lifted the cap off the motor, their freedom so close she could taste it.

It was almost comforting to see the simple mechanism, one almost obsolete with the electrification of everything after the Gatherer. She understood how it worked, the fields that drove the propeller not so different than the fields she had played with her entire life. Except this one would now hurt and there was no time for the silver suit.

"Hurry!"

Maria's voice was strained with pain and fear.

She pulled the cord three times before it started, ready for the spike of pain from the spark of the ignition. The throaty growl of the outboard echoed over the drum of the rain as she stepped back from the motor, the agitation of the field vibrating over her chest and abdomen.

She undid the stern without pushing off, wary of what that current would do once they poked into it. She stayed close to the bow on her way to the steering wheel, aware of the vibrations of the motor's field that reached out to her. Sweat gleamed on Maria's forehead. Storm stayed standing as she eased back the throttle.

The current caught the stern immediately and the side of the boat scraped along the edge of the boathouse before it was finally free. They were swept downstream, the rain slamming onto the shining deck, soaking into her thighs and back. She pulled the cap tighter over her forehead as she turned the bow parallel to the current. The boat surged easily, smooth and powerful.

She steered into the centre of the river, wary of sand bars and hidden logs, and kept an eye on the row of shuttered cabins and the hollow, yellowed window of the house. Only a few tendrils of smoke from the cellar survived in the rain.

The river curved right after they slid past the main house, the tip of the boathouse the last piece of the camp to disappear as they turned the corner. A deadhead poked out of the water close to shore and she gave it a wide berth, easing the throttle faster as she got a feel for the boat.

"Made it."

The words barely went farther than her lips, the force of the rain consuming them and anything in its path. She ducked under the bow to adjust her coat back over Maria. She had curled into a ball, her eyes shut tight, a compact ball of suffering.

When Storm looked back to the river again, a long deep dock floated at the river's edge and a gray steel Quonset hut sat back from the water partially hidden by trees. The tidy, organized yard was so different than the house and cabins she at first thought they weren't connected. Except the road was there, leading up the hill, and the foot path opened onto the flat loading area by the dock. A forklift was parked on a diagonal at the top of the ramp that led to the dock, abandoned mid-job, and the large rolling door of the hut was closed tight.

Her hand came off the throttle but it was too late. The motor would have announced them as soon as she started it and the current had already pushed them half way along the extended dock. The interrupted emptiness of the place unsettled her. Even now she expected someone to run from the hut and wave them down, or train a rifle on them unless they stopped at the dock.

She pushed down on the throttle as far as it would go, feeling the power of the motor as it engaged, the bristle of the field on her back. The hull lifted and settled as the bow flattened out. The hut and dock, whatever their purpose, were already behind them and the waves from their wake were dissipating against the shore, whatever disturbance they would have made smoothed over by the rain.

EIGHTEEN

Storm searched for obstacles in the shallow river, the splash of the raindrops preventing her from seeing much of anything on the agitated surface. They swept downstream, the motor rumbling behind her in warning as if the occasional bite of its electromagnetic field on her back wasn't enough to keep her pinned to the windshield. She adjusted the throttle, searching for a balance between her fear of being pursued and the field that pulled the hairs on her neck whenever she pushed too far.

Maria said something that was drowned out by the rain. She lay with a lifejacket under her head, the space beneath the bow just big enough to keep her out of the rain. Storm bent her head below the dashboard, grateful for the momentary break from the rain's onslaught.

Maria had pushed aside the sleeping bag and had the rifle in her hand with it open to where the bullets slid in. She was removing the bullets and placing them into her pocket. She nodded towards a long metal box, a shining silver padlock locking it shut.

"There could be something useful in there."

She handled the rifle with precise controlled movements, her discipline leaving her functional, if looking pale, her mouth set in a tight grimace. The only sign of distress was the fast rhythm of her breath through clenched teeth. She tucked the final bullet into her pocket and snapped the rifle shut.

Maria lifted the rifle to smash the stock against the lock and Storm returned to the wheel, steering them back towards the centre of the river. She braced herself on the top of the windshield against a wave of weakness as the driving rain muffled the crash of the rifle against the lock. She shook with cold, her body shrunken and drawn inward as it tried to shelter its core. They needed shelter, food, and warmth, and none of that was likely to come anytime soon.

Maria's banging had stopped, and when Storm looked underneath, she was lying back against the lifejacket, her hands gripped around the rifle. The remains of the smashed lock hung from the bent clasp.

The bow swung suddenly to the right and Storm stood to find the boat sideways to the current and being pushed downstream. She jerked the wheel and with a smooth sedateness the bow tracked back upstream. A curse came from beneath the bow but Storm resisted looking, steering around a fallen tree that reached far into the river. On a relatively straight stretch she ducked her head back under. A colourful tangle of lures, hooks, fishing line and sinkers lay inside the box. Maria leaned back on the lifejacket again, the red square of a tiny first aid kit held in her hands along with the cylinder of a flashlight.

Storm drew the kit from her hands and opened the small red bag to find a couple of useless band aids the size of a thumbnail and the shiny packet of an emergency blanket.

Maria's eyes had turned to a dull gray.

Checking their course again, Storm tore open the blanket and laid it between Maria and the sleeping bag.

Maria flinched as Storm accidentally brushed her leg. Sweat shone on her forehead and despite her prone position she held her body rigid.

"How bad is it?"

"I'm fine."

Her words were clipped and rough, her breathing shallow.

"We need to find a hospital."

Maria laughed, almost a gasp.

"And you're going to take me there?"

Storm stood, readjusting their course. She hadn't wanted to think about the city. They had been focused on staying ahead of their pursuers, but they hadn't actually talked about what they would do when they got there. Storm had had some vague idea of Maria helping her contact her mother in secret, an argument with her, and then Storm resuming control of the operation to shut it all down. A ridiculous plan, especially given the state she and Maria were in.

She ducked her head back down, one hand holding the wheel.

"I'll need your help won't I? So we need to get you something for that leg so that when the time comes you'll be able."

"Don't worry about me. I'll be ready."

The woman was infuriating but Storm didn't push it. For now they needed to get away from that compound.

Storm eased the throttle forward, stopping when the motor's field took bites out of the skin on her back. She returned to her course down the centre, equidistant from the trees and shallows that threatened to catch them. A few kilometres back there had been a split in the river, one leading to the interior, the other towards the coast. Storm had taken the larger branch towards the coast without consulting Maria. They were more exposed on the larger river but it was their most direct route to Rima.

The river bent to the right, narrowing as they rounded the curve, the forest pushing thick and close to the banks. Darkness was already falling, blurring the details of the land and water. The shadow of a dock emerged, and she steered towards it until the light of a window broke through the trees.

She scanned the trees and sky for wires. This far out it could have been solar, a generator, or a Gatherer. She kept their speed steady. It was too late to hide.

"What is it?"

Storm had hoped Maria was taking whatever rest she could get. Instead, she was alert enough to notice Storm's hesitation on the throttle.

She crouched down, holding a finger to her lips. Maria's voice would travel across the water, above the rumble of the engine. Maria struggled to rise.

Storm waved her back down.

"It's just a light. There's no one there."

Maria rose to one knee.

The current drove them hard downstream and they swept by the empty dock and single lighted window.

When it disappeared behind them, Maria collapsed back under the bow without a word. The river felt darker after the light, the obstacles harder to see. Storm navigated by the lightness of the water compared to the shore.

The rain had seeped through her coat and she fought with all her willpower to stay above the circling fatigue. She could barely see beyond the next few feet of black water, and her body ached with a full, deep exhaustion.

Something solid brushed on the right front. She spun the steering wheel left as the boat slid to a stop, lodged in a sandbar. The pitch of the motor rose as it churned against it.

She checked upstream as she shifted her weight forward and back. She turned off the motor and scrambled for a paddle, startled by the depth of rainwater that had accumulated in the back of the boat. She jammed the paddle blade into the sand and pushed. Her arms were slow to respond. She searched for more solid ground and pushed again as Maria moved beneath the bow.

"Stay where you are!"

Maria's tangled hair appeared first, followed by her shoulders and hips. She was crawling, grasping the back of Storm's seat and the dashboard to help her rise to her feet. She held tight to the top of the windscreen.

"You need to save your strength."

"So do you."

Storm climbed onto the bow, the deck slick with rain, and held onto a cleat as she lowered her legs over the edge. The water raced fast along the boat, its depth shrouded in blackness.

"What are you doing?"

"It's fine. I'm good."

"You don't have the strength."

Storm gasped as her feet touched the water. It was impossible that this icy flow had ever contained warmth.

She lowered slowly, her arms straining as pain shot into her feet and ankles. Mid-calf she could hold herself no longer and dropped into the water, panicked that there was no bottom until her feet sunk into grainy sand. The sand shifted and moved beneath her, the icy water at her mid-thigh.

"Get back in the boat!"

Maria hopped to Storm's side and leaned over the edge.

Storm pushed and pulled, feeling for where the boat was stuck in the sand. She rocked it up and down in wider swings as her feet and calves ached. Maria hopped clumsily to the other side, using her weight to increase the swings. Rain ran down Storm's back, blending her into the river.

The boat moved, shifted downstream. Another give and it floated free.

Storm grabbed the cleat and tried to haul herself up onto the bow. She rose a half step before her arms gave way. She slid back into the water, the boat pulling her downstream and off the sand bar. The water was just below her groin, getting deeper as she reached the edge of the sand shelf. If she kept hold she would be pulled off the sand bar and unable to hold herself on the boat.

"Jump!"

A sharp, strict order from Maria. Storm would have given anything to be able to carry it out.

She let the boat go, the current seeming to rush in with renewed strength. It whisked the boat far beyond Storm's reach as it swirled faster and harder around her legs. The speed with which the boat floated away astonished her, powered by something beyond the current. She heard Maria curse. The current pulled the sand from beneath Storm's feet. She stumbled backwards, to the top of the sand bar where the water reached her mid-thigh. Still stumbling and re-adjusting as the sand shifted beneath her, she paddled her hands in the frigid water to keep her balance. The river banks were far away, beyond the distance she could survive in the water.

Already her feet were numb, the air movement across her skin like tiny, icy blades. How long could she survive? Five minutes? Ten?

The boat had turned to an indistinct shadow against the downstream river bank. She couldn't even see Maria's shape inside it. She walked a few steps towards the distant shore. The water got deeper. The sandbar was an isolated island, not a bridge to shore.

"Maria!"

Her voice was a croak, not even reaching above the noise of rushing water. Her knees were numb, their strength wavering against the current.

The engine started far away. She couldn't see it in the darkness, her body equally hard to see as it was drawn into the river's icy cold.

She stepped towards the bank, going deeper into the water.

The lights were on in the boat, a tiny beacon moving impossibly slowly towards her. The current was winning, pressing against her legs. She moved her arms, trying to wave them but they barely came above her shoulders, like dead weights at the end of a string.

The sky was huge above her, hard and black, pulling and stretching out the landscape so that she grew even smaller, the distance between her and the boat farther. She felt like she could slip down. The water wouldn't even feel cold. Float on the surface. Watch the stars and let the current carry her all the way to the sea. Already she felt less cold. A slow warmth spreading through her.

Then there came the brightness of a light in her eyes. Her arms were so heavy, her legs like weeds stuck in the sand and bent before the current.

Tough hands looped under her armpits, a sucking feeling around her ankles.

"Move your feet!"

She was too heavy. Maria was too weak. Until suddenly her feet broke free and she was rising up, her stomach scraping over the side of the boat. She was on top of Maria unable to move and colder than she had ever been in her life.

* * * *

Maria's calf was on fire, a balloon of pain inflating to her entire leg, each hop to the steering wheel sending up a new jolt of agony.

"Take off your wet clothes. And your boots."

Storm had hauled herself onto her knees but hadn't done anything further. It was almost a relief to see the big muscular shaking as Storm's body tried to re-warm itself. So much better than the minute tremors she could do nothing about.

Maria steered the boat close to shore and into the opening of a small tributary. She coasted close enough to grab hold of the branches of a fallen log and turned off the motor. Her foot touched down as she pulled the boat next to the log and pain ran from her leg to her spine. The pain she could manage. It was the chill of infection already running in her blood that would be the problem.

When she had the boat tied to the tree, she lowered herself gingerly next to Storm, who hadn't gotten any further than loosening the laces on her boot. Maria undid the laces and helped her strip off her pants and underwear. She had boney hips, white thighs like sticks, and a dark patch of hair between her legs. There was the same dismissiveness of her body that Maria had seen at the cabin, as if it could no longer be Storm's concern. Storm rolled under the bow, her arms shaking so badly Maria had to help her pull the sleeping bag and the emergency blanket over her.

The rain had eased, more a mist than drops, as Maria handed Storm a bar from the pack. She had wrapped herself in the bag, the top pulled over her head, only her pale moon face visible.

"Not hungry."

Her words were clear and Maria felt a rush of relief. They might have a chance of keeping Storm from hypothermia.

"That was a stupid thing to do."

Storm's face was blank, her gaze averted from Maria.

"The boat was stuck."

"We could have got it out together."

Storm pulled the sleeping bag tighter around her.

"You were injured. I took care of it."

"And almost got yourself killed."

Storm's hostility didn't abate though she didn't argue Maria's point.

The narrow tributary shone silver, a relative brightness in the soaked grayness of the night. There were no lights in the distance, no sounds carrying over the river. How hard would the boat be to see from the main river? Was anyone even following?

"Move over."

The space was small, and they were pressed close together. The emergency blanket was wrapped over Storm's legs, the sleeping bags over both. Together they managed to generate a small core of warmth with the night air doing its best to steal it from them. Eventually Storm stopped shaking and Maria allowed herself to rest. Her leg throbbed and despite the heat between them, Maria oscillated between hot and cold, the wound in her leg the source of a white, hot heat.

NINETEEN

Storm woke to the putter of a boat moving slowly in the dark, men's voices audible above its motor. Her body was sluggish and sore and she stumbled as she crawled out from under the bow, the air stripping the warmth from her bare legs. The beam of a spotlight raked the tree trunks on the opposite shore.

She couldn't get her bearings, the river so much smaller than she remembered. The light panned across trees on a farther shore, and the smaller tributary off the main river took shape.

She untied the boat from the log, getting tangled in the branches in her haste, and by the time she held the untied end in her hand, the rumble and voices had moved up the main river, a final flash of light across the blank water their parting gesture. She crouched with the damp rope in her hand, but the threat had moved away, leaving her with a wildly pounding heart in the quiet of the forest. The trees on the opposite bank had fallen back into darkness, their outline darker against the luminous cloud backlit by the glow of the moon. A single star shone at the top of an unusually tall tree, before being overtaken by the mass of clouds.

"Who was it?"

Maria's voice was weak and when Storm bent to check on her, she had raised herself to her elbow but no further.

"I couldn't see."

In the light of the flashlight, Maria looked drained, her skin the washed out paleness of porcelain. When Storm touched her forehead Storm's hands were blocks of ice compared to the hot burn of Maria's skin.

"It's the infection."

Maria spoke plainly, without pain or suffering, and her lack of concern frightened Storm more than anything.

"Now we definitely need a hospital."

"No."

Maria dropped back onto the life jackets, a dull glaze to her eyes.

"We don't have a choice."

"The fields will kill you."

Storm tucked the sleeping bag back over Maria's legs, rhyming through all the drugs in her head that could fight the infection. None of which she had.

"And the infection will kill you."

Maria's eyelids were already closing with fatigue and Storm was grateful to not have to argue with her.

"Watch out for the sand bars."

A brisk wind from upriver drove the cold deeper into Storm's bones. She zipped her coat to the top and put on a life jacket for warmth. She slid on her pants, the cold of the river still clinging to them.

The river banks streamed past, the spindly tamaracks and white spruce clustered together so tight no light showed between them. At each curve she expected to see the boat coming back towards them or hear the higher pitch of a faster boat overtaking them. Yet the fast-flowing water carried no other travelers, and the day brightened and the bite of the wind lessened without seeing another person.

She frequently dipped her hand over the edge and wet Maria's face and neck. The icy water did little to break the fever's hold and Storm pushed the boat faster, pressed against the windshield to stay away from the motor's stronger field.

She had filled up the tank three times since the start of the day, and the two jerry cans lay empty on their sides. The day had waned, the darkness coming early and fast, the river's bends revealing more stretches of unbroken shoreline. The landscape drew her forwards, pulling her through the waters that ran beneath them from a seemingly endless source—at times deep and shielded, other times a slight shallow stream racing above the speckled sand. As night drew in, the shoreline changed, stretching out so the river widened, the banks steepened, and hills loomed in the distance with the peaks of a mountain range behind.

She slowed at the first cabin, closed up for the season on a brief patch of open shore. Curtains were pulled across the windows and water ran through empty boat houses. At a narrower, swifter section, an aluminum fishing boat was anchored in an eddy, hidden until it was too late to flee.

A weathered, stooped man sat as motionless as the rod he held over the water. She got no response as she nodded to him, and hoped his extended scrutiny was admiration of the boat rather than confirming she was the woman those men had been looking for.

She was feeling faint by the time they were out of sight, and would have found a place to stop, maybe eased the fatigue in her shoulders from hours of driving, but the man's scrutiny renewed her sense of threat.

When darkness was almost full, a long bend opened into the mouth of the river. The familiar outline of the hills formed a dark border around the open water, the peaks silhouetted by the last rays of light fading from the sky. The rippled water reflected the faded yellow light, so that it formed a plate of dimpled steel, its outline cut against the forest that rose upwards. On the far shore, the large smear of Rima formed a glowing band between the water and the mass of the mountains.

At one time the lights would have been reassuring, promising a place of rest and the comfort of arriving home. Instead, it felt as if the lights had suddenly turned towards her.

She didn't move and gripped the throttle as if the glow were reaching for her across the water. When a light lifted into the sky at the northern edge and the turbulence of chopper blades reverberated over the water, she finally eased forward. The helicopter seemed to be standing still, the clear rod of a searchlight extending below it. She switched off the running lights and steered north, aiming for the thicker darkness next to shore.

TWENTY

The lights had stopped a kilometre back and Storm had been paddling silently through a zone free of light and fields, as if they had flipped the breaker on a whole section of the city. This absence had allowed her further into the built up area than she had hoped. She had spent most of her time around the university and later the Gatherer compound, this concrete canal and where it led unknown. Shadows on the bank shifted and the occasional sounds of voices were the only indications that life existed in the darkened zone. She pulled the paddle silently through the water as the cracked concrete of the industrial dock slipped past. Her arms were heavy and her shoulders ached, yet she didn't know what else to do other than lift and pull. Maria hadn't spoken since they had left the river, and her stillness made Storm pull harder.

Up ahead streetlights lined a boulevard, the first line of the electricity that spread in a great swath on either side of the dark strip of river. It felt strange to think of this hostile place as cover, this unexpected patch of darkness the only thing that had allowed her to enter the city at all. Not far beyond the streetlights, a brighter area glowed like a stage or a spotlighted statue. Her anxiety rose with each lift of the paddle, anticipating the first burn of a field, her skin tingling in false alarm several times only for the burn to disappear at the brush of her hand over the skin.

A blocky, narrow structure loomed against the river's concrete walls. A boathouse or some kind or storage space perched over the water. She paddled next to it, feeling for a hold she could use to keep the boat from slipping downstream. The wood was rough and warped, and the holds it offered up were crevasses only big enough to grasp with her fingers. The skitter of some small animal, probably rats, made her take up her paddle again and continue upriver. She was amazed she could still move, the memory of the helicopter overriding the weakening muscles in her arms and the ache across her shoulders.

A log or some kind of floating object scraped along the side of the hull, briefly dragging the boat to one side. It was too dark to see anything but the faintest outline of the mass of splintered wood and discarded sheets of plastic. How many times had she imagined coming back here, choreographing her return from exile with all its fanfare? She'd imagined her mother would be there, and Daniel, the whole team reassembled. Even after she knew the team was dead she had kept them in her mental rehearsal, as if clinging to that fantasy would bring them back. How much more fitting for her to be slinking back through a stinking canal, now that she, and almost everyone, knew what the Gatherer had truly delivered.

A square patch of light broke the darkness beside the river. She stopped her paddle mid-stroke until she recognized the orange, flickering glow that spoke of candles rather than electric light. She paddled carefully over to the river wall below the light and the concrete staircase that led up the wall.

She had grabbed the rope to attach it to one of the metal rings cemented into the wall when a man yelled above her.

"What do you want from me?"

She looked up, expecting a threatening form above her. The top of the wall was clear. A woman's voice responded with equal ferocity.

"I didn't ask for this."

A door slammed and the night returned to quiet. Storm let the rope fall back into the boat and picked up her paddle. She was careful not to scrape the gunnel as she slipped away into the river, now more wary of who might inhabit the river bank—some friendly, most not. She would need to be careful figuring out which was which.

The shape of a small boat emerged out of the shadow of the retaining wall. Her paddle was at the back of her swing and she kept it in the water, pressing down to slow their momentum. It was a bare metal boat, open to the elements, not even a motor attached to its transom. She lifted her paddle when she knew it was empty, moving carefully past.

A dock jutted into the river forty metres ahead. She would stop and see if she could find a drug store, though she was reluctant to leave Maria or the boat, since both of them offered her a kind of safety. Beyond it, the glow of the city rose up in a great wall of brilliance. A Ferris wheel twinkled at the height of it, marking the center of downtown, spinning slowly in that other world. She had no idea how she would find medication for Maria in that solid mess of electricity. The abundance of the Gatherer would have jammed every available space in the city with something electric. Headlights streaked across the glassed wall of a building, and she gripped the paddle against the urge to flee, the darkness and the futility of even being there pressing in.

A movement flashed in the darkness at the top of the bank. When she looked for it, it wasn't there. She steered the boat away from the concrete edge, staying within the shadow of the wall. It felt as if she were gliding along a narrowing path, with more danger and stronger fields waiting upstream.

She craned her neck to see into the blackness above the bank, the unlighted warehouses and unidentifiable silhouettes of storage yards providing an infinite number of places to hide. She checked behind her with each stroke, scanning the tops of both concrete banks. Reflections of the distant lights gleamed off steel containers wet from the earlier rain. She dipped her paddle and pulled.

The height of the pier slowly rose above her, the concrete sides higher than her shoulders. She pulled herself along the pier until she reached a rusted ladder that ran down to the water. She tied the boat to the second rung and leaned down to check on Maria.

Her skin was hot to the touch, her hands icy and her leg ballooned with infection. Storm checked the two hundred dollars in her pocket and hoped it would be enough. The ladder creaked when she put her foot on the first rung.

"Where are you going?"

Maria's voice was hazy, blurred.

Storm stepped off the ladder and back into the boat. Maria made scuffling sounds as she tried to rise, her movements slow and clumsy.

"I'm going to get you some antibiotics."

It pained Storm to watch Maria struggle.

"I don't need them."

"You're getting worse. We have no other choice."

"I'll go."

Maria tried to turn onto her hands and knees. Her back hit the underside of the bow. There was a restrained whimper as she tried to crawl from under it that cut straight to Storm's fear. She placed a hand on Maria's shoulder.

"Stay here and rest. I won't be long."

"It's not safe."

Maria collapsed back onto her nest of life jackets and sleeping bags, winded from her brief effort. Storm ignored her own wave of crushing fatigue.

"We're in some kind of dark zone. I'll be fine."

Maria's gaze flicked behind Storm, to the restricted view of the concrete bank.

"Take the rifle."

Storm placed the rifle across Maria's chest. Her hands curled instinctively around the barrel.

"I wouldn't know what to do with it."

"You'll keep to the shadows? Come back if you sense any kind of field?"

There was a panic to Maria's gaze that Storm had never seen. She rested her hand over Maria's where it gripped the rifle.

"I've done this before."

Storm felt Maria's grip on the rifle tighten.

"Not very well."

Storm stood quickly, not wanting Maria to see her fatigue. Dark patches appeared in her vision. The rusted metal of the ladder was rough beneath her hand, small flakes digging into her palm. Six rungs to the top, as high as any skyscraper. It seemed ridiculous that this ladder would be what stopped her when it could have been so many other things. Her hands could barely hold the rung, her foot fumbling to find the first step. She had visions of falling backwards, landing half on the boat, half in the decayed, terrifying water. She hooked her elbows through the rungs and started climbing. She didn't think of the water, or the boat, or the shaking ladder. Instead, she focussed on moving her arms to the next rung, lifting her feet and breathing enough air to feed her pounding heart and lungs.

The edge of the concrete at the top of the ladder was solid, rough, and damp to her touch. She only had to climb over the top. She rested her forehead against the rusty metal, willing for her heart to slow, her body to find the strength. Two steps, two rungs and a final scramble over the edge and she was collapsed on her back, panting, the cold dampness of the concrete beneath her. The glow from the city permeated the sky, blocking her view of the stars.

She struggled to her feet, stumbling until she found a slow, steady gait. One foot in front of the next. Her body felt hollow, starved, its depletion far beyond this single day.

A dark road led to the left, the glow of the city at its end. The drug store, and medication, would be somewhere within it. Warehouses extended the length of the river bank, floodlights illuminating the yards beyond the bridge. It had seemed an easy plan: enter Rima, get the meds Maria needed. But faced with the great swath of electricity, the plan seemed doomed to failure and all kinds of pain and suffering.

With a final look back to the boat, she chose the road leading away from the docks. The pavement was uneven and difficult to see in the dark, her path guided by the light at its end. Alleys opened up between warehouses, only a few steps visible before darkness blocked her view. It didn't make sense that there was no light here, that she hadn't felt the brush of a single field. The strength of the fields in the lighted area would be overpowering, a lethal force against her. Yet here, there was an absence as welcome as it was disturbing.

She moved close to a warehouse to read the sign hung above its door. Spray painted graffiti obscured the letters, the slashed lines of paint extending onto the metal siding. The door below had been boarded over, dirt and old leaves accumulated at its base. The window beside it had not been so lucky, the glass smashed, a crate placed below by whoever had climbed through.

She stopped as a wave of dizziness wobbled through her, walking again when it had cleared. She passed through a crossroads where two large laneways intersected, choosing to continue straight on for no other reason than that it was the direction she had been going. Her experimentation had been like that. Follow an idea because it was there. Let it take you where you needed to go.

She had gone several blocks, the river far behind, when she felt a singe on her skin. She stopped and retreated several steps. The shape of a tall fence emerged less than ten metres ahead of her, blocking the road. Its metal posts gleamed in the darkness, the field it was generating far more effective at stopping her than the chain link fence and the inward slanted rows of barbed wire at the top.

The barrier continued between warehouses on either side.

"Don't go any closer."

Storm started, alarmed at being so unaware. A small figure emerged out of the shadows. It had a nest of tangled hair, a thin jacket over a sweater, and what looked like a pink tutu over a pair of jeans.

"Are you new here?"

The voice was young and had an ease to it that seemed out of place in their surroundings.

"Were you dropped off?"

Storm stared at her, trying to reconcile the child with the threat of the barrier. Who sets up this kind of barrier for children?

"What is this place?"

"You should get off the street."

The street was dark where Storm had come from. The river and pier were out of sight, the voids between buildings filled with infinite places to hide. The girl was already disappearing into the shadows. Storm followed after her, her pulse high in her throat, her body protesting against the rush of adrenaline.

"Why?"

The girl stopped before the next street, a shaft of moonlight glinting off the top curled layer of her hair.

"People come here at night."

The girl moved to step into the relative brightness of the street. Storm reached out her arm.

"What people?"

The girl cocked her head, the outline of a small nose and wide-set eyes appearing below the mass of hair.

"How did you get over the fence?"

"I didn't. Is there a drug store in here?"

She frowned. The childish pout of her lips seemed out of place with her calm certainty.

"Somewhere I can get medicine. For when you have a headache."

"I know what a drug store is."

A metal gate or door clanged shut. The girl looked in the direction of the sound, waiting for the reverberations to end before crossing the street. The shadows between buildings had deepened. Storm saw movement where there was none. What kind of place had she stumbled into?

"Is there one in here? My friend is sick."

"My mom is sick."

Storm bit back her frustration. The girl was leading her further into the labyrinth of warehouses and Storm didn't know if she would be able to find her way back to the boat.

"Can you show me where your mom gets her medicine?"

"Medicine doesn't help my mom."

It explained why the girl was out at night in this awful place, the mother too sick to keep track of her.

The girl led her through a series of alleys and Storm became aware of people sitting in the dark. Some had their backs against the wall, so still that Storm wondered if they were alive at all. The girl paid them no attention, and occasionally one greeted the girl as Megan. A bright name, out of place in this strange, dark maze.

They turned onto a larger throughway lit by torches on the walls as if they had stepped into the living core of the place from an earlier, more primal time. Firelight flickered off drawn, tired faces, and one group held cards in their hands. Conversations halted as they approached, and surprised, excited whispers started as they passed.

A warm yellow light streamed from a doorway. Storm grabbed the girl's shoulder and bent to speak into her ear.

"Where's the drug store?"

The girl pulled away as if Storm's touch had hurt her.

"You said medicine."

The lighted room was high and cavernous, once a warehouse. Storm hesitated in the draft at the entrance, wary of the fields that came with light and heat. Beds filled the floor, some in rows, others stacked in makeshift bunks. Some were empty, but many had people lying still, eyes closed though Storm didn't get the sense that they were sleeping. They were as thin or thinner than she was, and the space reeked of sweat, sickness, and too many people living in close quarters.

Megan skipped away from her to a woman with straight, gray-streaked hair pulled back in a ponytail, and a stretched-out sweatshirt and saggy pants that looked like they had been worn for many days in a row.

The woman smiled at Megan and rested her hand gently on top of the girl's head. Megan's hair was sandy blonde, her face dirty, and she was around ten years old. A group of younger children watched from a sectioned-off play area filled with toys.

"She needs medicine."

Megan pointed at Storm as Storm felt the pressure of people drifting into the room behind her, following them in from the street.

The woman's tired, worn eyes widened when she looked up at Storm. Storm tried to move back but the arrival of the people behind her kept her in one place. Her weight loss and the cropped hair had not been enough. The woman rose and walked stiffly to Storm. Storm tried to flee sideways and ran into the wall of people arriving from the sleeping area. The woman laughed as her warm, smooth hand grasped Storm's.

"Miracles do exist."

Storm's name was being whispered in the crowd behind her and she could see people sitting up along the rows of beds as the word spread.

"Welcome."

Already people's expectations filled the room. More shockingly thin people continued to push in through the door, spilling on either side of her. Up close the tremors were obvious. A red rash spread out and down from one woman's ear. A man struggling to sit had the same tortured look as

Mac and a child of no more than three jerked its head to the right every few seconds. Storm felt ill, the last threads of her energy stripped away.

"I need antibiotics. For my friend."

The woman frowned, half smiling in confusion.

"Antibiotics won't help us. You should know—"

"It's for an infection. Not the plague."

Referencing the plague in front of an audience made it hard and tangible, no longer just stories that Maria had told her, but a real horrible thing that she had created. She was light headed, the hours of paddling and not eating rushing into her in a wave of nausea and shame.

The woman's grip tightened and she moved one hand to Storm's elbow. A chair was placed behind her and she was lowered into it. A glass of water was pressed into her hand along with a sharp-edged tablet. The crowd loomed around her.

The woman nudged Storm's hand upwards, encouraging her to take it.

"What is this?"

The woman was warm and welcoming, but that benevolence didn't ring from the crowd. A definite undercurrent of hostility increased her desire to run.

"It's fast absorbing electrolytes and minerals. Your body will respond to it as soon as it hits your tongue."

It had similar ingredients to the concoctions she'd created. The tablet was so much more practical. The crowd was silent, though voices and whispers continued further back. She would need something to get her back to Maria. They couldn't have been waiting for her with a poison pill when they hadn't known she was coming.

She touched the pill to her tongue. Sweet. Sour. She washed it down with the water, finishing the glass. Maria needed this more than her, and she looked around for the source to refill it. The pill was no miracle cure but she did feel a subtle lightening, her body's systems running smoother.

"Where is your friend?"

Megan hung close to the woman's side, gripping the woman's hand in both of hers. She seemed shyer in the light, younger, less like the girl who had led her through the dark.

"At the river."

A murmuring in the crowd as the woman frowned.

"Where?"

"The Pier."

A small group of people disappeared out the door. Storm followed and found herself struggling to keep up in a pack of quick footed, silent ghosts, floating unheard back through the alleys and empty warehouses. The air felt crisper and harder, as if the corners had gotten sharper, the walls more unyielding. Megan ran beside her, an easy, sure-footed gait of someone who had spent a lot of time running.

Storm's fear grew as they ran, the few mentions of 'gangs' and 'trollers' she had heard as they left repeating with the rhythm of her feet striking the ground. They reached the river downstream from the pier, the group staying tight against the abandoned buildings as they ran. One by one they dropped off, each taking up a position along the river. The pier looked as it had when she'd approached it, concrete sides rising out of the dirty water, the outline of the railing jutting above the top, and no boat tied to its base.

She was out of breath, shaking and off balance when she reached the end of the dock, each rung of the ladder clearly visible. The inky restless water churned against the concrete wall as if it had swallowed the boat whole. She checked the opposite side of the pier and lifted her gaze to the dark recesses of the river that led deeper into the city. She had been stupid to leave her, thinking the darkness would provide protection. She leaned over the top of the ladder, hoping for a flash of chrome and the impossibility of a boat waiting in the shadows. The water looked as hard as ice, the black brittle kind that allowed no light to pass through.

Megan stood next to her, her attention upriver as if she could see something Storm couldn't. She saw only lifeless river banks and the water's unyielding surface. Storm needed something she could chase or run after, something other than the silence of the empty river.

The girl kicked a chip of concrete. It rattled across the pier and over the side, the plop where it hit the water absorbed into the wall. Storm felt the burning heat of Maria's skin, saw the rifle clutched in her hand, and remembered her strength when she had carried Storm beneath the hydro line. She was too strong to just disappear.

One of the runners came onto the pier, his steps truncated, reluctant to be exposed above the water. He was tall and lean, with wavy black hair that swept back from his forehead.

"We can't stay out here too long."

He took hold of Megan's hand and drew her back to the bank.

Lights flickered and headlights moved in the distance. The starless sky arched away from her.

"Who took her?"

Megan and the man had reached shore, moving back the way they had come. The air stirred, the beginning of a breeze delivering the smell of garbage, asphalt, and progress. Had they taken Maria upstream into the light? To a hospital that hummed with electricity. Storm had a sharp ache for the busy calmness of it: machines humming, surrounded by the comforts of power.

"Storm!"

Megan called from the entrance of the alley. With a final look at the spinning Ferris wheel, Storm jogged away from the pier, checking several times over her shoulder for the shape of a drifting boat or water lapping against a hull. She felt as she had when she had walked away from the lab the final time. Nothing the way it should be. She shouldn't have left then, and she knew she shouldn't be leaving now. She stopped at the entrance to the alley. Megan and the man neared its other end.

The moon was a brilliant, clear cut disc in the sky, yet its light was not strong enough to show her where Maria had gone. It was darker closer to the buildings, the light in the distance brighter, mocking. She turned and stepped into the now empty alley.

TWENTY ONE

Storm wanted to push the faces away. Some trembled openly, their skin as thin as rice paper, others gazed curiously from bright eyes above cheeks that held colour. Most of the people in the warehouse had come to see her, shaking her hand or simply laying a fingertip on her arm to see if she was real.

She had expected blame and accusations. Instead, the same reverence surrounded her as when she had left, but now for a different reason.

Megan pushed through the crowd, her pink tutu ragged at the edges, and placed a warm bowl of soup in Storm's hands. It smelled rich and heavenly, lentils, carrots, and celery floating on the surface. She sipped gratefully on the hot broth, wishing she could share it with Maria.

Marty, the gray-haired woman who seemed to be in charge, had said there were plenty of antibiotics donated by the medical community. Drugs that could be racing through Maria's blood right now, soothing the inflamed flesh, if Storm hadn't left her.

"Are you organizing a revolt?"

"Where have you been?"

"Why are you here?"

It was the same as when she had been surrounded by reporters. Questions coming faster than she could answer, their persistence in getting an answer feeling personal. They made assumptions that made her into something she wasn't and gave her intentions that were so much more pre-meditated than they actually were. Except this persistence wasn't about getting a good story. It was about finding hope.

It was too much after the silence. The loneliness. She was entirely unequipped to deal with this, and she longed for Maria to step in.

Megan stood, putting her small body between Storm and the accusations, as she took the empty bowl from Storm's hands.

"Thank you."

The girl slipped into the crowd, her pink tutu the last thing visible between the bodies.

"Did you destroy the Gatherer?"

The question hung in the air, surrounded by the quiet. What felt like a thousand pair of eyes focussed on her. She had ignored the question since they had returned from the docks, her crude, effective method of compromising the Gatherer's mechanism in Three Rocks having been embellished in the days since into a well-engineered terrorist act that was to be the first of many. The beginning of a revolt. Didn't they understand that the Gatherer was what had happened last time she'd tried to save people?

"How did you do it?"

It was the tall dark-haired man, his near black eyes examining her every move. Was this the answer to getting rid of the Gatherer? Sending out an army of sick soldiers to nearly kill themselves trying to destroy a single device? There had to be a better way, yet she couldn't see what it was.

She let the soup's warmth and energy seep into her veins, the warmth bringing a blanket of drowsiness with it. Maria would have stepped in by now, herded these people away so she could think.

"It's a matter of interrupting the process."

The crystal bowl was half art, half energy harvester, the real beauty of it in the structure of the crystals. An intricate web that had to be precisely laid out for it to gather the minute, reclusive energy.

"Can you show us?"

The room watched her, broken only by the hum of a distant propane heater.

She wanted to say 'No.' The urge to protect her creation was as strong as when she had first laid out the network of crystals that would bring such power and energy to the world. Each crystal had to be laid precisely within the lattice and energized at a specific frequency. As intricate and simple as the mechanism for the first light bulb she had seen at the National Museum of American History, delivering the same unforeseeable change to the world.

"You have to get inside the Gatherer to do it."

Feet shifted. People glanced at one another. All of them were aware of the risk that would entail and none of them willing to get that close to a Gatherer that was drawing energy into itself—the moth that is drawn to the light only to be destroyed.

"I need to find Maria first."

"Did she help you?"

The smell of burning wax was thick and close and a dull ache had formed behind Storm's eyes. The flickering flames of candles and torches created patches of abandoned light in the cavernous space. Of course she had helped her. Without even being asked.

"Yes."

Better that they thought Maria was critical to destroying the Gatherer.

The black haired man had his head bent in conversation with a man about Storm's age whose arms trembled, and a tired-looking woman with short cropped hair, her arms crossed tight over her chest.

"Where have they taken her?"

It didn't feel as if she were in the same city where she had lived, the darkness and danger not part of the city she had known. Some of the crowd moved away, shaking their heads, her ignorance or her fear stripping away that moment of hope. Some walked quickly as if being chased, swallowed into the darkness between the candles.

The two men and the woman had stayed, the woman's arms still crossed tightly.

"We don't know."

"But you know who's taken her."

The man shrugged, came forward and offered his hand.

"I'm Romero. This is Trevor and Bev."

Romero's hand enveloped Storm's. Trevor's and Bev's were as emaciated and sharp as her own.

"You aren't sick."

He was out of place amidst the waifs that shifted and whispered in the shadows. She envied his easy movements, free of the fear of an invisible attacker.

"Not all of us are."

The woman laughed, her arms gripping her sides, as if afraid of letting something out.

"He and Marty are the only ones. Everyone else got here on their own, or was dumped."

The children had gone back to playing a slow, unenthusiastic game of *Sorry!* Most were younger than Megan, all of them casting occasional hopeful glances in her direction. It made her ill to see their thinness, the tension around their eyes that spoke of an understanding of pain. They were the same signs that had been in her team, if she had thought to look—Jana's growing fatigue, Callan no longer able to pull an idea out of the air, Ari's growing absence. The rawness of it was too much, her carefully packaged guilt torn open, each pair of eyes taking the shape of her team's.

"We heard that you had found a cure."

The thick smoky air caught in her lungs and she was coughing, the coughs doing nothing to dislodge the irritation at the back of her throat. Romero moved away and returned with a bottle of water, holding it beside her. His fingernails were trimmed, the back of his hand smooth, plump in comparison to the ridged tendons that streaked the backs of her hands. It took several gulps before her throat eased.

"So you have found one."

Bev's brow was drawn over dark pupils, their recesses a mix of anger and fear.

Storm thought of her regime of diet and isolation that had helped her manage her illness, but not cure what she had created. She wanted to tell them she could fix it. Maybe, for an instant, see the same wonder as when she had unveiled the Gatherer.

Bev turned away at Storm's hesitation, her shoulders hunched from the force of her arms around her. Romero stopped her.

"We already know this."

Bev's pointed shoulder blades poked beneath her thin coat, the roots of her hair gray at the base of her neck.

An accusation would be better. Something Storm could defend herself against. Except there was no defense. Nothing that could justify the suffering of these people. Free energy. Limitless amusements. Everything anyone needed at the flick of a switch.

Bev's shaking had gotten worse, her face distorted by suffering. Storm had to look away. Romero led Bev towards the completely dark area at the back of the warehouse. Megan rose from her place in the play area and followed, her steps so quiet it was as if she didn't touch the ground at all. A bedraggled angel that floated among the sick.

"Groups of teenagers come into the blackout area at night."

Trevor had wide bones of what must have once been formidable shoulders. His hair was long and shaggy, his beard overgrown in patches. He gestured to two plastic chairs near the entrance.

"It's a game for them. Hunting down the weak ones, like wolves."

His trembling was nearly constant and she clenched her fists against the sympathy tremors racing up her arms. She hadn't shaken in months.

"Or at least that's how they see it."

He unrolled his sleeve over his hand, and rolled it up again, stroked his beard, and leaned over to pick up a torn scrap of paper off the concrete floor.

"The police let them do that?"

He folded the paper into a tiny, scrunched square and tossed it away from him.

"They're afraid to come in here. Worried they'll catch something."

"Don't they know it's the Gatherer?"

It was good to say it out loud. Accept it as common knowledge so that she could find a solution instead of being perpetually drawn into the pit of her own guilt. Actually take a breath of air.

"We do. Out there, they aren't so sure."

Storm was aware of the great churning of the city around them. Whirring, spinning, broadcasting, glowing, speeding around them in a great wheel of electricity. As bright and shiny as gold. It was so much easier to keep your eye on the light than on the darkness it created.

"But they use the fence to keep you in."

The warehouse had settled into quiet as if the excitement of her arrival had exhausted the inhabitants. The empty quiet of the rafters lay over the low murmur of the sick. Several candles had been snuffed out and she and Trevor sat in an isolated pool of light. The trembling of Trevor's hands made no noise at all.

"They know what our weaknesses are. The debate is over what is causing it."

She remembered how effectively the field had stopped her, any passage through that strength of field enough to incapacitate if not kill her.

"What do the teenagers do when they catch someone?"

Maria had had a rifle. She shouldn't have been overpowered. Yet the space below the pier had been empty as if the boat had never been there at all.

"Is she sick?"

"She's got an infection, the handle—"

The task of having to explain how they had ended up in the cellar overwhelmed her. The bomb. Maria's deterioration as they had fled up the river.

"No. Sick like us."

She could still feel the boat beneath her, her body rising and falling with the lift and roll of the water, her exhaustion inseparable from its rhythm.

"Not like us."

This place where they had arrived was beyond anything she had imagined. Had Maria known what she was delivering her to?

She crossed to the door, her legs heavy like when she had been in the river, except this time it was Storm who would have to come to Maria. Her hand was on the handle when Trevor reached her.

"You won't find her."

His eyes were blue and clear despite his illness, his core not yet compromised. He looked back over his shoulder to the sleeping room and shook his head at someone she could not see. One of the corners on his lip had split.

She tried to shake off the fatigue crashing towards her. She hadn't been struck this hard since the first early days. She struggled to stay above it as she remembered Maria's hand tight around the rifle, her unusual sense of panic.

"I have to."

She turned the handle, but her dry skin slipped on the smooth metal and the latch did not release.

Trevor slid a bolt into place, clicking a padlock shut. She would have fought against him, but there was no strength, no energy to do anything but gaze at the shining metal.

"It's too dangerous at night."

He moved between her and the door so that she had to turn away.

Romero stood behind them and she wondered how long he had been there.

"Come. I have a place for you."

TWENTY TWO

Daylight penetrated through the opaque walls of the upper warehouse, flooding the expansive room with a soft, bright light. The space was bigger than it had appeared in the darkness, the ceiling three stories high and the cots and partitions extending the length of a football field before a brighter light outlined an open bay door.

For a moment Storm couldn't place where she was, the brightness and the peace of the place pulling her back into the days before the Gatherer had been created. The lab filled with morning light. The silence filled with possibilities. She would have loved to travel back to that point in time, to not make the error in the lattice that would lead her to discover the principle behind the Gatherer. To have that moment float by, maybe as part of someone else's life, and to allow her to continue scraping by, the fame and the impact of the Gatherer never touching her or this world. She had tried many times to imagine what that life would have been like, but it never took shape, that reality not one she was ever destined to see.

She rubbed her face, trying to clear the fog from her thoughts. Excited voices sounded from the far end of the warehouse where she had first come in. An agitated group had gathered, shifting and jostling for position as they tried to see into the centre of the crowd.

Storm stood and braced on a metal column. She wove her way through an extensive layout of cots and low barriers. Halfway to the entrance she paused. She stood along the exact centre of the building, the beds and barriers laid out symmetrically on either side of the mid-line. What had once appeared as a random cluster arranged itself into smooth curves arching outward. The partitions acted as neat dividers, segregating the curves into smaller sections, like the careful structure of a beehive, every branch designed for a specific purpose.

The grand structure enveloped her and the rows of cots. In her daze, she had wandered to the centre of it, her muscles lying smooth and close against her bone and the fog gone from her head.

"What do you think?"

Romero stood behind her.

She opened her arms, lifting them out from her sides, waiting for the fatigue to return, the sense of well-being to leave. She felt as she would after a long illness, drained and weak, yet out of the danger zone.

"How does it work?"

Romero lifted his face to the ceiling, to the glow of the natural light. There was pride there and also a resistance to share.

"It's strongest when all the cots are full."

The cots were maybe half filled with people, the soft light permeating the barren room as if the morning sun were rising at the far end of the warehouse. She had tried to make her own shield to protect herself from the currents of the Northern Lights but had been too blind to see the power of taking it a step further. By connecting the fields of many humans into a larger network, Romero had created something greater than the whole. She wanted to rest forever at the centre of this unseen thing, let go as it held her gently in its subtle power. There was a joy to it, low and fragile, with the potential to grow into something more.

"Does it cure people?"

Romero gazed around the room, following the lines of the web he had created, as real as any column or pole.

"Maybe. After a few years. If people could stay here long enough to be rebalanced."

Two empty spaces broke the symmetry of one line of cots, and another single space interrupted a row further out.

"Is that where people—"

She didn't say the word out loud, for fear of disturbing this fragile joy, but Romero understood.

"Not at all. The empty spaces make the web stronger. Give it space to adjust to the larger structure."

The noise grew from the end of the room and the web tightened around her. Was he baiting her? Telling her what he had discovered?

He pointed to a thin copper wire that ran up one of the poles. Each column had a similar wire, and the walls had wires running a foot apart. He wasn't looking to her for a response, merely basking in the pleasure of what he had created. Had he stumbled on the need for the imperfections on his own?

"Was it you?"

He spoke low enough so that only she would hear. She looked at him, not understanding, frightened of his sudden intensity and the familiarity of it. She felt the joy slide away. Other scientists had been some of her biggest detractors, spending hours discrediting her online, espousing on how the Gatherer couldn't possibly work, even when it had.

"The headquarters. It's on the news."

She tried to hide her confusion but he had seen it. His focus shifted along with something in his understanding.

There were catcalls and cheering as the crowd closed the space. Romero searched her face, his expression wary as he looked to see if she was lying and she tried to understand what was happening. The crowd paraded towards them, more animated than they had been since she'd arrived. Bev led the pack, beaming, a changed person from the previous night.

They crowded around her and Romero, eight to ten deep, the peace of the web broken by their manic energy. Trevor stood next to Bev, not shaking. Their faces were bright, as hopeful as the small impoverished communities where they had delivered some of the first Gatherers. The crowd clapped and grinned, some of the younger men thrusting their fists in the air in victory, their exuberance strangely threatening. She flinched as a few slapped her back too hard.

"Three cheers for Freeman!"

Storm flushed, hating the attention and confusion. She had only ever seen photos of the new headquarters, glimpses of its glass and steel façade on videos of press conferences, her mother poised and in charge in front of the microphones.

"Can you show me?"

The crowd parted as they moved through. She wanted to pull away from where they touched her, but there were too many, and whatever had happened at the headquarters had wiped away their distrust.

A rough steel cage encased the computer screen, a marked radius of open space on the floor preventing anyone from getting too close. Trevor and Bev stood next to her as Romero brought the news clip up on the screen. The restless crowd closed in around them.

Smoke billowed from the front of the Gatherer's headquarters as people in office clothes milled around. Lights from fire crews and police cars flashed erratically over the scene, as fully clothed firefighters directed the frightened flock of workers away from the entrance. Storm searched for her mother in the crowd before a young female reporter with flawless makeup blocked the screen. Her mother stood beside her.

"Thanks for speaking with us Ms. Freeman. This must have been quite a shock for you."

Her mother's hair was styled, clothes neat.

"I wanted to let everyone know that Gatherer Inc. is fully operational and that this blatant terrorist attack will not stop the good that we are bringing to the world."

Several workers wandered across the screen behind her, looking off into the distance.

"Was anyone hurt in the explosion?"

"At this stage it looks like there are very few injuries. We have some of the best security in the world and I don't suspect this to slow down our production."

Her mother's reassuring smile was out of place.

"Do you know who is responsible for the attack?"

The camera zoomed in and her mother's face filled the screen. The slick, professional veneer vanished and the iron will Storm recognized slid into place. It was as if she were in the same room with her, sensing the anger before it broke.

"No one has claimed responsibility."

Her lipstick was bright red, and the eyeshadow she had never worn when Storm was young looked professionally done. A renovated version of her mother. Storm wondered whether any of the original structure remained.

"There are rumours that your daughter, Storm Freeman, the inventor of The Gatherer, has attacked and destroyed a Gatherer. Could this attack have come from her?"

Storm felt as if she stood in the path of a tornado, the first edges of the cyclone about to pull her in.

"It's too early to say who is responsible. I'll let the police and fire crews do their job."

The quiet thickened in the warehouse, a solid stillness surrounding her.

"Have you been in touch with your daughter? Is it possible she is responsible for this?"

Her mother's expression didn't change, her face frozen in that odd smile. Storm could feel her mother asking the same question.

"My daughter brought a great gift to the world with the Gatherer. I don't believe she would intentionally destroy what she created."

Was that meant for Storm? Did her mother assume she would be watching? She had to know Storm had left the Yukon, whoever was in that jet giving her regular updates on their failure to find her.

"But you aren't sure."

Her mother's gaze flicked off screen before she was pulled beyond the camera's vision. Black smoke rose out of the entrance as jets of water from thick hoses dosed the blackened crater where the door had been.

The image changed to an early evening view of the central square in Three Rocks with Storm's silver-clad figure making its erratic path towards the Gatherer. It had felt like her skin was being peeled back, the draw of the Gatherer leaving her depleted, a sense of doom lying so close to her she hadn't thought she would make it out the other side.

The view changed, showing her hacking away at the side of the Gatherer with a crowbar. In between strikes she looked up towards the camera and the sight of her own face shocked her. It looked gaunt, the skin stretched tight over bone—but it was her mindless purpose that most frightened her, a beast determined to stop whatever was causing it pain. She barely remembered those minutes, the entire journey through the square a haze of pain encased in the certainty of death. No wonder her mother had been so cagey. Anyone seeing this would believe Storm had lost her mind.

Romero turned off the screen, powering down the entire console.

The quiet was thick enough to suffocate her. She stared at the blank, washed-out display waiting for her mother's image to return and answer the question.

"Is that how Kowalski got hurt?"

Romero sat next to the screen as if it and the computer were as inanimate as a chair. No one else went close. The crowd had made a space around her, forming into a loose semi-circle.

"You said there was an explosion."

Their explosion to get them out of the cellar had been small and personal compared to the magnitude of the one at the headquarters. The hole in the cellar roof had been designed to get them out. The explosion at the headquarters was something else. A line had been crossed. The shine finally falling off the Gatherer, that gaping hole giving credence to the rumours and feeding the panic that people would have been trying to keep at bay. The situation was far beyond what she had imagined, the great work of the Gatherer hemorrhaging at the seams.

"There was."

She would never be able to make them believe she hadn't been responsible.

"And you didn't take her to the hospital."

She tasted fury at their accusations. A deep, humming annoyance that they believed they had the right to judge her.

"It's no secret Maria and I have been accused of terrorism. A hospital isn't a safe place for her."

"That's where they've taken her."

It was a young man, the same age as Trevor, though skinny, with a patchy beard.

"How do you know?"

The boy looked to Romero.

"We haven't cut ourselves off from the city around us. We simply filter what gets through."

"Have they arrested her?"

Romero paused before he answered.

"Not the police."

Storm felt a sudden break in the connection to Maria, the rope that had connected them coming undone and slipping away, all their efforts disintegrating as soon as they were apart. She tried to picture Maria being held, but in her imagination Maria broke free, kept moving forward.

She would need to move forward on her own, despite the distraction of the attack and the worsening situation. Those were symptoms. She needed to keep her focus on the solution and the connection she had with the Gatherer.

"What are you going to do?"

The crowd had moved back but she was aware of them listening, faces turned only partially away, conversations truncated or not existing.

Her path was strangely clear, the explosion and her mother's distorted interview bringing it back to what had only ever mattered, her and the Gatherer and that connection. There was only one other person who understood it as well as she did. He had disappeared even before she left, retreating to the lab he had set up. He hadn't wanted it soiled by the fame that followed her. It hadn't mattered. The strain of the release had already pushed them apart. His accusation of self-importance and irresponsibility still showing up in her dreams.

"I need to find someone."

Romero sat next to the inert monitor. His health shone from beneath his old clothes, no amount of disguise able to camouflage his strength.

"Do you know if he's alive?"

She paused, for he spoke as if he knew it was Daniel. She felt the insidiousness of fame again, of people knowing so much about her life and so little.

She shook her head, wondering who he was with his intricate web and how much she could trust him. He was running tests on his patients. Benevolent tests but tests, nonetheless, and she wondered how much they knew.

"Are there other blackout areas?"

"Three. None of them as large or as sophisticated as this."

He waved his hand to indicate the layout of the beds, the children's play area.

"Do you know the people there?"

"Some but not all. Their setups are less structures. People come and go."

He didn't need to say that they died. It was understood.

"Does everyone come here by choice?"

She felt the recoiling, the wound she had touched still raw. The smell of burned wax hung in the air, a charred underlayer to the light flooding in the high windows.

Romero answered.

"In the beginning people came on their own. Later, as soon as they started showing symptoms, they were dropped off."

Like a modern day leper colony.

"So if someone was ill they would be in one of the areas."

Daniel had shown only the smallest signs of fatigue, and a habit of forgetting things. She had attributed it to stress but he could have been sick, like the others.

"Not necessarily."

Trevor's voice was rough, carrying the same anger she had heard from Bev.

"Some families keep them at home, believing that the doctors will cure them. They become prisoners, trapped by the fields, often so deteriorated that to escape to us would be fatal."

Storm had been a coward. She had known what was wrong and had let her mother convince her she was the only one.

"And staying where they are is fatal as well."

An open space surrounded her as if she emanated a lethal field.

"Can you show me where the other areas are?"

A shift of bodies and Megan emerged from the crowd wearing tattered fairy wings and carrying a magic wand, ready to grant wishes.

"Only Romero goes to the other areas."

She sat cross-legged on the floor next to Storm, a few curls sprouted above her matted hair, having not yet been consumed by the dirt and oil.

"Trevor goes too."

"Megan!"

Everyone looked to Trevor, his anger confirming Megan's words. At the edge of the group where only Storm could see, Romero glared at the girl, his malevolence gone so quickly she might not have seen it at all. Maria would have seen it, if it was there.

Trevor ran a trembling hand over his face.

"It's how I got here."

Storm waited. Megan lifted her smooth, young face to Trevor's.

"It's not a surprise to anyone here. What they don't know is that it almost killed me. I thought the tunnels would be free of fields but they weren't."

He looked down at Megan though he didn't see her, reliving whatever suffering had got him here. His broad shoulders were more wasted than the previous night, the illusion of breadth gone in the daylight.

"Let's give Trevor a moment everyone."

Marty appeared and drew Trevor away. He didn't resist. His departure seemed to take the air out of the rest, his weakness too much a reminder of their own. There was no one here with enough energy to fight for even the briefest of time.

"The best way to beat this is to stay healthy."

Romero had raised his voice, addressing the receding backs—a bedraggled, worn group once the excitement from the attack on the headquarters was gone and she had not been the saviour they had hoped for. Megan drew invisible stars on the concrete with the end of her wand.

"I've been down there."

Megan's small mouth was set in a determined line, her wand filling the cracked concrete with dozens of stars.

Romero closed his eyes and Storm understood that Megan was using her as protection.

"Down where?"

Romero looked like he wanted to swat Megan.

"The old subway lines."

"Aren't they electrified?"

"The city shut them down last year, once everyone migrated to the electric rail above ground."

"So they're empty?"

"People live down there."

Megan leaned forward to collect a piece of broken concrete, the tip of her wing rubbing against Storm's hand. Tiny copper wires were woven through the wings, a child's attempt to keep back the fields.

"Maybe you should check on your mom."

It was an attempt to get rid of Megan, Romero not appreciating her contribution. Megan didn't flinch.

"She's resting."

She wondered what else she might learn with Megan's help.

"Like who?"

Storm addressed Megan and a tiny muscle at Romero's temple twitched.

Megan lifted her chin to where the crowd had been.

"People like them. Or some who are afraid."

Her curls bounced.

Romero had stood, unconsciously or not, positioning himself between her and the door.

"The tunnels are dangerous. Some of the lines are live, and the gangs of teenagers hunt down there as well."

Bev had appeared behind him, arms crossed, her glare filled with enough anger to raise the hairs on Storm's arms. Megan watched with her wand half raised, stopped in the midst of casting a spell.

"How do I get to the tunnels?"

She focused on the possibility of being able to move beneath the city. The opportunities that could deliver. She might be able to find Daniel or learn where he was.

"If you're like the others, the fields will kill you."

"I'm not like the others."

Hadn't that always been her problem? So determined not to be like everyone else. Instead, she had made them all exactly like her.

"So you have a cure?"

She felt the closeness of this place, the navel gazing of the sick. The same navel gazing that had trapped her in the Yukon.

"No."

Romero stepped forward suddenly and she got the impression that he had been waiting for this, for whatever had just happened.

"We could find one. If you stayed. Your knowledge of the Gatherer. My success with the webs. We could do it. Save people from this."

She saw the excitement in him, the desire to be the one who found the cure. It wouldn't be about the cure or helping these people. It would be about his brilliance, and hers. How they had brought this to the world. The back of her legs bumped the table behind her. Glasses rattled and a stack of papers fell to the floor.

"It wouldn't turn out how you expect."

If they ever even found one.

He paused. She had momentarily distracted him from his excitement. It returned quickly, not easily dissuaded from how he saw this playing out.

"But we would have the cure. It would save people."

He was an earlier version of herself. Blinded to anything that didn't fit with her vision.

"And if the wrong people got it?"

"We would have control of it. Distribute it through our own network."

His certainty angered her. You couldn't predict how anything would turn out.

"We don't need a cure. We need to stop the Gatherer."

That was the only certainty.

"So you're going to leave without helping?"

His idealism saddened her. He believed a cure was going to solve this. She had known the moment she walked around the corner in Three Rocks the Gatherer had to be stopped. It had just taken a while to realize it had to be her.

"I'll take you to the tunnels."

Megan had slipped her hand into Storm's—warm, small, her grip firm.

"It's too dangerous."

Megan held Storm's hand tighter.

The city drew closer, its churning presence a living, breathing threat.

"I know my way around."

Storm would never be able to outrun it. It followed her wherever she went.

"It's dangerous here too. If the area turned on. You'd all be incapacitated or worse."

"They won't."

"How do you know?"

Megan had lifted her face to the ceiling, seeing the light beyond the opaque windows. A bird flew high in the rafters, making tight manic circles as it sought a way out.

"We could find a cure."

"It won't stop the Gatherer."

"Neither will you if you go out there. You'll be turned back before you reach the downtown."

A squeeze from Megan. Was he lying? Or did Megan know another way?

"Then you take me. Show me how to get through."

The bird circled towards the back of the warehouse as Romero threw out his hand in a gesture of frustration.

"I'm not getting myself killed. I am needed here."

The accusation was obvious. That she was needed there too and that risking her life was irresponsible.

"Then let Megan take me."

"She is a child!"

His exasperation and disappointment were complete. Whatever admiration she might have had lay dead on the floor between them.

"I can't stay here."

"No. The great Storm Freeman would not bother herself with the mess."

The sudden calmness of his fury frightened her. His distaste for the person he believed her to be turned to loathing in an instant.

She let go of Megan's hand as he strode forward, bracing for whatever attack would come. Instead he brushed past her and snatched a map from beneath a pile of papers. He sketched quickly and concisely, the tunnel's darker route emerging over the grid of city streets. He put in labels and junction points, all of it on the perimeter, none of it coming close to the university or the compound. Megan's face was close to the drawing as she watched.

"These are the other dark areas."

He pointed to a section to the south, close to the water, and a slightly more central area below Bell Park. She and Daniel had been to a concert in the park, on a rare summer's night when they had been out of the lab. Its lush greenness had been a welcome contrast to the sterility of the lab.

Romero handed her the paper, letting go even before she had taken hold.

"You'll get yourself killed."

It could have been a warning or a threat.

"Nowhere else is going to be safe but here."

She had the sudden memory of waking up on a good morning in the Yukon, feeling the protection of the landscape, the certainty of being safe.

"I still have to go."

"Wait until tonight, so that no one sees you enter the tunnels."

He turned, dismissing her, and disappeared back into the warehouse and the intricate web he had created. He charged through it, immune to whatever calming smoothness its threads created.

The rough route showed a potential path that could get her to the next blackout area, closer to the headquarters and maybe closer to Daniel. She turned her head, listening to the thrumming city she could not hear. His pulse could have been part of that larger churning, or she could have failed to notice when it stopped.

Megan's face was close to the page.

"I can show you the way."

"I thought it was dangerous."

She shrugged. Her brow pinched as she traced Romero's route on the page. She stopped at one of the junction points.

"Not if you know which way to go."

TWENTY-THREE

There was the easy chatter of women's voices, disturbances in the air as people passed close to Maria, and an absence of pain below her knee. She squinted against the light, its brilliance aggravating the parched, hungover ache of her head. The faceted lens of a fluorescent light shone over her, one in a row that extended end to end down a long corridor. She saw white walls with an opening to an adjacent corridor just beyond her feet, a white sheet over her legs.

She heard a sharp intake of breath above her head and creaking rustling as someone shifted on their gurney. Further up, someone delivered a muttering monologue. She was part of a long row of stretchers that, like the lights, extended down a long corridor. There had been rain and fever and a cold that shook her every bone. She struggled to sit. Where was Storm? A nurse in a brightly coloured uniform came out of the adjacent corridor and walked away from her. An arrow on the wall pointed towards Radiology. Keys clicked on a keyboard, and a telephone rang.

Maria collapsed back into the pillow, light-headed. She let her heart slow and her breathing rest light and shallow. She felt the snug light pressure of a bandage over her calf, the clear tube of an IV running into the back of her hand. Her mouth so dry she couldn't swallow.

They had been in a boat approaching Rima. She arched her neck to look for her chart. Her name would be on an admittance list. The military protocol told her to wait for help and that someone would come for her. But there was no one that would care enough to come for her, other than the military or the police. Even if Havernal weren't sick he wouldn't be dropping everything to seek her out. He had a wife and family. If he was even alive.

She lifted herself onto her elbow, waiting while the vertigo settled. A sharp scent of rancid alcohol wafted from the direction of the moan. Had this been Storm's plan to get rid of her? Dumped at the hospital so the military would find her?

"Hey sleeping beauty!"

Her gurney shook.

Maria turned her head as far as she could. The boot that had kicked her gurney was worn away at the toe, the sole detached from the tip. It was attached to a pair of grimy tights that had once been red and the folds of a stained and torn skirt. The woman wore enough layers of coats and sweaters to form a solid genderless lump. She watched Maria from a sagging weathered face surrounded by a mane of crusty, clumped curls.

"They've been talking about you."

The voice was sing-songy, threatening, like a kindergarten teacher in need of a sick leave.

"Who's they?"

The words were rough, misshapen by the dryness of her mouth.

The woman tilted her head back and forth, her smile on the darker side of creepy.

"People."

Shouts came from down the adjoining hall and were silenced quickly like a candle being snuffed out. Beyond the woman the corridor ended in a set of swinging doors with a circular red sign that read RESTRICTED. Maria was cold again, traces of her fever still active in her veins. She swung her legs over the side and sat up, nearly keeling over from the pounding pressure in her leg. She lay back down, fists clenched at her sides as she waited for the pain to subside.

"Clipped your wings. Clipped your wings."

The old woman tittered.

A nurse strode down the corridor, her steps quick and efficient. Maria forced herself to relax and feign sleep. The military wasn't here yet or there would be someone posted at her bedside and she wouldn't be stuck in a corridor. She jerked at a gentle touch on her arm. A young nurse stood over her, fresh-faced, blonde hair pulled back in a ponytail with a tinge of pink in her bangs.

"Welcome back."

* * * *

The stretcher wheels rolled over the hospital's tiled floor, the squares of fluorescent lights between ceiling tiles rolling past like the telephone poles outside a car window. The hushed murmuring of the emergency ward had been left behind and they passed countless doors and arrows pointing back to the Emergency Room and Diagnostic Imaging, until the signs stopped. The nurse continued to roll past doors marked only with numbers, the labyrinth of brightly lighted corridors seemingly endless so that Maria lost track of the twists and turns, unable to keep the map in her head.

It felt as if she were speeding through a silent subway line, the lights on the ceiling the brief flashes of the stations as they hurtled past. She shook her head, though it was more of a lolling from side to side, the drugs used to take the pain away having clogged up the synapses in her brain so her thoughts wouldn't connect together. She had a brief thought that this would be how Storm felt during an attack, before the thought was whisked away and it was the lights again, sliding past in that endless rhythm, counting the beats to the end.

Occasionally a face floated by, looking down at her with blank curiosity. They would know who she was, all of them part of a conspiracy to whisk her out of sight, deliver her back into the hands of the military.

She grabbed at the gleaming silver railing when they turned a corner but she missed the mark, her hand falling uselessly beside the gurney. The nurse tucked Maria's arm back under the sheet, tightening it around her shoulder without slowing. They never got close enough for Maria to reach again.

"Where are we going?"

The words were thick, hard to form. She lifted herself onto her elbow, nauseous from the motion of the stretcher. The nurse pushed her back down, humming a nameless, repetitive tune.

"This will be a better place for you."

"I liked the old place."

The girl laughed, a young tinkling laugh as if no one ever liked the bustle and chaos of the emergency room. At least there had been people, witnesses.

She must have dozed off. Had there been an elevator? The corridors were colder, less bright, the doors functional and unmarked like a morgue. She was being wheeled to a slot in the wall where she would slowly die before anyone found her. She struggled, but couldn't move, straps tight across her hips and chest.

"Help!"

It was an unformed moan that echoed inside her head and went no further. The woman patted her shoulder to say she was okay and in good hands. She squirmed. She wasn't in good hands, didn't want to be in anyone's hands.

She heard the thud and clang of an emergency door opening, a rush of cold air, and the sudden exposure to the dark sky. She didn't want to be out here, needed to return to where the people were.

She saw more faces above her, no longer the polished cleanliness of the hospital staff. A bearded man looked familiar. She sensed the exchange of words, a handshake, something transferred, then a sudden lift, vertigo, the push of metal across a dirty floor, and the inside of a truck that smelled of cattle. She could hardly move against the restraints, called for help without effect.

Where was the nurse? Her tuneless humming echoed inside Maria's head.

Doors slammed. The bearded face floated over her in a harsh overhead light. Not military.

An engine roared, she smelled diesel and the world shook.

The sudden prick of a needle jabbed into her thigh. She twisted, flailed uselessly. A warmth rushed into her toes and up her thigh like water overflowing a bathtub. It spread through her abdomen and she lifted her chin as if she would be able to keep her head above water. She felt threads of dizziness, the first trickle, and then the deep flush of oblivion as it flooded over her.

TWENTY-FOUR

Storm stood in the darkness at the canal's edge, her gaze lifted to the glowing horizon of the city with the same unease as when she had approached Three Rocks. She stood within the shelter of the darkness, trace currents whisking and pulling across her cheeks.

The electrification started benignly enough, a few decorative lanterns along the water's edge and the glint of cars in the distance beneath higher, brighter lights. Beyond that monstrous digital signs flashed incessantly and an electric train streamed by, its windows a chain of glowing squares. At the center, the sparkling ring of the Ferris wheel spun lazily.

"My mom never comes here anymore."

Megan had skipped easily along the river, skirting around featureless stacks piled on the banks, pulling Storm into a cramped alley when a group of teenagers had sauntered past.

"We used to come and watch the lucky ones."

Storm's respiration was too shallow, her attempts at breathing slowly doing nothing against the taste of fear and the certainty that if she went in, she would not come out. She focused on each breath, imagining her heart beating slowly—all the techniques that were useless against this kind of fear.

"You can go back now."

It had been a game for Megan when they had hidden from the teenagers, more a bout of hide and seek than the possibility of violence, even though Marty and Trevor had warned them repeatedly to avoid the groups.

The river flowed black and silky beside them, its faint rotting stench smelling more of chemicals than plants.

"I have the map."

Storm patted the stiff rectangle on her chest where the map of the subway network was tucked inside her suit.

A police car, blue and red sirens flashing, skimmed across an overpass.

"It's not the same."

"You saw Romero draw it."

The city pulsed and shimmered, a sparkling mirage that dominated her vision.

"He didn't draw the safe ones."

Storm pulled her gaze from the shining distance to the shadows where Megan stood beside her. Megan looked back behind them, away from the brilliance of the city.

"On purpose?"

Megan's shoulders lifted, the back of her matted hair lighted by the glow of the city.

"He says we can't trust you."

Storm's gaze returned to the shimmering city. She tasted the fear, the bitter acid of a seizure.

"He's probably right."

Megan started walking, closing the distance to where the world turned on.

"My mom is sick."

Storm didn't follow, wary of the vibrating fields that would reach their tendrils towards her. Bev wasn't only sick, she was angry, her bitterness eating her alive as much as her disease.

"Did she tell you to do this?"

The girl disappeared between two crates, and Storm heard scraping and sweeping sounds until she emerged carrying a long metal bar. A slender reed in the dim light, she strode to a metal door at the back of a newer commercial warehouse and inserted the end of the bar between the door and its frame.

"She told me to help you."

Megan grunted with effort, leaning her tiny body against the bar.

Storm moved to help, her face turned from the city's light. She wrapped her hands around the cool bar and pulled.

"You can't come. It isn't safe."

The door gave way and Storm stumbled back, Megan falling on top of her. She weighed next to nothing, every part of her boney and sharp. Storm steadied her as Megan got to her feet.

"I'm not safe here either."

Megan held the flashlight as they descended into the subway, its small field not strong enough to touch Storm. They passed through cavernous foyers that Storm felt rather than saw, the awareness of wide open spaces extending up from the narrow beam of the light. The hair on Storm's arms rose as they descended down the jagged-edged steps of frozen escalators, aware of the powerful motors that lurked beneath them, ready to spring to life at the flick of a switch. At the third station the hum of a lone escalator echoed throughout the high ceilings. Megan guided them around it without Storm saying a word, her features solemn in the glow of the flashlight, focused on her role as guide.

The route was lined with evidence of people, garbage cans turned over, the searched contents strewn across dirty tiled floors. They passed empty kiosks with their gates intact and others with them torn open, the metal in twisted crumpled balls still partially attached. Electrical plugs hung from digital signs behind where the cash register would have been. Powerless monitors didn't announce train arrivals. In their second station one bank of monitors had been left on, their dull grey screens casting a deadened glow into the forgotten space.

Megan led them across the damp concrete barrier to the opposite track. Storm had the sense of traveling in the wrong direction, as if, like the spinning escalator, there was a lone train circling incessantly along the same repeated path.

They entered the somehow darker confined space of the tunnel, the metal rails gleaming in the narrow beam of light. They were so smooth and polished she could imagine the current that drove the trains still pulsed beneath the surface. The echo of their steps moved with them, a bubble of disturbance that passed, the dark and quiet closing in behind them.

"My mom and I rode the trains."

Storm had been in these same tunnels when they'd been brilliant and light, the people flowing along the corridors in parallel with the current that fed the lights, monitors, cash registers, and ovens of the businesses that inhabited the tiny cave-like cubicles. There would be a yard somewhere, the defunct trains pushed together in a corner, waiting for a better day.

A hundred or two hundred meters from a platform Megan stopped and pointed the flashlight at her feet. Ahead, the glow of a flickering light filled out the circled roof of the tunnel. Voices floated towards them, one male, the second indistinguishable.

Megan turned and retraced their steps, pausing every few feet to scan the side walls, running the beam up to the ceiling. Storm's pulse ran faster, its beat echoing against the silence.

"What is it?"

Megan held the beam on a small trap door, then moved on.

"People."

"Are they sick?"

They were almost back at the platform when Megan pulled on a metal utility door. It swung open easily, revealing a bare, narrow corridor perpendicular to the tracks. The voices were getting louder, approaching along the tunnel.

Megan climbed into the corridor and Storm pushed in behind her, pulling the door shut. There was nothing to lock the door or jam the handle. Storm listened but the solid steel blocked all noise and she didn't know if the voices had passed, stopped, or waited outside the door.

The corridor was full of narrow, bare conduits running along the roof, leading into the tight closing darkness. The flashlight didn't extend far into the corridor and Storm had the sense of it growing smaller, feeling that if she gave in to her desire to run, she would be trapped.

Megan walked lightly ahead, her slight shoulders leading Storm into pitch blackness. She would be lost in darkness without her tiny guide, forced to take her chances with whoever controlled that square of light behind them, products of the Gatherer who might not be as welcoming as Megan's group.

"Are we close?"

Romero had shown her the second blackout area on the map, yet she wanted Megan to say yes, that this shortcut would somehow bring them out of this tomb earlier. Several doors led off the corridor, yet they continued straight on, the air thicker and damper as they left the brightness of the subway platform behind. When Storm felt as if the pressure of the darkness around them would crush her, they passed through a metal door into the lifeless quiet of an abandoned mechanical room. A large boiler sat at its centre, pipes sprouting at odd angles like the legs of a beetle and running out and up into the darkness above them.

Storm stopped. Somewhere in the room would be a panel, the gateway for all the electricity that would power the incessant churning of these machines.

"It's not live."

Megan backtracked to stand beside Storm. The boiler's bulk towered above them.

"It was at one point."

They passed the smooth faces of the control panels, small dirty windows showing stopped dials or newer digital faces gone blank. Storm dared not breathe, afraid that any breath would alert someone of their passage and let in the fear that rode on the back of her neck.

Another entrance, wider, led to a finished hallway of drywall and musty carpet. The light revealed their ghostly reflections in the glass windows of empty offices, chairs, desks, and telephones all abandoned, waiting for people to return.

There was a sudden crash of metal falling, a boulder tumbling through a metal culvert. They ducked into an open door, the flashlight out, and waited, stricken, in darkness. Storm was overwhelmed by the smell of candles on Megan's hair, the desperate search for a piece of light to hold onto, and the reverberating crashes coming out of the darkness. Megan slipped her hand into Storm's.

The clanging stopped, its vibrations echoing through the corridors, rattling the empty spaces out of their silence. A brief draft of cool fresh air blew past. There was no sound of footsteps or retreating voices, simply the end of the noise.

Megan slipped her hand from Storm and Storm reached for her in the dark, unseen threats looming closer. The arrival of light from the flashlight cast distorted shadows up from the floor, turning her from a child into a frightened cadaver.

Storm re-took Megan's hand in hers.

"Keep the light in your other hand. It was something in the ventilation system."

Megan's hand was soft and malleable. When they reached the new blackout area, Storm would send her back, above ground. It was ridiculous to have brought her here.

"How much farther?"

"We're almost there."

They had passed through four subway stations and were likely below the old rail storage yard. At the end of the corridor a staircase led up. Looking up through the centre of the railings, the glow of either daylight or electric light shone several stories up. Light at the end of the tunnel was not a good thing.

"That's not the way."

"You have to go back to your mom."

"I don't want to go back."

She spoke with the certainty of a child, her gaze unyielding. There must have been a dad at some point. Other family members who had walked away.

"You've brought me far enough. I don't want you to get sick."

Megan smiled and shone the light across her fingertips. A chill spread down Storm's back. It was faint, almost not there, yet the fingers trembled at a fine, delicate frequency that was impossible to fake. Storm wrapped her hand over them to make them stop as a dam released within, waters crashing and tearing through her, ripping away the excuses she had built up, her justifications like broken weeds in the wind.

Megan flinched as Storm squeezed harder.

"Look at me."

She tried to pull her hand away.

"I will make this better."

"Romero says you won't."

She felt a surge of irritation at Romero's insolence, that he would expose a child to such futility. Though it was the Gatherer that had levelled the playing field for everyone.

"Well, we'll have to prove him wrong."

"Then I better come with you. The place he wanted you to go is right ahead of us. You won't know it is coming."

TWENTY-FIVE

The daylight reflected off the stairwell's tiled walls, bits of it sneaking through the metal railings. The light had the softness of early morning and Storm wanted more than anything to step out of the darkness of the tunnels into its fledgling warmth. They had stopped on a landing two floors below street level, and Megan looked down at her from a few steps above. She had one foot on the next stair, her body twisted back towards Storm, her brow pinched as she fought against her need for sleep.

"It's okay to go this way."

Whether imagined or real, Storm felt the city coming awake above her, a slow ramping up of its radiation as trains glided along rails, coffee shops turned on their pots, and ventilation systems pushed air through the boardrooms and open concept floors of hundreds of office towers—along with the underlying pull of the network of Gatherers as they stripped away the world's peripheral energy for fuel.

"How do you know?"

She shrugged, as if it was something she had always known. The tips of her hair glowed in the light.

"I came here with Romero."

"Does he know you're sick?"

She looked up through the centre of the staircase and shook her head.

Storm handed her one of the hand-made snacks Marty had given her before they'd left. Megan sat on a stair and Storm took the spot one step below her. The crinkling of their wrappers echoed in the bare walls, the sound of her chewing loud inside her head. Storm drew the map from inside her suit and laid it across her lap.

They had walked for at least half an hour after the last staircase, heading further underground before rising up through several stories to this place.

"Can you show me where we are?"

Megan traced their route with her baby finger, a few crumbs falling across the creases.

"This is where we went into the small tunnel."

Megan's finger moved perpendicularly away from the line Romero had drawn. She continued following their route, changing directions where they left the first stairwell, until she stopped at the intersection of Dunthorn Avenue and Bell Street. The green area of Bell Park extended out from the intersection.

"That's the dark zone?"

Above them, the muffled sound of a car horn beeped. Megan tilted her head side to side, chewing.

"It's where some of the sick people live. It's not really dark."

Storm followed Romero's red line with her index finger. It ended half-way down a street in the centre of a tight grid.

"Where does this go?"

Megan took her time to peel off her remaining wrapper.

"It's a dead end. There's nothing there."

Storm held out her hand for Megan's empty wrapper and folded the two together before sliding them into the pack. The jar of tablets Marty had given her didn't fit with the water bottles and she readjusted them until they all fit in a straight line along her back.

When she sat straight, Megan was pushing a thin black case back into her pocket.

"What is that?"

Storm held out her hand and Megan turned, shielding it with her body.

"Give me that."

Storm reached for it and Megan pulled it away but not before Storm's fingertips warmed where it touched.

"It will make you sicker."

Storm's voice echoed in the stairwell, making it louder, harsher.

Megan had her head bent to the screen.

"I don't care."

"Yes, you do."

Storm grabbed for it, hating herself even as she overpowered the girl and pulled it from her hand. She glanced at the screen, the ache bleeding into her fingers.

It was a photo of Megan with a happier, smiling Beverley and a beefy, grinning man.

"Did you tell them where we are?"

The small icon circled endlessly, searching in vain for a signal. Thank God. A few steps higher and they would have found them. The imbalance of the small field made her nauseous.

"No."

Megan was defiant, chin stuck out. She reached for the phone and Storm let her take it. Storm lowered herself onto the step, her eye on the sleek black device. She remembered the heat around her car during phone calls, its constant seemingly innocuous presence.

"Why do you have that?"

"So my mom knows where I am."

Who else would be waiting for Megan's text, or the tiny ping that would show their location on the screen?

"Can she use a phone?"

Megan stood with her back to the railing, the phone clutched in two hands, away from her body. Her wings were tattered, the frame bent, strands of copper trailing off the bottom.

"Marty takes messages for people."

Whoever was watching from the warehouse would know they had changed their route.

"Where were you supposed to take me?"

Megan had been so calm when she had led Storm back to the platform. It hadn't felt like they were fleeing.

"Where the voices were coming from."

"Who were they?"

Megan slid her back down the railing until she was sitting on the step. She laid the phone carefully two stairs above her and rubbed her fingers together.

"Does it hurt your hand?"

"It feels weird."

Storm nodded. Megan's nerves were healthy enough to feel only a slight irritation. The pain would come with time.

"Rub your stomach like this."

Storm demonstrated by circling her flat palm clockwise over her solar plexus.

"Sometimes it helps."

Megan did as instructed, the motion of her small hand more triangular than circular.

"Anything?"

Megan shrugged and left the phone where it was. The icon circled.

"Why didn't you take me there?"

"I thought they might hurt you."

The phone lay between them, the screen dark for the moment.

"I need you to turn off the phone."

Megan's look was suspicious, the first sign she had shown of distrust.

"My mom will be worried."

Storm looked upwards through the railing, listening for the sound of footsteps below them.

"If they know we took a different route they'll come and find us."

"Why do they want to hurt you?"

Megan's eyes were a clear, deep brown, the lashes small traces of blonde. She would be beautiful when she got older. If she had the chance.

Storm stood, her foot raised to climb up, though down might have been safer.

"I made everyone sick. With the Gatherer."

"On purpose?"

She almost laughed. As if anyone would do this on purpose. The moment when she had understood what they had created, it had been like holding the answer to life itself in her hand. The power to change the world with a delicate web of crystals, like a piece of hot burning coal that would blister her skin if she held on too long. It could shut off the diesel generators in Northern communities, bring electricity to the impoverished around the world, a pump for a well, light to work by after dark, heat on cold winter nights. She had seen it all spreading out before her, a beautiful domino of benefits that they would release onto the world.

Others had seen different potentials. Almost no one had seen the dangers, except Daniel, the follower of rules, the one checking under the bed for monsters. She still didn't know if he had started the fire. It could have as easily been Maria. Or someone else she was too blinded to see.

"No. That's why I have to fix it."

Megan powered down the phone and slipped it into her pocket.

Daniel had been with her the night of the fire, working at his terminal while they'd waited for a test to run on the Gatherer, the gathering rate on a setting far beyond anything they had tried before. She didn't know what they had expected to find, the finish on the walls melting or reality altered. They hadn't figured out yet that the damage the Gatherer created was hidden—the slow wearing away of health, like the erosion of cliffs by the ocean, the damage unseen until the cliff collapsed. By the time symptoms showed up—tremors, diarrhea, nausea, foggy head—the damage had been done.

She had fallen asleep while they'd waited and woken to the lab filled with smoke, so weak she could barely stand. She'd dragged herself to her feet, coughing, tasting chemicals. She'd barely been able to see the lab bench where Daniel had been sitting. The test area had been filled with flames, as if their test had spontaneously combusted and was taking the whole lab with it. It had burned her skin and shattered the protective glass.

"Daniel!"

Smoke had blocked every path. She'd dropped to the floor, covered her mouth with the soldering rag and crawled toward the door. There had been the sound of cracking and falling, and the great whooshing as the fire drew everything towards it. She'd scraped her way across the floor, focused on one hand in front of the next, found the stairwell, and stumbled down, grasping the railing as clearer air filled her lungs and the echoing alarms attacked her ears. She'd met firefighters at the ground floor, the flashing trucks crowded on the street.

"Is anyone up there?"

She had looked up to flames licking out of the window, their floor the only one on fire.

"I don't know."

She'd searched for Daniel in the small crowd across the street, scanning profiles for the slight lift of the chin, the righteous determination of his shoulders. They'd sat her in the back of an ambulance where she'd watched the flames move to each window, stubbornly resisting the firefighters' jets of water. She had laid the prototype so carefully at the centre of the web. Hours and hours of time invested into its tiny pathways that had likely been the first thing to disintegrate before the flames. She'd kept seeing Daniel at the bench, refusing to look at her, the rift that the Gatherer had formed between them deeper with each argument and their certainty in their own points of view.

"Where is the prototype?"

Callan's face had suddenly appeared in front of her, flushed, his large hands gripping her arms.

Water had poured into the shattered windows, alone enough to ruin the delicate structure even without the fire.

Callan had moaned, lifting his hands towards the burning building, and dropped to his knees.

TWENTY-SIX

Storm held tight to Megan's hand as they reached the top of the stairs. The small landing was flooded with a soft, weak light through a wall of windows that faced the rising sun and the faded treetops of Bell Park across a concrete square. As Megan had promised, the safety of the park's expansive lawns and tended gardens was within sprinting distance, no more than a hundred meters to the road, a few steps beyond that to the green.

"You're hurting me!"

Megan pulled her hand away and Storm realized how hard she had been gripping the girl's hand.

Dust floated lazily in the rays of sun, unconcerned by the intense fields that raced past with every car, or the possibility of a WiFi network and a silent attack. It would be like walking into a video game with only one life remaining.

Already her breathing was too fast, shallow.

Storm stood close to the glass. It was too early for the main rush of traffic, and only a single man with a leather case over his shoulder strolled between two flower urns, the brown leaves and stems drooping over the sides.

She lifted her gaze to the corners of the office buildings, searching for the telltale transmitter of a cell phone network, or worse, a tower with transmitters on multiple frequencies.

"We follow those."

Megan pointed towards the park, through a series of wide, low concrete steps that ended at the road.

"The steps?"

Megan pointed again, the tip of her finger pushed against the glass.

"The red arrows."

At first Storm didn't see the faded red chevrons spaced five or six large strides apart in a long curved path to the road.

"Who put those there?"

"They're all over if you know to look."

"And you've followed these before?"

The park looked a long way away across a sea of concrete filled with invisible sharks. All they had to guide them were a few spray painted arrows that could have been left over by a farmer's market.

"Ones like them."

A faded chevron showed on the landing beneath her feet, pointing out towards the square. Below it, 'Almost There,' had been printed in block letters and beside it a triangle overtop of a square. The universal symbol for shelter. She tried to picture the person who had drawn this path and had the forethought to add that bit of encouragement.

There had been an army of people stepping up to help the afflicted navigate a suddenly hostile world. It sharpened the loneliness she had felt in the Yukon. She could have been here, among people, getting better and stepping in before it all went too far.

"Okay, let's go."

The emergency bar clanged as they pushed out, releasing them into the cool dampness of the morning. A few trace currents crossed her cheeks before they found the path. They walked in single file, following the chevron's path closely, trying not to think of what swirled around them.

Half-way across a dull ache ran down her right side, her arm growing warm as if she were too close to a fire.

"Keep moving."

Megan had slowed and Storm pushed her faster. Speed was their friend here. The girl had hunched her shoulders, cowering away from the trace fields, and Storm understood she was sicker than she let on, the protection of the dark area masking her symptoms. Storm held on to Megan's shoulder, trying to protect the girl with her body though it would do no good. The stairwell was fifty paces back. The park equal distance ahead. It should have been just another early morning, the sun slowly warming the trees, drying off the concrete, the start of a new day.

They stopped well back from the road. Electric cars had their own special kind of power, like a moving lightning bolt that could kill on contact.

The chevrons pointed to a very specific path across a darker patch in the road. A willow tree stood at the top of a small rise on the opposite side.

They waited for eight, nine, a dozen cars before a large enough opening arrived.

"Go!"

Megan's arms pumped madly, her pack bouncing wildly on her back. Storm's legs were sluggish, a tight pain searing across her chest when she reached the road. She didn't stop, even as a long sword of pain jammed up her spine so that she was flung forward, stumbling over the opposite curb, hearing her own cry even as she kept moving, putting her feet in front of her to get as far from the road as she could.

Behind the tree she collapsed, sucking air and curled into a ball, her nerves vibrating with the aftershock of whatever that had been. There were flashes like lightning on the inside of her eyelids, a keening scream rattling her ears.

She crawled towards the sound and found Megan by feel, her head arched back in full seizure. She rolled her onto her side and held her, whispering low and calm, telling her it would be okay even though she wouldn't hear.

After a long minute or two, the girl's body relaxed, collapsing heavily against Storm. She continued to hold her as the agitation slipped from her nerves and a low ache spread up her legs.

Cars sped past below in increasing numbers and the sun cast shadows of willow leaves across their huddled bodies. No one came, and when Storm eventually could sit, Megan woke, her brown eyes frightened until she saw Storm.

"You're okay."

Megan started to cry. Storm held her close, letting her own frustration and fear flow with the girl's tears.

"Sorry."

Megan pulled herself away when her crying had reduced to sniffles.

"No need to be."

"Is that what happens to you?"

Storm gave her a tablet from the pack and a bottle of water for the little good it would do. She had brought her too far, underestimating Megan's illness. It was the same vulnerability she had seen in Jacob—obvious symptoms present yet an ability to keep going, their bodies more resilient to the imbalance until faced with something like this.

"It used to."

She didn't know why she had been spared this time. The shock had been strong enough, her nerves stripped.

"I don't like it."

Storm smiled.

"Me neither."

Megan's colour returned and they watched the traffic as they ate. There were no spaces between cars big enough for them to cross. The cars bumped over the off-coloured strip in the road. It must have shielded them from the worst of the field, but it wasn't a crossing that she would do again.

Storm lifted herself from the ground and they walked over the top of the hill. Megan stayed close, eyeing the trees and paved pathways as if they might harbour a painful field. At the crest they stopped. The landscape had been bleached white. Translucent leaves hung from tree branches, pale grasses lined the path, and faded, wilted flowers filled carefully structured gardens. A pond at the base of the hill dully reflected the pale blue sky, but they saw no flutter of wings and heard no skittering animals.

The park was beautiful in the same way a statue or a building was beautiful, without life though its form and structure were exquisite. She felt the roiling sickness of it and the harsh helplessness at seeing something destroyed.

"Are all the parks like this?"

Megan barely lifted her head.

"There was a big Gatherer here. They moved it to the other side."

"How can you tell?"

The damage to the area was uniform, starting as soon as they had crested the hill, the entire landscape bleached white.

"We used to live here."

She lifted her chin towards the street than ran to the north, the tops of condos and brown apartment towers visible through the faded treetops. Megan slowed further and Storm took her hand, needing to touch something alive. The Yukon's Tundra had pulsed with life compared to this crystal wasteland. A bluebell drooped on its stem, only the faintest trace of blue visible on its petals.

"Did no one notice?"

Megan's hand had gone limp in Storm's. Her expression had a kind of blankness that spoke of loss and anger too fierce for a child of her age.

"They said that it hadn't been set up properly. That they had fixed it. My mom still wanted to move but my dad didn't."

Megan had lifted her chin to look at the back of one of the apartment buildings. Three windows showed between branches and Storm didn't need to ask where Megan had lived.

"Is he still there?"

The shrug came again. There were dark circles under her eyes and her curls lay flat against her skull. Storm had mistaken the girl's innocence for strength. She wrapped her hand firmly around Megan's and led her downhill. The grass along the path was cut short, neatly trimmed when it had stopped growing. The reeds in the pond were white stalks above the still water, the grasses that dipped into the surface like pale, flowing hair.

Megan's weight pulled her backwards. Storm slowed further but Megan lagged, stumbling on the slightest unevenness in the pavement. Her clumsiness seemed out of place in the stillness, each scuff of her foot a break in the lifeless perfection.

At a park bench Megan sat and after a few moments lay down. Storm checked for a fever, alert for tremors but all it seemed to be was fatigue. She didn't blame her. Storm should have been feeling the same way, yet she was wired, alert to the slightest shift in the air.

She moved her pack onto her front and squatted next to Megan so the girl could climb onto her back. She was light, easy to carry and almost immediately relaxed into the heavy weight of sleep. Storm had expected her to be more of a burden, to struggle more beneath Megan's weight, yet her steps felt more solid, her back warm from the girl's heat.

She followed the path into a white wooded area. It was hard to breathe in the thick quiet and Storm's ears buzzed with her effort to hear warnings of an approach. Her arms were beginning to tire from holding Megan's legs when she saw the boy lying on an open patch of forest floor as if he had lain down for a sleep. She knew immediately he was dead, his pallor matching the drained lifelessness of the forest, his stillness not of the living. She stopped and leaned forward against Megan's weight, holding her tighter against her back as her legs shook. His hand lay curled at the end of his oversized sleeve, with either dirt of a bruise discolouring his thin neck.

She forced herself to go closer, the fallen twigs snapping beneath her feet. How could a child have been left to die in this ruined forest? Had the world become so damaged to think that this was permissible, every man—or boy—for himself?

His head had fallen to the side, his face turned from the path. It was dirt that was smeared down his neck, the action that had left it there unknowable. He was slightly smaller than Megan, though she didn't know if that meant younger. His dark hair had grown to his collar. His scuffed boots were splayed apart.

Could she have really done this? Been so blind as to not see this consequence?

She lifted her head, searching the forest, hoping a different place might exist for him. Two people stood on a rise in the path. A man and woman, thin and haunted like herself. They walked slowly, intentionally, with no urgency at the condition of the boy.

"You've met Andy I see."

The woman's tone was hostile, leaving no doubt as to her understanding of Storm's identity and her guilt. The woman didn't look at the body, and the man was watching Megan. Storm turned her away from them.

"What happened to him?"

They wore copper bands around their wrists and necks—necks that had started out wider, judging by the diameter of the bands. The man's right eye twitched rhythmically, and when he saw her watching he turned his head so she wouldn't see. The woman's only sign of illness was the folds of flesh hanging from her jaw, the remnants of a much larger woman.

A disinterested shrug was the woman's only response, as if Storm had asked a question for which she should already have known the answer. Storm adjusted Megan's weight, the girl heavier now.

"Is Megan hurt?"

Storm held her tighter.

"We all know who Megan is. We won't hurt her."

Their shoulders nearly touched, and they had their arms folded, right over left. Their dirty and worn shirts were threaded with silver, misaligned rows tracked up their chests. The man repeatedly pushed greasy, overgrown hair out of his eyes.

"How do you know her?"

The woman's gaze flicked to Megan with the briefest softening of hostility.

"What's wrong with her?"

Their clothes were dirty, of people living rough, their paleness at one with the ghostly forest. They carried nothing with them.

"We've been up all night—"

"In the tunnels."

The man finished for her. Storm pressed her lips tighter.

"Can you get her back to her mom?"

The woman pondered Megan's sleeping form. They obviously cared for Megan, though that welcome definitely didn't extend to her.

"Yeah."

It was the man who answered, his loathing less complete than hers.

"The kids will be happy to see her."

He could have been speaking about his own or the ones in the dark area.

Storm lowered Megan to the ground at the base of a tree. Her eyelids fluttered in the new position and Storm briefly smoothed the curls across her forehead.

The woman snickered.

Storm stood slowly, experiencing a sudden clarity inside her.

The woman's mouth was closed tight, and Storm could see the muscles in her jaw flexing. If hatred were visible it would have been seeping out of her eyes and nose like blood. Storm was almost relieved, finally receiving the recriminations she had believed were her due.

"Is there someone called Daniel in your community?"

"You expect us to help you?"

The woods were quiet, as if they had been plucked out of the city. It was likely why they had ended up in this place, with its illusion of distance.

"We know who he is."

"You've seen him?"

She felt hope, relief, the smallest flash of blue sky.

"Photos online. From the beginning."

Old news. Nothing that would help her now. The two of them had probably been smiling, maybe even holding hands raised between them. There had been a photo like that, jubilant, very popular for a while.

"If you can tell me anything about where he might be…"

"Get out of here!"

The woman's eyes were bloodshot and tiny red dots covered her skin.

Storm felt surprisingly calm, as if fate had finally settled on her and this was something she deserved.

"Can you carry her?"

She stayed close to Megan and focused on the man.

He nodded, though he refused to meet her gaze.

Turning away from the woman, Storm slid the powered-down cell phone from her pack and slipped it into Megan's hand. She hated to give it to her, but that, if nothing else, would get her back to her mother. She filled her lungs and stood, letting the soothing calm of inevitability flow through her. It felt so good not to be struggling against it anymore. Someone had finally accused her. She half-smiled as she faced the woman.

"You think this is funny?"

Seething rage coursed through the woman, her body shaking with it.

"No."

The closeness of the forest suffocated her and she had the welcome desire to move forward. This was a place to hide, not to find solutions. Or Daniel.

The straps of her pack were damp with sweat as she picked it up. It felt lighter, empty of so many things she had started out with. She threaded her arms into the straps under the scrutiny of the man and woman, her every move proving her guilt.

"What about the boy?"

The man had already bent to pick up Megan and held her close in his arms. She was so small and thin, it seemed impossible she had withstood the force of the seizure.

"Someone will come for him."

It was a body alone in the woods, though it was unlikely any animals existed here to scavenge it. The open area was close to the edge of the woods, located so people could come retrieve the body without having to get too close.

They watched her leave, as if after that reception she would try to sneak back in. The path dipped before sloping back to the park and her legs burned as she began to climb. She hoped Megan would forgive her for leaving. She allowed herself that hope, a small blip in the vast pool of blame she was sinking in.

The tops of the apartment buildings appeared above her and fear gathered in her chest, its low familiar hum preferable to the anger boring into her back. She let the fear settle, ready to use its stability and consistency as her guide.

TWENTY-SEVEN

Maria tried to lift her hand to see where the IV hanging from the post attached to it, but she couldn't move against the pressure of restraints on her upper arm and wrist. She moved her good leg, more hesitant with the injured one, feeling the same pressure on her thigh and shin. Strapped down like the soldier that had been evacuated, his hold on reality snapped by whatever he had seen. She wasn't crazy though. The muddle of the fever was gone, her mind clear, her body returned to its normal size without the bloated inflammation of infection and pain.

She saw a white stucco ceiling, framed photos on white walls, a lamp with a decorative shade. It was all encased in a muffled quiet, as if she were sealed in a cocoon with the stench of her own body overlain by the smell of coffee brewing. Her stomach dipped with a craving for the bitter liquid, her mouth so dry her throat caught when she swallowed.

The sound of voices came from the direction of the coffee, one angry, the other calmer, appeasing.

"She's awake."

She startled at the woman's voice close behind her head, older, without a trace of warmth. She craned her neck to see who it was, but the woman was beyond her view.

There came a scraping of chairs and footsteps on tiles, then muted on carpet. A man loomed above her, sporting slicked back black hair, a bushy beard, and a tired determination. She would have moved back if she weren't strapped down. It was the farmer from the railroad tracks, facing down a train with a hunting rifle the last time she had seen him.

"We meet again."

He sat next to her cot. The second man was younger, with rosy cheeks and a long mane of tangled blonde hair held back by a pair of glasses perched on top of his head. He held a tablet in his hand.

"Sorry to snatch you like that, but we had no other choice."

A kidnapper that started with an apology. How quaint.

The woman came into view behind the farmer, and any quaintness vanished. It was the woman who had carried the torch outside the train, her robot-like blankness setting Maria on edge. She had seen it in soldiers on patrol, too broken to engage with the world, and dangerous in their willingness to carry out any order regardless of consequences.

"Your fever's broken and the swelling in your leg has gone down. Dorian looked after it."

Maria recoiled from the thought of the woman messing with her leg while she'd been unconscious.

"We should have you up and walking by tomorrow."

"Might be difficult strapped to a stretcher."

The bearded man started to undo a buckle at her side and the pressure on her thigh loosened.

"Don't."

Dorian moved to stop him. He pushed her hands away. There was an intimacy there, not of lovers, or husband and wife, but something shared.

"She isn't going anywhere."

Maria flexed her toes, feeling the tight skin around the wound. Could she run if she had to?

The straps loosened one by one before he lifted them from her body. Neither the boy nor Dorian offered to help, wary to come close as if she were a rabid tiger about to be unleashed.

When the final strap fell away, she struggled to sit up. She wasn't as strong as she had hoped. The bearded man supported her back through a wave of dizziness.

"Can I get some water?"

Slowly, to let everyone know she wasn't anyone's servant, Dorian moved towards the source of the coffee. There was the easy, tantalizing sound of water rushing into a sink. The man turned his head to the boy.

"Let them know she is awake."

The boy tapped rapidly into the tablet.

Her cell was someone's living room, a plump white sofa and chairs filling the space, and sheer gauzy curtains obscuring a bay window. Her stretcher had been laid across a coffee table and the house was too warm.

She drank deeply when Dorian returned, the taste of chlorine sharper than the clear earthiness of the water she and Storm had drank.

A big screen covered one wall, the control panel for the house's monitoring system glowed in the hall, and somewhere upstairs an electric motor whirred. Anxiety gathered until she reminded herself that Storm wasn't there and had most likely left the city. She couldn't blame her, now that she had seen Storm's suffering up close.

The man took the glass and rested it on an end table. If this was someone's living room it wasn't Dorian's, the white sterility not matching the woman's stony broodiness.

"Can I go now?"

The man extended his hand towards the foyer and the exit. Like pulling a band aid off, she swung both legs over the side. Her bare feet touched soft carpet as spikes of pain burst from her calf and an icy chill spread like cold rain down her back. Black spots swam before her. With both hands she lifted her injured leg back onto the stretcher. She closed her eyes against the pain and to block out Dorian's spiteful smile.

"How did you do it?"

Maria opened her eyes.

She and Storm had been linked inextricably to the Three Rock's Gatherer's destruction like some kind of miracle avengers. She could have laughed that anyone thought she had the brains to manage it.

"You got the wrong person."

"Yes, we understand that."

Maria's pride rankled.

"But we thought it best to take both of you."

Maria levered up onto her elbows.

"Is she here?"

The bearded man watched her coolly, more calculatingly that she had given him credit for.

"She will be soon."

Maria tried to imagine how long Storm would last in the overlapping fields. There wouldn't be a safe place for her.

"You can't bring her here."

Something in the way the boy turned away and a darkening of Dorian's blank face told Maria that in some way Storm's arrival was controversial. Perhaps they hadn't all thought it was a good idea. The boy showed Dorian something on his screen. A Bluetooth device bulged from inside his ear.

"That isn't your decision."

The feeling of it was so familiar, of decisions being out of her hands. She'd once had such faith in that process and the comfort that as long as you obeyed the orders it would all work out. She had obeyed every single one until they had stopped her and Havernal from investigating the evidence around the Gatherer's health effects. A directive that had come from higher up, as though they were completely uninterested in what they had found.

"Killing her isn't going to help you."

The man remained still, his gaze lowered as if caught by a powerful memory. White lines from many hours in the sun spread out from the corners of his eyes. The frayed edge of his collar rested against skin that had spent its life outdoors.

"We aren't in the business of killing people."

From the way he said it she understood that there had been killing at some point and he did not rest easy with it.

"Is it true?"

Dorian's expression had barely changed but for a slight opening of her mouth.

"That she's dying."

Maria paused, starting to speak the denial that lurched from her chest, yet didn't. For what else had she been witnessing on their journey but the slow draining of Storm's energy, the depletion of whatever force kept her going?

"No."

They waited as she struggled to sit.

"It's just the fields."

She tried to put her feet to the floor again but the man stopped her with a hand on her leg. The pressure was calm, steady with a gentle firmness as he guided her leg back straight. She kept her good foot on the floor.

"You have to get her out of the city."

The man exchanged a glance with Dorian and she nodded. The boy's thumbs clicked on his tablet as the woman slipped out of the room. There was the suck of a door opening and silence when it shut again. The boy lowered his glasses, which were more of a visor, clicked something on, and left into the kitchen.

The man offered her the remains of her water. She drank, urging her body to take what it needed so it would heal faster.

"How sick is she?"

She hadn't thought of Storm as sick, only exposed to the wrong environment. Keep her from the environment and she would be safe, except Storm had willingly immersed herself deeper in this world. Maria cursed her injury, her weakness for not being able to overcome it, and her stupidity at being caught in the cellar in the first place.

"When I last saw her we hadn't reached the city yet."

He pushed himself to standing and turned towards the kitchen. His head almost touched the top of the door frame.

She considered the option of dragging herself across the carpet, somehow making it onto the front lawn.

"Who are you?"

He returned to the doorway, his thick broad shoulders and strength at odds with the white carpets and the soft pastels of the house.

"You can call me John."

"Is that your name?"

He smiled and turned away to the sounds of drawers opening, cutlery clanging.

She considered the exit again, the two steps down to the foyer. She put weight onto her good leg, testing whether she had the strength to carry herself. Even if she could, she would be like a cobbled horse, easy pickings for anyone who wanted to catch her.

A few old decorating magazines lay on the table beside the couch, a remote for the screen next to them, china knick knacks populating a glass case. It was a standard suburban home with no signs of military intelligence or organization. Except for the absence of the owner, they might have been stopping by for tea.

The man returned carrying a plate of food and her hunger took over. It was a cold mixture of canned pasta and beans, and as good as anything she had tasted.

"You won't get any money for her."

He resumed his spot next to her, watching her eat.

"It would be easier if this was only about money."

She jabbed at an escaped bean at the side of her plate.

"So what is it about?"

"More?"

He took her empty plate.

She nodded, surprised to be taken care of but willing to take what was offered. The slow tide of fatigue gathered around her as she waited for him to return. He brought her another plate of cold food that she ate more slowly.

"So how did you do it?"

She shoved another spoonful into her mouth, worried he would take it away if she refused to answer.

"You were there when she took out the Gatherer."

He was leaning forward, a newer, more demanding note to his voice.

"It was a homemade bomb. Nothing special."

He pulled himself closer. His face over her plate.

"The outer shell was intact. Only the internal workings were compromised."

She heard the continued whirring from above.

"I wasn't with her then."

"You were on the video."

Maria balanced the empty plate on her good leg. The room was brightening, its growing white shine in contrast to her grimy clothes and beleaguered state. John didn't fit much better in his worn, faded work clothes. They were like a poorly altered image where the people don't fit with their surroundings.

"When did you give up stopping trains?"

The curtains blocked any view of the outside and she felt again the tightness of a cocoon. She hoped at some point to metamorphose and be allowed to emerge. Her leg throbbed dully, whatever they had given her starting to wear off.

"It wasn't making a difference."

"And this is?"

He regarded her calmly, a slow methodical examination as if time was all he needed to know her secrets. His patience disarmed her. No wonder people had followed him. He gave off a reassuring stability that even made her feel calmer, with an underlying strength that could be called upon when needed.

"What was it you and Ms. Freeman were planning on doing? If she is as sick as you say she shouldn't be anywhere near the city."

How had they thought that Storm would survive the city? She could be incapacitated somewhere, what was left of her health draining away. Yet there had been no other choice. It was through the Corporation that the Gatherer had to stop. With Storm the one who would have the ultimate control.

"Is she safe?"

He lifted the plate, holding the fork with his thumb. In the kitchen he spoke again with the boy. The talking stopped for several minutes before he returned, and when he sat, more time passed before he spoke.

"We don't have her."

A surge of pain in her leg accompanied her panic.

"Who does?"

If the Corporation had found her, they could already be dictating what she could and couldn't do.

"We were going to intercept her but she never showed up."

Maria again tried to lift herself, cursing her leg; she would have cut it off if it meant she would be mobile. There were too many scenarios of what could have happened. In most, Storm didn't come out alive.

Maria gripped the sides of the cot. It took her a few moments until she was able to relax her grip. She had to believe Storm was still free.

"What do you even want? You can't catch a sick woman, but you've got some conspiracy to profit from the situation? Is that what this is?"

Anger flared now, so fast it couldn't have been far below the surface.

"At least we're doing something."

The boy appeared behind the man, tapping him on the shoulder. There was more discussion out in the kitchen out of ear shot as Maria reviewed her hopeless escape options.

The boy didn't have his tablet when they returned and stood far back, one hand behind his back. John walked slowly, not looking at her, his thoughts far away.

He had her pinned onto the stretcher and his knee pressed into her good thigh before she could react. She struggled, screaming at him to let her go, but his grip didn't ease, his soothing voice telling her to 'take it easy' as if she were a spooked horse. The boy jabbed a needle into her thigh, his hold on her leg as strong as the farmer's.

She gasped at the cold rush of the drug. John released her, and though she tried to sit, she couldn't gather her muscles into a coherent effort. The last thought she had was how brutally she was failing at what she had set out to do.

TWENTY-EIGHT

Rain soaked Storm's shoulders and ran from the cuffs of her shirt. The path felt wide and empty without Megan beside her. She should have taken her back to her mother and made sure she was safe. Yet going backwards on this route wasn't an option, all her energy needed for moving forward.

She was relieved to reach the edge of the damp, pale forest, disoriented by its whiteness. At the path's junction she stopped. To the right lay the willow tree and the dangers of the road, to the left more park and eventually the downtown. And not a single red chevron to guide the way.

She chose the unknown path and climbed a long slope of soaked grass. The tops of apartment buildings peaked above a grove of bleached trees, a few lights glowing on the upper floors. She walked away from the buildings, their very existence a barrier, yet she couldn't circle forever.

The rain had eased to a light drizzle when she arrived at the crest, an extended flat area open below her with the movement of a single figure at its centre. She retreated down the path out of view until she could just see the figure circling, a pinpoint of flowing motion in the lifeless scene of white.

He glided and jumped, skating on the ground where she had once watched the concert with Daniel. He lacked the abandon of a young skater, yet he made up for it with skill and grace. The slice of his blade into the ice and the scrape of his pick when he jumped floated in the still, misty air. It was a decadence she hadn't foreseen, having an ice pad available all year round.

She searched for what she knew must be there, and found it behind a stand of bare birches, like looking through ghosts. A Gatherer, smaller than the one in Three Rocks, but large enough to power the refrigeration system that would maintain the ice all year long.

She felt a flash of pride at how sleek and clean it looked, immediately snatched away by its dirtiness and legacy of sickness. A white swan tarnished by tar, the blackness never coming clean. She gave the skater and the Gatherer a wide berth as she moved south.

The morning haze blurred the edges of the rooftops and the grid of streets that led to the cluster of office towers in the downtown. Daniel might have been out there, or he might have died like the rest of the team. It was a relief to move towards the towers, even if it meant she would die the way they had. At least it wouldn't be alone in the Yukon, hiding from what she had done.

The open hands of the Gatherer emerged above the haze, the logo's clear elegant lines gracing the tallest tower. They had been dubbed Wings of the Angels by the media, but to her they were nothing more than hands grasping for whatever they could.

Her mother would be up there somewhere, looking down from her high tower. Could she sense that Storm was close? Or was she too consumed with running the Corporation to care, Storm no longer shiny enough to hold her attention?

Storm could remember the first time her mother's attention had fully turned on her, beyond the distracted ministrations of a busy parent. It had been at a school science fair, her mother arriving too late to see the displays but sneaking in during the last half of the awards. No one had been more surprised than her mother when they'd called Storm's name for first place for a tiny microgrid of solar energy and windmills. Even then it had always been energy. There had been graphs, charts, and balancing calculations, and her mother standing proudly beside her in the official photo. Storm remembered her mother's arm clasped tightly around her shoulder.

After less than a half kilometre, two perpendicular streets marked the boundary where the park ended and the houses began. Big, elaborate houses fit for the prestige of fronting onto the park, though that prestige would have faded with the fading green.

She brushed water off a wooden bench, the rain having stopped, and sat facing the houses. The heavy clouds had trapped the morning in dusk, and more than a dozen houses had their lights on. Streetlights shone. The city was dense here, every path as hazardous as the next. It would be as good a place as any to go in. She flexed her fingers against the ache in her hands, already picking up the overlapping fields of the houses.

A woman emerged from the house at the corner of the two roads with a small poodle on a leash, her head bent to a cell phone. She was around the same age as Storm, maybe a bit older, and Storm envied her energetic stride and the swing of her ponytail with each step. The dog sniffed lawns and cable boxes, pulled away by the woman's quick pace. She longed to lay her hand on Blue's solid back. The woman turned at the first side street, away from the park.

If she had asked for help would the woman have given it? She might have recoiled at her obvious status as one of the afflicted, or would she have recognized her, her notoriety hanging around her like a shining cape so that people no longer saw who she was—only the brilliance of the Gatherer, or the shame of its creation.

Daniel had hated the fame and the people who had wanted to know him when they had passed over him before. Professors who suddenly had projects they wanted to collaborate on, posting photos of them together on social media. He had withdrawn into his brand-new lab where he ran test after test, failing to see that their work was done.

"Why don't we go for a walk?"

He'd had the greasy, gaunt look he got when he had been in the lab too long, and Storm had hoped a walk would help with her fatigue that no amount of sleep seemed to touch.

"So we can see some of your adoring fans?"

"They're your fans too."

Daniel had carried a rabbit in a cage into the test area. Soft white fur, a fluffy ball for a tail, and fierce black eyes.

"What are you doing?"

"Running a test."

His cheekbones, once the base structure of a beautifully sculpted face, had looked too large and his natural restlessness had ballooned into an agitation so that he'd stood to start the test on his computer, paced while it ran.

She'd moved closer to where she could see the rabbit through the glass window of the test area. It had sat in the same spot in its cage, twitched its ears, and looked no different than it had when it sat on Daniel's bench.

"What are you looking for?"

She'd known it wasn't impossible that the Gatherer's process would cause minute changes in cell function, but figured they would adapt. It was like taking a drop of water off the top of a bucket. Daniel had stood beside her.

"Changes. Decreased function. Anything that would indicate damage."

He was taller than her, all angles and hard edges and she'd missed that intensity, the joy at seeing it soften.

"You'll have to cut it open to know for sure."

The rabbit hopped twice, revealing a gray patch of fur on its opposite side.

"I have a control rabbit but I want to check over an extended period of time."

"How long?"

"Months. A year maybe."

A new wave of fatigue had rolled through her. She'd pulled a stool from beneath the bench and sat down, the desire to sleep overwhelming.

"You okay?"

She'd closed her eyes, the burn easing.

"It's been busy."

She'd considered moving to the couch but it would have taken too much energy to get there.

"Still want to do that walk?"

Daniel had laid his hands on her shoulders, and her need for him had rushed through her so intensely she felt dizzy, off balance. She'd leaned back into the hardness of his chest, absorbing the heat from him.

"Is anyone here?"

His answer had been to run his hand up the back of her neck, pulling gently on the roots of her hair. His lips had touched the base of her neck as every cell turned on, the energy from that simple touch flowing through her. If only she could have created a Gatherer to gather that kind of energy. She'd spun her chair to face him and ran her hands up the taut muscles on the sides of his spine. She had thought briefly that he was thinner but as his mouth had found hers the thought was pulled away.

It had been like it was in the beginning, the rest of the world busy beyond the walls. A space only for the two of them.

She'd kept her mouth on his, held him close longer than she normally would, the need for him beyond anything the fans could offer. When he'd come up for air his hair had fallen over his eyes, and she'd felt again the thrill of being at the centre of that intense focus, as if he meant to consume her.

He'd rolled the stool towards the couch, his hands tucked beneath her hips. She'd touched her lips to the salty skin of his neck. It had surprised her when he'd lifted her to the couch, the weight of him on top of her exquisite, holding her firm to the ground. She'd lifted her hips to his.

"What about the rabbit?"

"The rabbit is fine."

A breeze blew dead white leaves around her feet and Storm stood, the back of her legs damp from the bench. She walked several steps down the slope to gain distance from the memory, those moments only reminding her of everything she had lost.

Wires hung on the hydro poles that ran the length of the street the woman had taken. She would only know if they were live once she got close.

She felt the final memory of Daniel's touch as a signal crossed her cheek. A man came out of a house further down from where the woman had turned. He tossed his bag into a bright green car and got in without looking up. Storm could have brought a whole army and no one would have noticed.

What sounded like a footstep echoed behind her and she looked up the hill. It was only the rustle of the trees, whispering for her to turn back, that no good would come from this.

In the end she simply started walking, her steps leading her downhill. The depleted grass gave way beneath each step. She thought she was resigned to this, but as she drew closer to the sidewalk her chest shook with the crash of her heartbeat, her breath shallow and fast. Would it be the passing of a car that would get her? Or a Gatherer she didn't see? She might not get more than a hundred metres.

She followed the same route as the woman, for no other reason than the possibility that the dog would choose to stay clear of any particularly lethal areas. She could hear Daniel's derision in her head.

"You're reaching if you think the dog has the answer."

"Too bad."

She spoke out loud, anything to release the fear that built with every step.

She walked on the opposite side from the wires, grateful for the inertness of the concrete beneath her feet. There was the sudden whir of a garage door rising and she hurried in the opposite direction, her footsteps echoing in the still morning. The hum of a car came behind her and she veered off the road, coming within steps of a house by the time she had fled far enough away.

She cut back to the sidewalk, walking faster. It was fourteen blocks to the Gatherer's office and she had covered half of one.

Storm adjusted her pack and rubbed her hand clockwise over her solar plexus as if that small gesture would protect her against what waited for her—her own version of making the sign of the cross in the hope that God would help her get through whatever she had taken on. Yet it wasn't God she was asking for help. It was her tired body, asking it to fortify itself for the suffering to come.

She checked the top poles for cell phone transmitters, their pulsing signal more a potential threat than the isolated bullets of the cars. Her skin tingled, tuned for the first burn from the rake of cell phone data over its surface, like trying to navigate blind through an ocean of stinging jellyfish.

She crossed the road to avoid a square green transformer case on the front of a lawn. Many communities had used the Gatherers to form small microgrids, the transformer boxes no longer necessary, but she wasn't going to take the chance. She crossed back at the next set of lights, walking mostly on lawns, a balancing act between the passing vehicles and the WiFi networks that reached out from the houses.

The houses were closer to the street in the next block, the easement narrower so that she had to constantly jump away from the road when a car passed. Twice the tingle of a WiFi network warmed her shoulder and arm. Her path was getting narrower. A map wouldn't have done any good. It might have a grid of carefully named streets, a few cultural landmarks, but nothing that would indicate that here she would have a seizure, or only a jitteriness in her nerves if she went here. It was something she would have liked to do before this started—map out the electromagnetic fields of the city. At the time it would have been to show people the wonder of electricity. Now it would be to show them the city where they really lived.

She felt the transmitter before she saw it. It came as sudden bursts of pain on her skull, a few pain-free moments before the next burst. She walked back the way she had come, turning onto an alley behind houses where she could see across well-tended back yards, through to people sitting at breakfast tables and standing at kitchen counters. A movement caught her eye at the end of the lane, whatever it was gone by the time she turned her head.

She moved past scraps of garbage and rusted non-electric cars. Wires mounted on a pole at the end of the lane seared her left shoulders before she hurried past, nearly stumbling in front of a car in her haste to get away. The car honked and she straightened, turning her back so that the flowing flux from the car tore across her back and legs, like being whipped with a thousand tiny lashes. There was a stop light up ahead with a line of cars waiting for it to change. The painful pulse of a cell transmitter broadcasted from the corner of an apartment building. She dashed across the street into the next alley, only to be forced out by a car coasting towards her. Back on the sidewalk she made for the stop light, pressed to the front of the not yet open shops, an illuminated sign prickling her scalp. The line of traffic started towards her. She sprinted past a butcher shop, carcasses hanging in a refrigerated display, the spasm in her chest so strong she thought her heart would stop. The cars passed before she reached the corner, each vehicle like a physical blow, leaving her reeling. Around the corner, she faced more stores and larger, bigger buildings with frenetic screens flashing in the emerging morning light. She looked for a sewer grate, anywhere she could crawl into. A service cover sat in the middle of the road, under the tracks of endless cars. A man passed her, ear buds in, stepping around her like she was a piece of trash. In the middle of the block was a small gate with green foliage. She stumbled towards it and unlatched the gate, feeling the earthy smell of grass, a sudden moisture to the air. She staggered up a set of stone steps, pushing through the heavy wooden door, taking in the cold stale smell of stone, the mustiness of age. Pale light shone through stained glass windows, illuminating the close nurturing of the stone walls. She moved further in, past the wooden pews to the centre of the church.

She collapsed onto a pew, her body feeling scraped and bruised, swallowing to keep from vomiting. It felt like the edges of her body were disintegrating, the vein walls starting to fragment as bits of her muscles tore free, no longer able to withstand the onslaught of the fields. She had the thought that this misjudged route could be her final failure, like an aged electricity network where a fallen tree branch causes a cascading collapse of the entire system.

TWENTY-NINE

The door opened and thudded shut. Storm was on her feet, scrambling along the pews, the walls of the vestibule blocking her view. She pushed through the only door available to find a small office, empty, a window above her head.

Unhurried footsteps echoed on the stones and stepped behind the door. The steps drew closer, no effort made to quiet them. The door opened towards her, pushed close to her nose.

"Storm?"

There was the same lilt in his voice as when he used to return to the apartment and check if she were home. Daniel stepped around the door and closed it behind him. His wide brown eyes were sunk in dark shadows, his white face floating above the black rubber suit that encased his body like a scuba diver's. He was beyond thin, his limbs like sticks.

The joy of seeing him overwhelmed her. She had imagined this so many times that this could have been another dream. She wanted to touch him, hug him, feel that he was alive, yet she barely had the strength to stand. The wall held her up as much as her legs.

"You're alive."

It was like a sigh, the dread she'd had of finding him dead streaming out of her.

He ducked his head in acknowledgement, the light from the single window shining behind him.

"So are you."

The relief at hearing his voice was unwarranted. Nothing in this situation justified her sudden sense that everything would be okay. Sweat gleamed on his forehead and he stooped at the shoulders as if he didn't have the strength to stand straight. A hood of rubber covered his head beneath a ball cap, the sleeves of the wetsuit poking out beneath a worn leather jacket.

He scanned her arms and legs, examining the suit, frowning as he reached out to rub the material between his fingers.

"I tried silver—"

His voice trailed off as his hand dropped.

"I didn't think rubber would work."

He shrugged, turned away, and leaned against the desk. His hand gripped the edge.

"Are you alright?"

He blinked slowly, half smiling.

"Are you?"

They couldn't ignore the depletion between them, their physical limitations tampering their emotional reactions. She had imagined anger, tenderness, even refusal, but not this struggle to function.

"Is everyone dead?"

He pressed his lips together as he dug in the fanny pack he wore around his waist. He drew out an electromagnetic field meter, watching the screen intently as it powered on. The sides of it had been encased in metal, the meter suspended inside it. He wore his emotions front and centre, and he had used his long hair and bangs to hide behind. Without them, he had left himself exposed, for all the world to see his shame. She wondered if he had done it on purpose. A penance for what he would have seen as his sins.

He wiped at the screen and adjusted a dial on its side. When he seemed satisfied he clicked it off and returned it to his pack. He handled it like an inert piece of wood.

He pulled off the hood of his suit. His head was shaved, the absence of hair making him gaunter, with harder edges. Her own body was equally tired, the fibres in her legs not coordinated enough to support her weight.

The walls of the office were of faded plaster, the surface rough, its imperfect ridges exposed in the angled light from the window. She passed close beside him as she moved out from behind the door, her undercoat of silver brilliant in comparison to his matted black. The aged chair squeaked as she lowered herself into it and the ache in her legs eased. It would only be a matter of time before the structure failed.

"How did you find me?"

He laid his palm flat against the desk, the wide, broad bones devoid of flesh.

"News spread fast that you had been seen."

A pause as he breathed.

"I didn't believe it at first."

Fatigue was spreading out from her chest, dropping her shoulders, collapsing her spine. She hated its persistent presence, an anchor lodged in the depths of the ocean floor that never let go.

"I didn't have a choice."

"Is anyone following you?"

There had been the presence in the park, and whoever Romero had sent likely hadn't given up. Plus the Corporation and the guy with the gun.

"You could say that."

She laid her head on the desk to rest for a moment. She imagined she could see through the wood, down through the stone floor to the dark pit that drew her downward.

"Come on."

Daniel's hand was under her arm, lifting her, but he didn't have the strength and it resulted in only half lifting her shoulders. She sat up, trying to shake off the fatigue.

"I'm fine. I just needed a moment."

"Stand up."

Her nerves were deadened, unable to sustain another attack. The effort to stand was unachievable.

"Come on Storm! Stand up."

His frustration pushed past her deadened nerves, sending a strike of pain into her heart. It was a voice from a different time, when his only impatience was at her not arriving fast enough when he wanted to show her what he had found.

Using the desk for support, she let him guide her away from it. She was as stooped as he was, the two of them like an old couple hunched with age.

"You need to lie down."

The floor was stone, cold, and the effort to lower herself down to it seemed hardly worth it.

"I thought—"

"You won't get there in this state. I can help you feel better."

He was digging in his pack, the idea that she might say no not occurring to him.

"Why should I trust you?"

He stopped. A tired lift of his head.

"Because I wouldn't hurt you."

His certainty almost made her laugh. It was so Daniel. He saw black and white while she saw gray.

"You need to lie down."

Across from the desk, Jesus hung on a cross. The only adornment on the empty wall, whoever owned this place preferring the world stripped bare.

Daniel struggled to remove his jacket and was breathing hard as he laid it on the floor. He kneeled beside it. He had always been the boy scout of the group, prepared for anything. That preparedness had been what had saved the prototype from the fire, Daniel having taken it home in the metal lunch box he carried with him.

"The lab isn't secure."

It was how he had explained why he had taken it on the night the fire had come, claiming he had gone home because he needed the rest. Of course he hadn't started the fire. He would never have done anything to hurt her or the Gatherer. How could she even ask that?

Every small imperfection of his skull showed through his shaved hair. In his hand, he held a bag of the tiniest screwdrivers.

"What are those?"

He looked down, surprised she didn't know what they were.

"Needles. For acupuncture."

She retreated towards the chair.

"And you want to put those in me."

He stopped her with a hand on her wrist.

"It will help you feel better."

Sweat formed in the deep lines of his forehead, his desperate brown eyes shining from a skull that was not far from a skeleton.

"I promise."

She sensed the reassurance of his grip on her arm, the voice that he had only ever used for her, and the fatigue so insistent it battered against her like the wind. She didn't have the energy to fight him, to tell him that it would be another false trail and this was a damage she would never be rid of.

She knelt and eased down onto her hip.

"Take off your boots."

"Daniel—"

She recognized her stern tone, their familiarity returning fast and easy, like the day they had met, both wildly excited to finally be at university, the connection as if they had already known each other.

"Trust me."

After a moment where she looked up at him, his brown eyes the only part that resembled the Daniel from before, she untied her boots, loosening the crossed laces so she wouldn't have to struggle to pull them off. The air was cold on her toes, her skin wrinkled. She placed the boots neatly beside her. Daniel always did what he felt was right, and if today he wanted to help her, she would let him.

She lay back, welcoming the divine release of the stone's cold support. "Will they help?"

A tiny distracted nod as he pushed up her sleeve and inserted the first needle near her elbow. His hands were warm, almost hot, and she felt the smallest of pricks as the tip pierced her skin. It calmed her to have him touch her, shifting over her as he administered his cure.

He inserted needles in her hands, calves, and feet with the final one delicately placed between her eyes. His face was close to her as he inserted it, hovering over her as he had so many times before. She would have liked to be in that other time, when their only concern had been to quench their need for each other. She wanted to touch his hand but her arms were leaden, the thought overtaken by her body's need to sleep. Rusted stained circles marred the plaster ceiling.

"How long will it take?"

She tried to sit at the sudden image of Romero barging into the small room, or one of the corporation's goons bearing down on her.

Daniel eased her back down, and checked that she hadn't dislodged the needles.

"I'll be here the whole time."

THIRTY

Storm's hands and feet were as cold as the stone beneath her back, yet she felt as if she was waking from a deep, complete sleep. She pointed her toes to warm them and flexed her hands.

"Hold on."

Daniel's voice was close beside her, and she remembered her flight, his gaunt face and the frightening power of her fatigue. Sunlight filled the ceiling as Daniel leaned over her, and she felt tiny points of awareness wherever he touched her. She lifted her head as he pulled the acupuncture needle from the web of her hand and felt a small prick of pain between her eyebrows. She reached for it but Daniel gently stopped her hand.

"Wait."

Carefully and methodically he drew out needles. As she waited, she realized she was impatient, eager to sit up with a freshness and energy she couldn't remember feeling, like a close friend she hadn't expected to see again.

"You know acupuncture?"

He drew the needle from between her eyes.

"I know a lot of things I didn't use to."

He offered his hand to help her sit, his skin deliciously warm. Her muscles were smooth, relaxed and each shade of the stone floor was finely etched.

"Does that even work?"

He sat back on his haunches, the shadow of a beard visible below sunken, exhausted eyes.

"You tell me."

She stood slowly and stretched her shoulders, feeling a small moment of vertigo that vanished.

"It's like I've been washed clean."

Lines appeared around his eyes as he smiled. He looked twenty years older than he should have.

"Can you do it to yourself?"

He was slow to nod, the way he often did when unsure of an answer.

"It's not as effective."

Storm reached her arms over her head, stretching from side to side. She was thinner, her muscles atrophied, but she felt as if her body were her own again. She grinned, starting to peel off the suit.

Daniel's mouth tightened. She stopped, one arm out of a sleeve.

"What is it?"

Her jubilation notched down.

"Once you're exposed to another field you'll be knocked out of balance again. Whatever the Gatherer does, it seems to permanently destabilize the body's electrical balance."

"But I feel amazing."

He pulled himself to standing, running a thin hand over his head as if his thick bangs still hung in his eyes.

"The needles rebalance it, but you're still susceptible to any other currents or fields. Once you're exposed, you'll slip out again."

She put her arm back in the sleeve, zipping up the front. She hated the feel of it, as if it carried the pain and sickness with it.

She lowered herself into the chair, fresh, yet now with the awareness of her new state's fragility and its need for protection.

The silence in the church was complete, only she and Daniel tucked inside its sanctuary. The loneliness of it was exquisite, a low keening that vibrated through the air and walls.

"What are you going to do?"

She frowned, confused and distracted.

"It's why you're here, isn't it? That's why you came back?"

His voice had only the slightest inflection, an attempt to keep it neutral.

"I couldn't have come earlier. I was too sick."

She wondered if that was true. In the last few months she had been focused on her experiments and an unrealistic goal of creating something so she could return without pain or suffering.

"You could have at least let me know where you were."

A thin crack of light outlined the door, an entrance to a different, brighter world.

"I didn't think you wanted to know."

There had been fights, screaming matches, Daniel accusing her of everything from betrayal, to using him, to her being an ego driven opportunist—some of it true, some of the wounds deep enough that they hadn't healed.

He stood and looked around the small room as if it might offer an alternate exit.

"It was hard on all of us. We were in way over our heads."

She remembered a specific morning when the lab had been filled with sunlight, each of them working at their stations, the combined energy of their brain power so strong she could have run her fingers through it. The energy had been so palpable she had believed they were being led by a higher power, their unique group brought together to make the world better.

It had been Maria who'd interrupted them that day with a sharp knock at the door. Even then she had been trying to protect her, as Storm thwarted her at every turn. Storm had released an unfinished version underneath the military's nose, thinking she was so clever when she had been naïve. Stupid. Vain. It still hurt to think of it. She turned her head in the direction of the door, wanting to be able to feel Maria's presence, know where to find her and thank her.

"Do you know how to stop it?"

The silence splintered, the room widened, the noises of the street suddenly there with them. Daniel stood below the window, looking up through it at the facing brick wall. From the angle of the sun it had to be past noon, its rays beginning to slant through the narrow gap between buildings.

"There are so many of them."

Storm felt the web of Gatherers that spread out from Rima, its birthplace, like a never-ending cascade, expanding its outer boundaries, intensifying at the centre. A slow, fatal consumption.

"Was it you who attacked the headquarters?"

He asked the question with his face still lifted, the cords on his throat exposed.

"No."

He was watching the brick wall, seeing something there beyond the mortar and stone.

"Do you remember the fire?"

The wall of smoke that had enveloped her, finding the stairs by feel, calling his name. Not knowing if he was caught with her in the fire or if he had set it. There had been burns on his hands, the smell of gasoline on his clothes. All of which he'd claimed to have gotten in the fire, and could easily have gotten from starting it.

"Every day."

"Water would have done as good a job. I don't think they really knew what they were doing. Water would have made more sense than fire. Disabled any Gatherers we had on site without the destruction or danger."

"They probably didn't understand how it worked."

He turned from the window, his face fresher, more alert.

"Or, it wasn't the Gatherer they were after."

He smiled a little, a hint of his old energy vibrating off of him.

"It could have been me or you. Or all of us. We knew that at the time."

It was one of the reasons she hadn't thought Daniel had done it. Destroying the Gatherer and its danger, yes, hurting anyone on the team, no.

"Once we lost the lab the Gatherer was too exposed. Ready for anyone to take it from us."

While she had been questioning whether they should have invented the Gatherer at all, he had been rehashing the events of what had happened, looking for a solution or forgiveness.

"We could have told people that everything was destroyed in the fire. Kept the prototype secret and worked on it ourselves. Released it the way we wanted to."

He could have been telling her what could have happened, or what he had planned. Either way, that wasn't how it had worked out.

"I'm more concerned with what happens now."

He stretched out his arms, trying to ease the tension of the suit.

"I know some people."

"What people?"

"That could help us."

The outer door thudded shut, followed by footsteps and hushed female voices.

Daniel pressed his eye to the crack in the door.

There was the creak of a pew and more shuffling on stone.

Daniel pulled back and put his hands together, nodding towards the nave to indicate the women were praying.

Storm had prayed often enough during experiments, when she had been caught in the fire, and when she'd thought the illness would kill her.

Daniel reclosed the door and sat carefully back in his chair. It was quiet for a long time and Storm wondered what they could possibly be praying about. Her pleas normally lasted little more than a few desperate seconds.

Daniel placed his hat on the desk between them, its white edge smudged with dirt.

She breathed carefully as she listened for sounds in the nave, and as the silence continued she checked in with the various parts of her body, carefully exultant when she discovered no pain or threat of spasms. As the time grew longer, her new well-being gathered into an impatience that she left untouched outside of herself, careful to protect her moment of strength.

When an eternity had passed, Daniel checked the door again, moving even slower. After confirming the women had not left, he removed his outer clothes, draping them over the back of the chair. A long string hung from the back zipper of the wetsuit and he unzipped it slowly, one tooth at a time, each tiny click as loud as the rap of knuckles on the door. There was the quiet sound of rubber stripping off flesh, and Daniel's ravaged emaciated body stood before her. His clavicles rose high out of boney shoulders, a spotty violent rash covering his right side. Boxer shorts hung on sharp hip bones, the hair on his legs dark threads on white flesh. She turned her gaze away, his deterioration so much worse than watching her own.

Unconcerned with her scrutiny, he laid the suit on the floor and slipped back into his outer clothes. Once dressed, he lay on the suit and drew a handful of tiny packets from his pouch. She watched in fascination as he gently inserted the needles into his feet and shins moving up to hands and arms. He had to pause on several of the needles when his hand shook.

He lay down and placed a final needle between his eyes. As it leaned towards his forehead, the women's voices started, louder than before. Storm moved to the door. The women were older, thick in shoulder and waist, their gray hair neatly coiffed tight against their skulls. As they made their way out of the church, they donned gloves, speaking with their heads together. The door thudded closed.

Daniel laid his hands lightly on his hips.

"Will you turn the needles for me?"

The request was strangely intimate, knowing as she did that there would be an exchange of energy between them, something baser and more absolute than sex or exchanging bodily fluids.

She knelt down beside his shoulder, the balls of her feet pushed tight to the wall.

"Just turn. Maybe five degrees. Back and forth."

Daniel closed his eyes and she could almost see the illness that spread through him. There was a heaviness to his shoulders, his feet splayed apart. His silver cross hung on a chain around his neck, a fixture since the day they'd met.

She started with his hand, turning so gently it barely felt like she had touched it at all. When he didn't respond, she moved to his elbow, making infinitesimal twists of the tiny needle. She didn't know if she had been expecting lightning bolts racing out of her fingers, but as she moved from needle to needle like a hummingbird hovering over him, she felt more calm than energized, with a complete, contented focus on each thin stick of metal.

When she had finished, Daniel was watching her.

"Thank you."

She nodded and sat back. His eyes closed.

He looked fragile on the bare stones in an office devoid of comfort, the stone and the metal legs of the desk speaking of hardness and impenetrable surfaces, like he had been banished from the softness of daily life.

"Don't leave."

The pull of something deep inside her resonated, of guilt, fear. She felt him slip away from her, dragged into whatever depth waited for him. Her legs were strong where she leaned against the wall, her body ready in a way she hadn't felt for months. And Daniel looked worse than her.

When his breathing deepened, she stood and, checking first that the church was empty, slipped into the nave. The air was colder, damper, the high ceilings and stone floor incapable of providing any warmth. The stone would stop any electric fields, but she was still tuned for the magnetic fields that could penetrate the thick walls and arrive from any direction or source.

She took in the dimness of the pews and the cross mounted high above it all. Red and blue light refracted through a stained-glass window to a single point of colour in the sanctuary. She ran her hand along the wood, recognizing the relaxed smoothness of her muscles at each step. It reminded her of standing in the middle of Romero's web, its energy holding her gently in its palm.

She craned her head to the high peaked roof, scanning for any kind of pattern in the pews. There was no web or grid, just the stone walls, wood pews, and the tiny flicker of two candles along the side.

She approached the shrine, drawn to the restless light, the drafts from the church buffering the small flames so they were never still. She lifted her palm to it, grateful for its small heat and the warm reflections on the stone. It reminded her of long nights in the cabin, the wood stove her small source of heat against a vast landscape, its light battling alongside her against the loneliness.

She stopped at the exit doors on her second lap. There was a whistle of air sucking beneath the door. It would be so easy to push open the heavy doors, take her momentary return to health and run with it. It made sense to keep moving, to make the most of this new energy while she had it.

She eased open the door, colder vibrant air rushing through the thin opening. The light was strong and clear, like looking onto a stage before a performance begins.

"Leaving again?"

She let go of the door. Daniel had dressed, his cap pulled low over eyes almost darker than they'd been before the needles.

"Will you come with me?"

* * * *

He took them down the alley beside the church into a narrower, tighter laneway that ran behind the businesses, the reek of old garbage and the skittle of an empty chip bag blown across broken pavement. They walked fast, their long strides easily matched, a fresh wind bringing the taste of salt.

Daniel held the meter in his hand, veering around fields that formed in their path. She tried to believe she would have brought hers if she hadn't left the cabin in such a hurry but she wasn't sure. Daniel had done a better job of looking after himself.

"Stay close."

They passed around the hulking hum of a refrigeration unit. When they approached power lines strung above the alley, Daniel took her hand and led her through as he watched his meter intently. He drew her under as if they were playing a game of double dutch. One quick hop and they were past, the field little more than a shadow over her skin.

They hung back from the end of the alley, beyond the direct sight of passersby. Daniel looked odd in his wetsuit, but it would be her silver suit that would be more identifiable. She moved several paces right, in the direction of the headquarters. The hand holding the device dropped to Daniel's side.

"You'll never get past security."

"I need to talk to my mother."

Daniel gave a sharp, dismissive shake of his head and shifted his feet, ready to move again. He had been against letting her mom get involved. Another instance where his vision had been clearer than hers.

"And you think showing up at headquarters will help that?"

Storm felt the sudden popping of a bubble she had been working so hard to keep inflated. She had always made excuses for her mom, the same way her dad had, yet her mother had known where she was. Even if she'd been busy, sending an email took almost no effort at all. She pushed her foot against the bottom of a faded plank fence. It gave beneath her force.

"Do you have a better idea?"

Two men passed on the sidewalk, wearing casual pants and light jackets. One glanced into the alley and Daniel stepped in front of her. They would look like two freaks to anyone walking by, anonymous unless the viewer knew what to look for. After the video, she was more exposed than she had been to the fields.

A car horn blared and she startled. An elderly man mid-block slipped a garbage bag into a can. She was a rat trapped in a maze, with some scientist or official just waiting for her to reach the cheese. She had to think. Not just follow the obvious path.

"We should go back underground."

For once it wasn't the fields she was escaping.

Daniel nodded, watching his screen.

"That's what I'm trying to do."

She matched his stride, faster this time, and she felt the energy from the needles softening, the depth of it not what she had hoped. It was hot inside the suit and she already needed water. Sweat rolled down Daniel's face, the neoprene suit worse.

They came out onto a street that fed into the busier area, a few businesses set up in what were once houses, a few broken sidewalk tiles and poorly tended planters giving an air of businesses that were surviving, if not thriving. She was grateful, as it meant less pedestrian traffic.

They crossed a large square, its concrete layout like the one she and Megan had traversed. She searched for red chevrons, scanning for the safe path. At the entrance Daniel held the door for her, his face an unhealthy red, the smell of sweat and rubber rising off him like steam.

They bypassed the elevator and followed the stairs down, traversing similar empty flights to those she and Megan had climbed. At the bottom of the first flight she paused and couldn't help but feel she was moving backwards. Another person entered the stairwell from above and Daniel waved her onwards, his hurried footsteps close behind her.

At the third flight, he stopped her with a hand on her shoulder, steering her into the parking garage. Her legs weakened at the rows upon rows of parked cars. He didn't stop, walking fearlessly between the gleaming red, blue, and greens of the cars. The place was lit up like the showroom of a car dealership. The cars looked to her like a battalion ready to deploy at any time. Lights reflected in expansive windshields, and an ominous bank of charging stations sat along the back wall.

She held her breath as she walked almost on top of Daniel, feeling as if he were placing down red chevrons with each step. She didn't speak, afraid the cars would hear her and suddenly come alive. They reached the end of the row and turned right, seeing more empty spaces now, some of the cars older electric models, their sheen not as bright.

"Through here."

They passed through another doorway and a smaller staircase going down, lit by dim emergency lights. There was dirt in the crevasses, a stale dark smell wafting up the stairs. She choked. The air tasted like they were descending into a sewer. They were already far deeper than the subway.

Daniel pulled back his hood, his scalp slick with sweat. Storm covered her nose. His eyes were haggard in a scorched face.

"It doesn't last long."

They were moving away from where they needed to be. They had once been inseparable, a formidable team, but now there was no way to know who side he was on. He could easily be aligned with the group Megan had saved her from.

"Wait."

She had her fingers over her nostrils yet she still smelled the stench.

"Where are we going?"

He leaned heavily on the rail.

"This is where I live."

For a moment she thought he meant the cold bare walled stairwell, yet he continued moving down, faster, letting gravity propel him. He reached the landing, turning down the next flight, but she hadn't moved. It felt wrong to be going underground, but she didn't know if it was the stench, the parking lot, or the feeling that she had gotten off track.

One flight down, Daniel stopped. She could hear him breathing.

"Storm?"

There it was again, as if he were calling her in an empty apartment.

"This feels like running away."

Dirt darkened the pockets in the concrete walls, a column of solid inertness rising above and below.

"The Yukon is running away. This is survival."

She pulled off her hood, the damp air cool. She listened, waiting, as if she would be able to sense whether this was a good place or bad the same way she could feel the fields.

His footsteps started moving, slow and tired.

She caught him easily, sweat dripping off his nose, his cheeks too red. She unzipped the back of his suit. The red welts had spread to the middle of his back, some of them oozing pus, all washed in sweat.

"We're almost there."

He was panting and his hand gripped tight on the rail. She slipped under his shoulder, his weight immediately falling on her.

"Tell me where."

They went down two more flights, most of his weight on her. The stench of sewage was thick and strangely warm. A key for a locked steel door was retrieved, and as the door clanged behind them the smell eased. Rows of vast blank gray cabinets rose to the ceiling. A cold wash of sweat trickled down her back. Daniel stumbled away.

Conduits fed out the top of the cabinets to run across the ceiling and vanish through holes in the walls. She didn't move, even as Daniel struggled out of his suit near a cot and makeshift kitchen. Hundreds, thousands of megawatts would have fed through this substation, the place alive with the hum from within each cabinet, the occasional click of a relay opening, the thin needles marking the power that surged through the wires before fanning out to the world above. It made her sick to think about what this room had once been, as if trace elements would lick out from behind the cabinet doors to tear a strip of flesh off her back.

Daniel grunted as he struggled to free himself from the wetsuit, too weak to pull his arms free from the sleeves, the top of the suit bunched at his waist. She moved to help, conscious of the looming gray faces of the switchgear as if they watched her, longing to be able to unleash their old power on her.

Daniel gave himself over to her as she pulled one hand, then the other from the tight sleeve, trying not to touch the red sores. He was shivering, cringing each time she brushed against them. He leaned on her again and she laid him onto a dishevelled cot so she could pull off the bottom. She worried that she would break him, his thigh's flesh hanging off bone, his feet white and boney like dead fish. She pulled a grimy blue sleeping bag up to his chin, his face so pale, lips tinged blue.

He lifted his hand briefly off the pillow, towards a second aisle between switchgear.

"Look on the bench."

He had set up a mini lab, with a bench and what looked like a test area. The whole area was lit with LED lights that had once been used for energy efficiency.

"I'm missing something."

He dropped his head and his face relaxed, the slightest bit of warmth against her cheek indicating he still breathed.

Her own heart raced as she turned and faced up against an unbeatable opponent. An accidental flip of a switch somewhere above and Daniel would have been snuffed out in a single, ultimate seizure.

She felt oddly embarrassed as she walked to the bench, trespassing into his private space. The lab was neatly organized, a contrast to the squalor of his cot and the makeshift kitchen.

She found notebooks labelled with letters and project codes she couldn't decipher. A well-stocked testing bench with tiny circuit boards and lattices of crystals stacked in cubby holes. A work station encased in a thick black box and a screen draped with copper mesh. And to her fascinated horror, a glass test area within which was the original version of the Gatherer.

THIRTY-ONE

It was amazingly crude in comparison to the sleek white Gatherer in Three Rocks. A shallow concave disc that housed the crystals, wires from the converter hanging out the bottom like the legs of a jellyfish. A fine mesh screen stretched across the opening of the dish, preventing debris from interfering with the crystal structure.

Daniel had added a frame of wooden blocks so that it looked like a bad version of the Olympic torch, or more realistically a neglected bird bath with burned out Christmas lights hanging out the bottom.

She circled, gently laying a finger on the rim of the dish, the stretched mesh delicate as a spider's web. It was an assortment of odd pieces that could have made something miraculous or nothing at all. She felt surprisingly protective of this early model, even knowing what would come after.

She traced the wires back to Daniel's work station, abandoning them when she saw the contraptions on his work bench. A row of three lattices, each the identical size of the one that formed the core of the original Gatherer. She couldn't see the imperfections in the lattice, but she knew they would be there.

Daniel had arrived at the lab shortly after the Gatherer had collected its first energy. He had paced between the screen showing a graph of the process and the inert Gatherer lying in its test bed.

"Show me again what you did."

She had checked the results again on the screen, not believing what she was seeing.

"I changed the lattice. Increased the frequency."

"How exactly?"

She didn't dare tell him that she had been distracted when she'd made the final adjustments, not expecting this test to be any different than the others.

"I'm not sure."

"You didn't record it?"

"I didn't expect it to work."

She lifted her hand to check another screen.

"Don't touch anything!"

"Relax. I'm not changing anything."

He came close, watching over her shoulder. The frustration and bickering of the previous weeks flowed through them, both of them gripped by the fear that they would lose this moment. She took a moment to breathe, focussing on the tiny blip on the screen that showed energy collected.

"It'll be alright. We can go back and recreate what I did."

It had taken hours to determine that the tiny imperfections she had accidentally created in the lattice were what had allowed the Gatherer to work. Only she and Daniel had been the ones to understand it. Had Maria known there was something she and Daniel had kept to themselves? Is that why she had sought her out?

Small wires ran from the three lattices on Daniel's makeshift workbench, the wires connected to a circuit board the size of her hand. An inspection showed the circuit was designed to deliver currents at different frequencies. He'd been testing different combinations of structure and frequency, looking for a safer configuration that would deliver the same energy without the consequences. Or was he simply looking for proof one way or the other of the Gatherer's culpability in the plague?

She lifted her hand from the bench and wiped it on her thighs. She had been trying to create a shield to protect herself and he had been trying to fix what they had done.

In the beginning of the darkness beyond the test area, in a continuation of the aisle between the switchgear, she found ruined carcasses of old Gatherers. The exploded crystals and burned out wires spoke to countless failed attempts. She could imagine Daniel toiling down here in his pool of light with no one to break the obsession and make him rest, the silent bulks of the switchgear the witnesses as one after the other of his experiments failed and the Gatherer slowly stripped away his health.

Those same witnesses recognized her inadequacy. For despite their flight to the headquarters and their determination that it was she who had to set this right, she still had no idea how to do that. The solution had not shown itself when they had trekked through endless marsh, remained elusive when they had wound upriver, and not once while she had slept, unconscious or otherwise, had it shown itself or provided even the faintest of way markers.

She turned from the ruined pieces, the lights feeling dimmer, and the darkness deeper. Daniel's cot made barely a dent in the expansive concrete floor, his kitchen a table with a camp stove and a few pots. It was heartbreaking that he tried to save himself from the discomfort of an electric hot plate in between running tests on the Gatherer.

Only the top of his head peeked above his sleeping bag, his body curled on its side, still in its utter exhaustion. Textbooks and manuals lay in toppled piles next to the bed, a notebook filled with scratched diagrams face up beside them. She didn't remember why it had seemed like a good idea to not take him with her.

He kept his food in a mostly empty Tupperware beneath the table. A bag of rice, several packs of ramen noodles, a single dusty can of tuna, and a stale end of bread. The stove hissed as she lit it with a pack of matches she found in the bin. A yellow, then blue flame flickered, a small stream of smoke curling into the empty ceiling.

She filled a small pot from a water jug in the corner, the hum of the gas increasing as she adjusted the flame beneath to a clear, deep blue.

While she waited for the water to boil, she lifted Daniel's notebook off the concrete. She sat on the only stool and flipped through the last pages. The entries were disjointed, some jotted notes, others larger exposition about connections and missing links. Despite the confusion, she found the progression of an idea. Diagrams of crystal structures, roughly drawn and scratched out. Calculations of micro-volts and current levels made for each adjustment. Graphs of harmonic signals and the resulting waveform when coupled with the output of the Gatherer.

He had been trying to force the Gatherer to operate within a certain threshold. One that would shut down the channel and render it useless.

She poured a cup of rice into the boiling water and turned the flames down to small blue buds.

Her mother had never given Daniel, or any of the team, their due, giving all the credit to her daughter. Storm had asked her to help the team, look after them, and Daniel lived like a rat in a sewer.

She flipped pages to the low hiss of the stove, following the progression of Daniel's experiments as he moved away from physically altering the crystal structure to short bits of computer code. He had never been a programmer and the code trailed off, stopping when it ran into the firewalls and layers of security that surrounded the Gatherer.

She turned off the flame, the room bigger in the quiet, and lifted the pot off the stove. Daniel's can opener was rusty and barely turned, but she managed to pry off the lid of the tuna and stir it into the rice. She spooned half into the only bowl and left the rest in the pot, keeping the lid on to keep it warm. With her food in front of her she opened the notebook at the first page.

She read slowly, stopping occasionally to remember the idiosyncrasies of Daniel's writing, and ate her first warm meal in days to the soft in and out of Daniel's breathing. She followed his train of thought, looking for the error, the smallest change in direction that could set them on their final path.

* * * *

Storm held the bowl out to Daniel.

"You need to eat."

He shook his head, eyes closed. He had slept for close to four hours and seemed incapable of lifting his head.

"Did you look at the crystals?"

She pulled the stool next to the cot and sat, the bowl of rice and tuna cold on her lap.

"I saw your notes."

His eyes opened, tight at the corners as he braced against some kind of pain.

"And?"

"Can I get you anything?"

He rose to his elbow, right hip twisted towards her. The silver cross hung at his clavicle, the neck that supported it so much thinner than before.

"What am I missing? Did you figure it out?"

She laid the bowl on the concrete, having a sudden image of rats coming out of the walls to fight over its contents.

"You were trying to shut down the channel. Using the imperfections."

His face reflected the gray of the cabinets, the stretched skin devoid of colour. His head dipped and he collapsed back onto the cot.

"I can't get it to close. Once it's open it won't revert."

"Should I get your needles?"

A slight movement that signalled no as his jaw hardened. His neck arched and the tendons rose out of his neck like the stressed guy-wires of a sailboat in a storm. She lifted the side of the blanket, releasing the smell of old sweat, and held onto his clenched fist. There was no trembling or shaking, his body as rigid and flat as the steel columns around them, his unseeing gaze locked on the web of conduits that snaked through the rafters.

She thought of the syringes left with Maria in the boat. They were probably at the bottom of the river by now, or shot into some undeserving kid's veins.

"Come on."

She whispered, a plea to whatever god could banish the demon running circles in his brain. There was a movement in his arm, like a spring popping and his hand rolled outwards, the tendons in his neck receding.

She adjusted the sleeping bag over him again and caught sight of the rash on his side, now migrated to his chest. She leaned in closer, trying to match it with the photos of rashes she had obsessed over when the spots had briefly appeared on her skin, disappearing after a few weeks in Three Rocks.

Daniel sighed in his sleep and she let the cover fall, mentally retracing the path she had taken to get here, knowing she would never be able to get him out.

She returned to the lab bench and picked up the crystal lattice lying in the cleared section in the middle. He had tried so many variations, each of them honing in on the specific frequencies and structure.

She waded into the wasteland of failed experiments, nudging charred structures with her toe, flipping mostly intact lattices out of their cases. She carried one back to the bench, but it was too small and she returned to the graveyard. His theory was good. She understood what he wanted to do, except closing the channel wouldn't be enough.

She returned to the stool and sat for a few moments. She was sticky and hot inside her suit and it chafed at her elbows. As she undid the zipper, she glanced at the gray sheer walls of the switchgear, trying to reconcile her instinctive fear with their blank, inert faces. She slipped the suit off her shoulders and felt the welcome release as it fell off her back, the cool air rushing into the damp creases of skin. The suit caught around her hips and she bent to tug it down, letting it fall to a crumpled pile around her feet. She dug beneath it to untie her laces, the thud of the boots landing echoing in the darkness. Goosebumps rose on her arms and back, yet she stood for a moment in her underwear, enjoying the touch of the air on her skin.

She ran her hands over thigh muscles she hadn't had in the Yukon and the ridge of abdominal definition close to the surface of her concave stomach. She would have looked as changed to Daniel as he did to her.

She moved around to the side of the cot closest to the wall. Daniel didn't stir. She lifted the bag and slipped into the pool of warmth, being careful not to touch the sores down his back.

Tucking the bag around her shoulder, she shifted closer, the same comforting smell of Daniel still there beneath the sickness. She rested her hand lightly on his hip, already feeling the warmth of their bodies combine.

THIRTY-TWO

Storm's voice echoed off the concrete walls, the dim dampness making her feel like she was at the bottom of a deep well. The chill air seeped under the edges of the sleeping bag, and she shifted closer into the pool of heat between her and Daniel's body.

"It needs to be in a firmware update or part of an upgrade."

Daniel was whispering, his voice travelling no further than the space on the pillow between them.

"There's no way you'd get close to it."

Partly gray stubble roughened his cheeks and he reeked of sweat. Yet the raw stench of it didn't affect the pleasure of being next to him.

"I thought maybe I could get Ari to do it."

He paused, deep creases in his forehead beneath his smooth, pale scalp.

"I know he's part of the corporation now but he has to see what's happening."

Storm rose up onto her elbow, the cold air rushing into their warmth.

"Ari's dead."

Daniel made a face, a quick flash of impatience.

"No. He's there."

"It was on the news. All three of them."

Daniel continued to shake his head.

"One of their latest upgrades had Ari written all over it. He's the one who made the expansions possible. I'm sure of it."

There was a moment of vertigo, remembering the cold shock of hearing of their deaths. Could it have been a trick? To protect them? Or to make sure they stayed separated? She slipped out from beneath the cover and sat on the side of the cot.

"Wait."

Daniel laid his hand on her forearm, pulling her back gently towards him. "It's good to have someone next to me."

"Someone?"

The full weight of his hand rested on her forearm.

"You. It feels good to have you next to me."

He lifted the cover to invite her back in, exposing the rows of ribs and a pointed hip bone.

"I have food for you."

She made a quick jog to the Tupperware through sticky, damp air, the concrete cold with broken and scaled pieces biting into the bottoms of her feet. She placed it on his chest, the fork angled out of it.

"In a minute. I want you beside me first."

"You need to eat."

"I will."

He lifted the edge of the blanket again. Still wary of rats in the darkness, she laid the bowl aside and slipped back into the heat. His breath was laboured and his scalp gleamed with sweat.

"What can I get you?"

She looked down into his hollowed eye sockets.

"Nothing."

He had closed his eyes and when she moved in close to him, his arm squeezed briefly around her shoulders.

"We need to get you out of here."

He lay still, the only hint of life the low thrum of his heartbeat beneath her hand.

"And then what?"

"Build your strength up, get you better."

The silence around them was solid, complete as if the world had ceased to exist. She found his hand, lacing her fingers in his.

"We can't physically destroy all the Gatherers."

"Daniel, we don't have to—you need to rest."

He turned his head enough to look at her.

"There's too many of them."

She moved closer so her body lay flush against his side, sores be damned. She laid her head carefully on his shoulder as he talked.

"If we shut down the channel, that would stop them."

"It doesn't stop them from making more."

They had added new processes and safeguards to the lab after she left, the production facility operating day and night.

"What about Callan and Jana? Are they there?"

A slight shake of his head, as if it didn't matter.

"So they did die."

Her arrival at the clearing in the Yukon had felt like a physical opening, a recognition that this might be a place she would heal. She hadn't thought of anyone else. That they might have needed a place like it as much as she did.

"Do you think it's the channel that's the problem?"

Storm nodded, distracted by an idea that had barely taken shape, afraid that if she so much as moved it would vanish before it was fully formed.

"The energy we draw off upsets the balance, which destabilizes everything around it."

The sores on his chest were wet against her forearm. She lifted her head off the sharp bone of his shoulder.

"What if instead of shutting it down, we open it up?"

Daniel cocked his head to one side, like he used to when she had caught his attention.

"Explain."

"You've been trying to limit the channel until it doesn't exist. What if we opened it right up?"

"It would destabilize everything."

He was staring into her shoulder, not seeing it, his mind following the stages as the Gatherer drew more and more energy.

"Including itself."

She didn't move, following the cascading failure of the Gatherer's structure. The simplicity of it fed her certainty, the violence of the destruction and the satisfaction of having it disappear into an implosion of its own creation. Her energy rallied at the possibility, a part of her still willing to fight.

"Do you think it's possible?"

His fingers on her shoulder had loosened, his second hand resting lightly on her wrist. A rush of hope ran like a current through her and into him, a perfect circuit that would heal their depleted cells. She imagined the agitation of the crystals as the power into the lattice increased. It would spread, fork at each node and ripple out into the delicate structure. It would be like a rumbling, the first tremors of an earthquake as the energy poured in. She rode with the power of it until she could feel it undermining the natural order of the field as it drew the energy of everything around it into itself.

He nodded slowly.

"There would be damage."

She pulled back, not letting herself get too excited. They would be careful this time. Do it right.

She looked for holes in the theory. Daniel might have been doing the same, or he might have been sleeping.

He suddenly lifted his head.

"What is that?"

Storm strained to hear through the silence, distracted by the potential of this solution to destroy. With a clench of fear in her bowels, she heard the sound of footsteps.

THIRTY-THREE

Maria woke to the smell of exhaust, the revving of engines, and voices arguing. Her head ached and her lower leg once again felt three times larger than it should.

She squinted at the bright expanse of blue sky shining through a set of open bay doors. She stopped breathing for a long moment before a rush of adrenaline ripped through her. A military transport vehicle was parked inside the doors, the source of the revving engine. She tried to sit, struggling against the straps that held her down at the hips and shoulders, every muscle primed for flight.

The shadow of a body moved in front of her, blocking her view of the truck. It was the nurse from the house, Dorian. The flap of straps and the pressure on her shoulders released, but not her hips. Dorian put her hand between Maria's shoulder blades and helped her sit. She was dizzy, her leg throbbing.

A group of civilians stood beside the truck in coveralls and work boots, dirty hands being wiped on oily rags. She strained to see who had come for her. The vehicle was older and had civilian plates. The canvas flaps at the back of the box were missing. More civilians hung near the open door, some wearing the camouflage of the wannabe, but no one had the disciplined posture of a soldier.

Dorian thrust a bottle of water at her and Maria wrapped her hands around it. She took a long drink as she found 'John', the farmer, in a smaller group off the back corner of the truck. His head was lowered to an emaciated young man gesturing wildly. If the military were here, this wasn't them.

She took a longer gulp of water and she shifted her hips back to ease the pressure off the straps.

High rows of shelves stacked with wooden crates extended into the back of the warehouse. Two idle forklifts were parked at the end of the nearest row, the whining rise and fall of a third audible from the dim reaches at the end of the aisle. The air smelled of earth and rotting onions, and there were stray cabbage leaves and broccoli pieces crushed on the floor. The bay doors looked onto a small airfield with a mountain range in the distance.

A television was mounted in one corner showing images of smoke spilling from the entrance of a large office building with firefighters herding office workers down the wide steps. She had almost placed the building, just needing a wider camera view to confirm, when Dorian spun the stretcher around, facing her away from the screen.

Maria squirmed further up on the stretcher. With a quick jerk, Dorian tightened the strap harder at the top of her thighs and a spike of pain ran into her calf. Maria made a show of collapsing back onto the stretcher, taking the opportunity to ease again out of the strap.

Dorian faced the open door, her attention on the group of civilians where John stood talking. Maria craned her neck, watching the small group from a sideways angle.

Judging from John's shaking head and set shoulders, there was some kind of disagreement. The young man repeatedly gestured towards her, the truck, and the distant mountains. Maria let her gaze slide to Dorian. There was a stillness around Dorian's eyes and mouth where there should have been life. A purpose that seemed devoid of thought.

Moving slowly, Maria turned her head so she had a tilted view of the screen. The smoking office building had gone, replaced by an announcer talking earnestly beside a photo of a young, top of the world Storm. She was so different than the woman Maria had last seen driving the speed boat that it was like watching another person, Storm's suffering absent from the photo.

She rolled further onto her side as her own photo replaced Storm's. One from her early twenties when she had just signed up. She looked young, angry, and fierce.

The words 'dishonourable discharge' appeared stamped across her photo and cold flushed through her, worse than the chill of a fever. Her world shrunk to that single photo, her throat tight and her mouth dry. She tried to read the lips of the announcer, to catch a word of meaning, but the shape of his mouth could have formed any number of words.

Her instinct was to shout, protest, and explain. Yet as people paused in front of the screen and leered at her out of the corner of their eyes, she knew that there was no one who would listen. Was Havernal alive, watching the same broadcast? It would be so much worse if he had been the one to order this.

She undid the strap, the pain in her leg renewing as her feet touched the floor. Dorian was too engrossed in watching John to notice and she took a step towards the screen as the announcer's lips stopped moving and a photo of Havernal appeared. She felt a sudden, jarring recognition of how far she had deviated from their original plan. Her flight with Storm hadn't been discussed, nor her complete absence of communication. She leaned heavily on a stack of crates, the wood rough and cold. Sunlight glared off the tarmac, the mountains obscured by a murky haze. It had felt like she was on track, that this was what he would have wanted her to do. But from where he sat, he might hardly have recognized her.

The newscaster moved on to another story, an awards ceremony, people shaking hands. Dorian was suddenly at her shoulder, her face set in grim satisfaction.

The news cycle repeated and every time her photo appeared with 'dishonourable discharge' stamped across it, people stopped, each of them inevitably glancing her way. Some smirked, others nodded as if what they had suspected had been confirmed or she had gotten what she deserved.

The image on the screen changed to a video of a Gatherer, one side blown off, thick, black smoke billowing out the top. At first Maria thought they were rebroadcasting Storm's attack on the Three Rocks Gatherer, but the trees in the background looked tropical and some of the spectators being held back by police were wearing shorts.

She tried again to read the announcer's lips and could make out nothing of the story. Another video of a damaged Gatherer, this one with the top ripped off, its delicate inside chamber exposed. Behind the torn Gatherer civilians were clashing with police. A woman whose hair obscured her face had been pinned to the pavement by a knee in her back. There were several photos of people she didn't recognize, and then the Prime Minister speaking with all the solemnity of a declaration of war.

The news story ended with a repeat of Storm's photo. Young, brilliant Storm Freeman who would save the world. Except the image looked darker, as if the smoke from the billowing Gatherers had stayed on the screen, stripping away the sheen of her radiant health.

Maria imagined she saw the announcer say 'whereabouts unknown.' Or at least she hoped she had.

People started gathering at the open bay door at the same time that Dorian walked towards it and stopped halfway, not quite leaving her post. Voices were rising, faces flushed, and people bumped against each other as they gravitated closer to the door, their necks stretched to catch a view of whatever was arriving. The distant sound of an engine and what was now a crowd of almost twenty pushed further out the door into the breeze of the tarmac. The emaciated young man strode a half dozen strides away from the building, waving his arms over his head.

The floor vibrated and the sound of the engine deepened, matching the sound of the one the men had been working on earlier. The crowd parted, fanning out as a truck coasted to a stop, people slapping its fenders and the Agri-foods emblem on the door to welcome it.

Dorian stood at the back of the crowd, barely aware Maria was there. She could have run for it, slipped around a corner into the depths of the aisle, but the power of whatever was in that truck drew her to it, as captivated as the rest.

The right-hand door at the back of the truck swung open and a man dressed in the camouflage of a hunter waved away the crowd. As he unlocked the second door, the angle of the sun prevented Maria from seeing into the interior and it wasn't until he stepped aside that she fully understood her new situation.

Storm was supported between two more men dressed in hunting gear, her shoulders rounded, her body curled in on itself. She stepped erratically, unsure where the ground lay. As they brought her into the light, she turned her head from the brightness, keeping her head down like a convict under arrest. She had gotten thinner in the few days since Maria had seen her, all trace of health gone from her face.

Maria felt sick as they led Storm through the crowd and people cheered, realizing as they helped Storm to the ground that the silver suit was gone. Maria started forward, stopped by Dorian's sudden grip on her elbow. She tried to tug it free but the woman held firm, pulling her back and opening the space between her and Storm. She could have neutralized the woman in a second, been at Storm's side in two, but a voice inside her head told her to wait. Not Havernal this time, but her own measured, calmer self who recognized that antagonizing this crowd would only put Storm in more danger.

Maria called Storm's name but she didn't respond, Maria's voice just another one in the crowd. Confused murmurings came from the group as a second person was unloaded. Carried in the arms of a young man, the second captive's shaved head lolled against the man's chest, the hand that hung limply at his side distorted by its thinness.

Maria had an irrational moment of jealousy that Storm had ditched her for another companion until the whispered name of Daniel carried through the group. She tasted revulsion in her throat. He was unrecognizable, his dark hair gone, nothing left to identify him as the rigid, brilliant young man who had been so determined to do the right thing.

Dorian's grip on her arm tightened as they carried Storm and Daniel away, pain shooting into her fingers. Storm didn't wince below the TV screen or avoid the forklift as it passed close by. Anger rose so fast and strong that Maria shook—not the erratic trembling she'd seen in Storm but a manifestation of the fury rising from her gut.

She let Dorian drag her back to her chair. The pounding in her leg was so strong she thought the skin would burst, but it was nothing compared to the frenzied pounding of her chest. She strained to see into the low block of offices at the far side of the warehouse where they had taken Storm and Daniel. The crowd milled around outside the entrance and she could see nothing through the door's murky half window.

There would be lights, computers, and printers, possibly a photocopier.

Maria remembered the sudden rigidity of Storm's body as she had carried her below the power line and her courage at enduring the field. She would have gone through worse to get here and it didn't make sense that she was still standing. Maria stopped moving, realizing she had been rocking back and forth. She hobbled a few steps towards the offices.

Dorian didn't bother to say anything as she watched with a bemused smirk. It was not surprising after what Maria had seen outside the doors. The close-cropped air field was bordered by open fields in every direction she could see, with the protection of the mountains or the distant clumps of trees a mile or more away. The range of mountains was familiar but not the individual peaks.

Two men lowered a case out of the back of the truck. They handled it carefully, making sure of each transition before they acted. A hard exterior, big enough to hold a barrel of diesel, yet their care indicated something else.

THIRTY-FOUR

The dried blood of Maria's pant leg cracked as she rolled it up. A dark stain of dried blood covered most of the bandage on her shin, the outer edges brown, the centre a brighter red. She lifted the tape and unwound the bandage, the gauze catching on the dried blood with each turn. As she got closer to the leg each turn pulled at the wound beneath so that she grimaced through the bottom layers, carefully pulling free the gauze.

The black, trimmed threads of six stitches had pushed into the dried blood and skin, like tiny bits of barbed wire embedded in the swollen flesh. The wound was raw around the entry point yet without the hot redness of infection. Whatever Dorian had been giving her was doing its job.

She leaned back in her chair, stretched her leg, and flexed her ankle to ease the stiffness, letting the air move over the wound, welcoming it back to the living. She dropped the ball of crusted gauze and lifted her gaze to the screen that acted as some kind of a commanding voice to the people passing beneath it. Dorian had her back to her, rocking from one foot to the next, a gun clutched across her chest.

The rising noise of preparations echoed in the steel beams of the ceiling, with men, women, and teenagers trotting out of the aisles with weapons and large wooden crates carried between them. They carried them excitedly, like new toys as they lifted them into the three Agri-foods trucks that had arrived shortly after Storm.

Maria's stamped photo flashed onto the screen, a wound so much deeper than the one in her leg, yet already she could feel it scabbing over, its blade not reaching as deep as she had thought. She let her gaze travel along the group of offices with its blinds lowered on windows and the single door guarded by one of the hunters who had brought in Storm and

Daniel. The roof was flat, maybe four metres above the warehouse floor. Skids had been stacked against one corner that made an easy ladder to the roof, but what then?

The screen showed her photo again followed by the healthy, powerful Storm, and the edge of her anger lessened. For the woman who had been Storm in that photo no longer existed and neither did the green, young, fanatic girl who had joined up. It was so simple, yet it was as if her disgrace had evaporated like mist that lifts from a morning lake and she could see clear to the other side. She had been in theatre, adjusting to the situation as it developed. They might have wanted her to make different choices, but from her position, she wouldn't change a thing.

She rolled her ragged pant leg over her calf, flexed her feet, and pulled them underneath her to stand.

"Stay where you are."

Two patches of colour sat on Dorian's colourless cheeks, like rouge on the skin of a corpse.

Maria sat back down, perched lightly on the edge of her seat, paying attention to the flow of people. She noted who was in charge and where the weak links were, suddenly wide awake.

The place was in chaos, the men who were in charge organizing it more like a weekend at a hunt camp than a successful maneuver. She itemized what they put in the truck: an assortment of weapons, mainly hunting rifles, the occasional handgun and boxes of explosives. John moved among the chaos, stopping to confer with some of the hunters. He fixed a stuck trigger on a rifle for a teenaged boy with long gangly arms and legs. Like a commander in the First World War, blissfully sending unprepared troops to their death.

There was a cry from the boy with the tablet as he pointed a remote at the screen, clicking through blank images until he arrived at a channel where the image cleared. YouTube. The bustling stopped and people drew in towards the screen. A ghostly image of Storm appeared. She seemed short of breath as the video began to play, and Maria's shock was as acute as a punch to her gut. Storm sat on a cot, knees pulled up, her back pressed into a corner. Her face was turned away and she had her hand held up against the piercing light of the camera that was recording her. Her head leaned against the wall at an odd angle, and the skin on her face and the hand she held up to the camera had the translucency of a worn handkerchief that could tear at any minute.

"Ms. Freeman. Did the Gatherer do this to you?"

The voice was young, excited, likely that of the boy with the tablet.

Storm stared into the camera with red, slitted eyes. Maria hoped she saw intelligence there, that Storm was choosing not to respond and not that she didn't have the strength.

"Is the Gatherer the cause of the plague?"

It didn't matter if Storm answered. Her thinness and her drastic decline said everything the recorder needed.

"Was this your intention when you created it?"

Thin and burned by the light, Storm looked like a creature that had been hiding too long in a dark place. Her weakness was obvious, the sudden close ups and drawing back of the camera distorting her dimensions so that she appeared otherworldly, living proof of the sickness she had delivered to them.

The video ended, Storm's image frozen with her mouth open as if she had finally decided to answer. The crowd started applauding and cheering, the kid who had taken the video grinning from ear to ear like he had won a prize.

Dorian pressed the butt of her rifle into Maria's back.

"Let's go."

"Where?"

"Don't make me force you."

There were too many people for Maria to confront her there. Dorian would have armed, over-excited backup instantly.

Dorian turned her towards the entrance to the offices where Storm and Daniel had been taken. Maria's leg hurt more than she wanted it to, and even as she tried to adjust her gait, the pain shot into her thigh as if the wound had expanded. They crossed through the flow of weapons and people, and Maria got a close-up of a case of explosives. Enough power to create some serious damage.

A young girl stepped into their path, no more than sixteen, her eyebrow and nose pierced. Maria let the girl's hatred flow over her. The girl needed someone to blame for what was happening to her world. An outlet for the fear and panic that ran like stray currents beneath the ground as people's worlds disintegrated from an invisible force.

Dorian brushed the girl aside, holding Maria back as two men passed in front of them carrying the case that was unloaded with Daniel and Storm. Black plastic, metal latches on the lid, and no markings at all to indicate its contents. The men carried it behind the offices into one of the aisles, away from the trucks.

The hunter at the door had had his nose broken more than once and there was a toughness to him that could have been military except for the jittery intensity of his gaze. He was the kind who tried to enlist but didn't pass the suitability test. He nodded to Dorian as he opened the door. He was twice Maria's size.

There were bright lights down a bare corridor and the sounds of an office in high activity. Dorian pushed her forward and pain spiked in her leg. Phones rang, keyboards tapped, chairs rolled back and hit walls as bodies changed directions. She tried to hop as they passed several offices, yet every time her toe touched down a sharp jolt of pain radiated far beyond the physical wound.

In the first office, three men crowded around a screen, a fourth bent over a table. She slowed her pace, increasing her limp, and tried to linger in front of the second room. It was crammed with a half-dozen computers, each one occupied, several of the attendees wearing headsets with microphones. They passed a darkened corridor before stopping at the end of the hall in front of a closed door marked 'Conference Room'. The gold enamel was missing from the letter 'N.'

Another guard stood at this door, the one that had carried Daniel, and without speaking he chose a key from an extensive ring and unlocked the door. He held it open for her as Dorian released her arm. The room was dimly lit, with a table crammed up against the wall and chairs crowded against it.

She felt a push between her shoulder blades and stumbled. The air was stale, smelling of dusty plastic and old carpets, and at first she thought it was empty. Yet there was another smell, of flesh, of something alive or at least once had been. The beam of light that had projected onto the table and empty wall narrowed and disappeared as the door closed behind her. Her eyes refocused to the LED lights mounted at either side of two end-to-end cots, like candles lighting caskets.

Storm lay closest to the door, curled on her side, with a silver blanket over her. Daniel lay on his back in the adjacent cot, the light gleaming off his pale, papery skull, the hollows of his eyes and cheeks deepened by the angle of the lights. There was a stillness about him that was too absolute, and the smell of sickness came from him.

The door locked behind her and she limped forward, the scuff of her steps slow in the strange silence as if she had entered the sanctuary of two Gods who had been laid out to accept sacrifices. She approached carefully, the edge of the light acting like a barrier protecting a valuable artifact. Time passed slower in this quiet place, the frenzy outside the walls squashed by something stronger, more powerful.

Storm moved, a subtle tuck of her chin, and the illusion broke. Storm and Daniel became the two broken bodies they were, clinging to whatever life still existed for them. Copper wires had been stapled to the walls in an erratic web that rose to the ceiling.

She knocked her leg against the cot as she knelt and Storm's eyes opened. They were pained, unfocused, her brows drawn down tight. She turned her face further into the cot, away from the light and whatever had disturbed her.

"Storm."

Maria shook her gently. The cot rocked with the movement.

Storm grunted.

Her voice was angry, the strength of it catching Maria off guard.

"How are you?"

The one eye Storm opened was blood-shot, the rim red.

"Your crew did this."

Her face was a bad white but for the too dark freckles that bridged her nose.

"You cheered at the sight of Daniel and me."

Maria sat back on her heels, the damaged muscles in her calf screaming.

"These aren't my crew."

Storm pulled the sheet close to her neck, her hand trembling. Maria would have to carry her. She didn't think what that would mean for Daniel, though she already knew.

"Then why are you here?"

The strength in Storm's voice was out of place in a frame that could barely support itself, her suspicion rallying tissues and cells out of proportion to her damaged systems. Her lips were cracked, with blood crusted at one corner.

Maria limped to the small sink in the section of cupboards in the corner. Using a paper coffee cup, she brought Storm a drink of water. Storm watched the cup Maria held between them, the swallow in her parched throat visible in her thin, shrunken neck.

"Do you want this or not?"

The cup was filled almost to the top and the clear liquid shifted, picking up the spill off from the lights.

Storm lifted a shaking hand to take it.

Maria put it into her fingers and helped guide it back to Storm's lips, holding it steady as she lifted her head for one, two gulps. She dropped her head and her hold on the cup at the same time.

Maria sat on the side of the cot, cup in one hand, her pounding leg stretched out at an angle. Daniel hadn't stirred, his skull so pronounced she could see the outline of his teeth beneath his lips, the sharp curve of his cheekbones beneath the skin.

"They took me from the hospital and were holding me in the warehouse when you arrived. That's why I saw you. And Daniel."

Maria offered her the cup again and Storm lifted her head for two more gulps. When she finished swallowing she spoke.

"How bad is he?"

Not a single sound of the frenzied preparations reached them. Maria pulled at one of the copper wires above the bed, the metal bending under the pressure. She tried not to let her gaze fall to Daniel's stillness.

"Your video has started a revolution. They've loaded guns and explosives. They mean to attack."

Storm's eyes closed, her suffering leaving no place for Daniel or this news.

Maria returned to the sink and drank a full cup. She'd seen maps with the dense areas of Gatherers across the middle latitudes, fewer at the outer reaches. They would need an army to destroy them all. She filled the cup again to deliver it back to Storm.

"Who's guarding them?" Storm asked.

Of course Storm would see how it would play out. The potential for injuries and conflict. She had always been good at seeing how events connected. Except when it came to her own health.

"The military. Police."

Storm closed her eyes, her eyelashes casting tiny shadows on her sunken skin.

"It's worse."

The words were barely a whisper, spoken from a place of pain that wasn't physical.

Maria lowered herself back onto the cot.

"You couldn't have known."

Storm rolled back her shoulder, partially lifting her face to the ceiling.

"You did."

Maria placed her foot under her injured leg, trying to elevate it.

"My orders were to bring it under our control. The military wasn't trying to save anyone."

A dull thud sounded from outside the walls.

"Neither will we."

Maria tucked a corner of the blanket back around Storm's shoulder.

"We'll get there."

It was hard to see right now, but Maria believed it. She wasn't about to throw away everything they had done to get there.

"You might."

There was a sudden lift to Storm's chin, indicating pain.

"I'm not going without you."

"You might have to."

Storm's eyes had closed again, her stillness not as complete as Daniel's.

Maria went to his side, feeling even as she drew close that he was so far from them there was nothing she could do. At least he was free of the pain that attacked Storm.

As she straightened the blanket, she felt the dim warmth of his skin. She checked for a pulse, knowing from his temperature that she wouldn't find one. She laced her hands one over the other to start CPR, and stopped, her palms hovering above his chest. The temperature of his skin had been too cool; this wasn't something she could pull him back from. He could have been dead from before she arrived.

She pulled the blanket higher, just below his chin, not ready yet to tell Storm. She bowed her head as the horror of his demise tore through her like a gale force wind, fearing it would overtake her. She laid her hands on his chest, not to save his life, but to honour it. To convey to him that he had done everything he could to fix the damage he and Storm had brought, even if she didn't know if it was true.

He was so small without his spirit to animate the flesh, as if it had never truly been a part of him at all. She stayed for several minutes, hoping he had at least been aware of Storm as he died.

Storm lay quietly when Maria returned to her side, and Maria had a moment of panic that she had slipped away too.

"Is he gone?"

Maria didn't speak. Storm's mouth stretched in agony, her features misshapen in grief. Tears rolled out of her eyes, past her ears, and Maria dared not touch her for fear of the pain she would cause. Storm began to shake and a pale curtain drew across her features.

Maria pulled the blanket off Daniel, his body so thin and frail, and wrapped it carefully around Storm. She scanned the room for anything else she might use as the door clicked open.

She positioned herself between Storm and the door. It was the guard, followed by Dorian. Maria waited for John behind her but it was only the woman. The guard exited and closed the door, leaving Dorian standing in the dimness, one hand in her big square pocket, the other holding her black medical bag. Her placid face was as blank as ever.

Maria held her ground, prepared to do what she needed to protect Storm but the woman went to Daniel first, looking down dispassionately at his exposed frailty.

There was a faint sigh, the first expression of emotion Maria had heard from the woman, though it was irritation not sadness that she communicated. Maria would have stepped forward to keep her away from him if it hadn't meant leaving Storm.

Dorian leaned over, circled a fist around the cross that rested in his clavicle and yanked it off his neck. She lifted his right hand and pulled the small metal ring off his pinky. Maria had to swallow against the revulsion and fury that welled up together in a toxic wave. Dorian slipped the jewellery into her pocket and patted it twice.

"Put them back."

Her throat ached with the effort not to shout.

Dorian turned, grinning a lifeless smile.

"Spoils of War."

It happened fast, Maria stepping forward to force Dorian to give back Daniel's remaining possessions and the flash of a knife from Dorian's pocket. Maria acted by instinct, jamming the heel of her hand into Dorian's throat and smashing the hand holding the knife against the wall, as she shoved the soft, toneless body against the wall.

Dorian slumped down the wall, eyes wide in panic, hands clasping her throat as she gasped for air. The guard barged in, and in the few seconds it took him to adjust to the dimness, Maria struck him in the solar plexus and knocked him on the back of the head. Maria felt the impact of him hitting the floor as she leapt to catch the door before it latched.

Wild, throbbing pain pulsed in her leg as she balanced on one foot and stretched, one hand on the door, to grasp for the back of a chair. Her fingers just reached and she had enough leverage to tilt it back until it fell to the floor. She dragged it across the floor, and after checking the corridor was empty, wedged its leg in the door.

Dorian was wheezing against the wall, her mouth opening and closing as she tried to call for help. Maria yanked the cord off the projector screen and tied Dorian's hands behind her back, being intentionally rough with her so that the woman protested with a wordless moan. If there had been more time she would have really hurt the woman.

Apologizing to Daniel as she did so, she peeled one of the socks from his foot. It was old, worn and hadn't been washed in a long time. She rolled it into a ball and kneeled before Dorian. At first the woman turned her head, keeping her lips pressed together, but after a few well-placed points of pressure Maria stuffed the sock into her mouth. Dorian gagged, and Maria waited to make sure it was only from disgust before yanking her to her feet and pushing her down to sitting where she could tie the other end of the cord to the table leg. When she was secure, Maria dug the cross and ring from Dorian's pocket and slipped it into hers.

Under muffled protests from Dorian, she dumped the content of the medical bag onto the carpet, grabbing pill bottles, syringes, and small bottles of liquid, anything that might be useful. She swallowed two pain killers dry, and took a third for good measure. She gagged on the bitter residue as she checked the hall again. There were voices from the offices, people moving past the open door to the warehouse, no one yet concerned the guard had left his post.

Storm lay quiet, her skin translucent and pale, the tiny blue veins visible at her temple. Bracing against the pain, Maria sat Storm up, crouched down, and draped Storm across her shoulder. She gasped and grunted before she stood at full height. The first step was agony, the second worse, no adjustment of weight making any difference.

She hobbled, under Dorian's baleful glare, taking strength in having Storm close to her again and glad to be moving.

One of the hunters was in the corridor walking in the other direction. As soon as he disappeared into the warehouse, and before she could think, she latched the door behind her and crossed the few steps to an adjacent hallway. It was darker in the short passageway, the bulk of a water cooler narrowing the path so that Storm's arm dragged against it as they passed the two doors of darkened bathrooms.

She paused at the second door to the warehouse, trying futilely to rise above the pain. It rose and twisted up her leg like the flames of a raging fire. The start of the aisles was ten, maybe fifteen strides away. She shifted Storm's weight, her arms locked around the back of her knees. A row of loaded skids lay between them.

"It's happening faster than we thought."

The man's voice echoed from the main corridor, a second voice responding.

"There will be more troops."

She yanked open the door, her leg threatening to buckle with each step to shelter behind a mound of full burlap sacks. Storm blocked her view on one side as she waited for sounds of pursuit. The noise was concentrated at the far end of the warehouse, where Maria had been before. Someone was speaking, with punctuated responses from a crowd.

She half-ran, half-hobbled to the closest opening in the stacks, ecstatic and astonished she had made it this far. It was dim and cool between the stacks, the sounds from the front warehouse muted. She tasted earth and rot on her tongue, the smell of it crowding her senses.

The aisle extended deep into the warehouse, its far reaches completely in darkness, twenty times the distance she had already come.

She settled into the excruciating rhythm, able only to put one foot in front of the next and letting go of the responsibility of not being seen to whomever or whatever had gotten them this far. They had just passed a halted forklift, its two-pronged lift flat to the ground, when Storm moaned. A faint scream, from a long way under, of the pain and panic Maria was causing her.

Five more paces and Storm had started to squirm, pushing weakly against Maria's back to lift her torso. Maria staggered under the shifting weight, grabbing hold of a stack for support.

"Keep still!"

Her words were a strangled whisper. Storm refused to calm, struggling against Maria, her movements increasingly manic as she tried to free herself. A strong sudden lurch and Maria's leg gave out, her arm pulling on her socket where she tried to hold the shelf. There was agony in her knees as she hit the floor. Storm's weight pushed her down further, her face against the cold dirt and concrete. Storm rolled off her, the blanket twisted around her.

Maria rose to her hands. Storm had covered her eyes with her hand, a turtle tucked into its shell hoping the world would go away.

"What can I do?"

Storm lowered her hand, looking up at Maria with bloodshot, infinitely pained eyes. The blue was darker than Maria had ever seen, the darkness not far in the distance.

There was the sound of feet running several aisles over. The shelves were too stocked full for Maria to see who ran. She waited, barely breathing, as the footsteps came parallel to them, and kept going. She leaned over Storm, preparing herself for the weight and pain. Storm laid her hand on Maria's forearm, long, white fingers, the touch so light it was almost not there.

"Don't," Storm whispered.

"You've been exposed too much already."

Storm's eyes closed, her chest slowly rising and falling as if they weren't about to be found at any moment.

"You need to find Ari."

Maria threaded her forearm beneath Storm's knees, preparing to lift her.

"I have to get you out of here."

Storm grabbed Maria before she could gather in her shoulders. The grip was harder.

"He's at the headquarters. Daniel says he's alive."

There was a rise of energy again with her insistence, though less this time, leaving her more depleted when it left.

"How does he know?"

The barest shake of her head came as her eyes closed, an assumption that her belief in Daniel would be enough for Maria. The muscles across Maria's chest and arms engaged, wanting to pick Storm up and pull her back from wherever she was going. Yet she didn't touch her, couldn't cause her more pain.

There were more footsteps and Maria was forced to carry Storm two steps into an open section of shelf. She laid her down as quickly as she could. Storm's eyes were wide with shock and pain, arms braced at her sides to ward off more attacks.

"It will take them longer to find you here."

Maria pulled a skewed edge of the blanket across Storm's knees. Not that it would do any good.

"There are imperfections in the lattice."

Maria looked into the shelves above, touching the rough sacks of grain beside them. There was nothing that would protect Storm.

"Did you hear me?"

Storm lay back, her head next to the shrivelled remains of a fallen cabbage leaf.

"I heard you."

The sounds came of people being marshalled at the front end of the stacks. A crowd had formed, each person being assigned an aisle.

Maria wiped the leaf away from Storm's head. It had been the same with Havernal, his weakness a detriment to what they needed to get done, his determination no less than Storm's. The expectation of it gathered on her shoulders, that she would be the one to keep going and they would travel with her.

She laid her palm gently on Storm's forehead. Her eyes opened.

"I have to go."

Storm nodded, her gaze hauntingly clear in its understanding. Maria wanted to find hope in the wisdom it held, yet pain clouded it, always threatening in the distance.

"You'll find him?"

Every part of Maria was rebelling against this. You didn't leave people behind unless you knew help was coming. And the footsteps that were echoing around them wouldn't be help.

"I will."

Something went out of Storm at Maria's promise, whatever strength she had been clinging to slipping away. Maria straightened the blanket a final time, fighting the overpowering need to stay.

A figure was outlined at the head of the aisle, backlit by the lighter area at the front. A woman, though it was hard to tell at this distance. Maria crawled through the shelf. In the next aisle another person stood at the head. She climbed through an opening in the shelf above her, up onto the second level. She could just see Storm through the slatted shelves, her eyes already closed, her cheek turned into the floor. Maria fought the renewed need to go back to her.

She wound her way around empty crates, reeking of old produce, and canisters of unknown liquids. She moved continually higher so that eventually she was six shelves up, moving through empty slots where the air was warmer and the emptiness of the rafters was above her, the distance between her and Storm stretching and attenuating like a rubber band that would pull her back.

A line of searchers had spread into the stacks, moving slowly, checking the shelves as they went. When they had almost reached Storm, Maria climbed lower, waiting for the moment of discovery before she risked crossing the aisle.

The shout came when she had reached the second shelf, and as people abandoned their searches and ran, Maria jumped to the floor, landing carefully on her good foot, the jolt sending partially muted sparks of pain into her leg. She crossed one aisle, two, and reached the final aisle before the end wall. It was wider, with space enough for two forklifts to pass. A current of fresher air flowed along the empty path. At the far end, away from the commotion of the searchers arguing, the red letters of an exit sign glowed above a steel door.

She stepped into the aisle. It would take the searchers a few minutes to regroup, now that they had Storm. Maria tried not to think about their ignorance and the lack of regard they would show her. She walked quickly, without a limp, a fleeing individual more likely to attract attention.

The warehouse rushed in on her, loud and clear, every movement of air, call of a voice, or sound of dirt scuffing on concrete registering and logged into her wide-open senses. She imagined she could hear Storm's cries of protest, the absence of them even worse. The letters on the exit grew larger, the red outlines burned into her retina, even as she scanned the aisle ahead, the shelves above, and marked each column that she passed. She allowed herself to look behind her once, then twice, each time expecting to see someone in pursuit or a running body about to tackle her.

Her pace increased to a jog by the end of the stacks, a full run the final steps to the door. She tried to block out the image of Storm lying in the shelf, crumpled like a discarded wrapper, the agony she would endure as they pulled her out. The need to go back to her was almost unbearable, a tearing at whatever had connected them opening a wound in her back like the exit hole of a bullet.

Her hands touched the cool metal of the push bar. There were no wires attached to the door to set off an alarm. She looked one final time behind her. The aisle was clear and long, the layer of dirt on the concrete still, the space as empty as anything Maria had ever seen. The release bar clunked and the latch released.

She felt the sharp, fresh touch of cold air and embraced the wide-open space of the sky. It was late afternoon, almost dusk, the glow of the sun receding behind a stance of trees less than the width of a highway away. The door shut. She paused as if it had cut the final tether that had held her to Storm and she was now freefalling away from her. She held tight onto the metal bar of the door handle, the sweat on her palms delivering the coldness straight into her skin.

With a force of will beyond thought, she released her hand. One step, two. She reached the edge of the tarmac and was running by her first steps through the long grass. The pain in her leg had shrunk, the cool air returning it to its source, and for the first time since the explosion, she felt a gathering of strength in her limbs. In twenty paces she reached the woods, not slowing as she ducked into the deeper darkness of their shelter. She stayed looking forward, the branches scraping across her face and hands, attuned to the distance between her and the warehouse.

The trees didn't last long and soon she was crossing a rough field, slowing to navigate the dips and hollows obscured by the tangled grass. An unbroken space of darkening sky stretched above her, the peaks of the mountains that overlooked Rima visible in the distance. For a moment, she faltered, consumed by the urge to turn around.

A barnyard light turned on in the distance, a point of focused light against the yellow backdrop of the setting sun. The dusk had deepened enough to make her hard to see, though anyone looking for her would still find her.

At a road paved in broken asphalt, she turned away from the barnyard and its light. She stepped lighter than she had in weeks, revelling at the ease of moving alone, her body adjusting around the information Storm had given her. Her mission was clear. She experienced the same certainty she had when she'd pressed the throttle on the train and felt the power of it move through her.

She almost didn't see the car in the dusk, its running lights off, the evening well past the point where headlights were necessary. She dropped into the ditch and crawled through the soaked decaying bottom, up the other side and into the shelter of the grasses. The dead stalks cracked under her hands, the sharper ones digging into her knees. As the car slid past, its windows dark, it slowed. She flattened to her stomach, her heart beating slow and steady against the ground. The dark shape coasted past the empty barnyard and blended into the horizon.

The first stars were pushing into the fading sky, bits of infinite energy from a distance that would take several lifetimes to travel. She rose to her feet, testing the strength in her leg, and on a diagonal made her way back to the road.

The city glowed to the north. She turned towards it, aware now of silent cars and the people that searched for her. Already the night was colder with an edge to it, her only comfort coming from the knowledge Storm had given her.

She turned back once, noting the place where she had emerged from the trees, remembering the layout of the outbuildings of the farm and the curve of the hill behind them. When she faced forward, the darkness was almost complete and the light of the city beyond brighter for it.

About the Author

Colleen Winter is a science-fiction junkie and uses her electrical engineering degree to create stories that walk the line between what is real and what is possible. In a previous life she worked as a journalist and now is a communications consultant in the Ontario electrical industry. She lives near Toronto, Canada, and spends as much time as she can hiking the beautiful places of the world with her family and her dog.